Praise for M. K. Wren
and her Conan Flagg mysteries

CURIOSITY DIDN'T KILL THE CAT
"Conan Flagg is an appealing sleuth . . . and there's atmosphere in the Oregon Beach resort and plenty excitement."
—King Features

OH, BURY ME NOT
"Something different, a detective story set in western ranch country with cowboy characters . . . Suspenseful and a challenge."
—*Publishers Weekly*

WAKE UP, DARLIN' COREY
"A nice job, written with compassion and buttressed with some sharp observations."
—*The New York Times Book Review*

DEAD MATTER
"A superb puzzler . . . Wren has a deft touch with humor and lively examples abound in DEAD MATTER."
—DOROTHY B. HUGHES

KING OF THE MOUNTAIN

M. K. Wren

BALLANTINE BOOKS • NEW YORK

Copyright © 1994 by Martha Kay Renfroe

All rights reserved under International and Pan-American Copyright Conventions. Published in the United States of America by Ballantine Books, a division of Random House, Inc., New York, and simultaneously in Canada by Random House of Canada Limited, Toronto.

Library of Congress Catalog Card Number: 94-94660

ISBN 0-345-39019-9

Manufactured in the United States of America

First Edition: January 1995

10 9 8 7 6 5 4 3

In gratitude to Connie and Clarence, who have graced our lives with courtly solicitude, generous friendship, and laughter.

CHAPTER 1

Conan Flagg first saw Mount Hood, like an odd cloud on the eastern horizon, when he was halfway between the Pacific coast and Portland. By the time he reached Oregon's largest city, fifty miles later, the mountain had doubled in size, its serene silhouette visible from any high point in the city.

But Conan didn't seek out its high points, and he would gladly have avoided Portland and its tangle of morning rush-hour traffic altogether if there were any other way of reaching the King lodge from Holliday Beach. He hadn't been at all enthusiastic at the prospect of leaving home just when the Weather Service was predicting an ocean storm, or of leaving the Holliday Beach Book Shop, which he considered his albatross and *raison d'être*, now that most of the tourists had departed and left it in blessed, if musty, tranquillity.

At least he could avoid the worst of Portland's traffic by resorting to its freeways. Thus the black Jaguar

XK-E purred along in the center lane on Highway 205, the top down on this clear, warm October morning. The car and Conan Flagg presented a dashing image that attracted curious glances: a rare car designed for speed and power; a lean, dark man in his forties, his wind-blown hair straight and black, the exotic cast to his features affirming his Nez Percé ancestry.

But those observations would be made from vehicles as they rushed past the XK-E, which was traveling at a less than dashing five miles per hour under the freeway speed limit. Conan had not acquired this car for its speed or power—he would have been perfectly happy with four cylinders—but for its beauty.

At length he left the freeway and, finally, the last of the fecund suburbs and drove east on a two-lane highway into the foothills of the Cascades, relishing the gold and scarlet of vine maples against deep green conifers. Even if he had undertaken this journey reluctantly, he found himself enjoying it; the landscapes of the Northwest were always a sensory feast.

Mount Hood hid behind near hills, occasionally emerging as he rounded a curve or came over a crest, and at every appearance, it loomed larger, more surprising. It seemed, in this dry season before the winter snows, like a chunk of the Moon dropped here to erode and settle into the Earth, its glaciers and snowfields pale as lunar maria.

This solitary, spectacular mountain was one of the pearls in the strand ornamenting the Cascade Mountains from British Columbia south through Washington to southern Oregon. Like its sister peaks, it was born of the fires in the bowels of the Earth, and although its primordial cone had been eroded by the implacable chisels of glaciers, Conan always felt the savage life dormant within it. Only a few years ago, one of its sisters to the north had wakened. And exploded.

As he skirted Mount Hood's flanks, it seemed to move from east to northeast and finally to north by the time he passed the villages of Rhododendron, Zigzag, and Government Camp, whose sole purpose seemed to be supplying and feeding skiers en route to the three ski resorts on the mountain. A few miles after he passed the junction to Timberline Lodge, he slowed so he wouldn't miss the small bridge over King's Creek. For a quarter of a mile after the bridge, the highway was paralleled on the right by a pole fence. He looked for the gate and the inconspicuous sign that read simply KING.

The gate was open. He signaled for a right turn, swearing at the log truck that hissed and roared like an impatient dragon on his back bumper. He turned onto a gravel road, while the truck rumbled on.

Log truck drivers, Conan thought bitterly, assumed they owned *all* the roads, highways as well as the thousands of miles of logging roads these trucks used to haul out the timber—roads built at taxpayers' expense. Most of the Cascades were National Forest land, although a stranger flying over in an airplane might find that hard to believe after observing the checkerboard of clear-cuts and the lace of logging roads. That stranger might reasonably assume that all the land below belonged to timber companies.

The property Conan had entered did in fact belong to a timber company: Ace Timber and Wood Products, Incorporated. This was one of the few small enclaves of private land within the boundaries of Mount Hood National Forest. Conan drove up a gravel road flanked by more pole fences and thickets of alders, with their pale, speckled trunks. The road climbed out of the trees as it curved left, and there, backed to a slope green with fir and hemlock, stood A. C. King's lodge.

It was, Conan had to admit, an impressive edifice, an homage to Cascadian architecture, its materials—stone and wood—drawn from its setting. The long, two-story building was aligned broadside to the north for the view of Mount Hood, and at its midpoint an octagonal structure rose through both stories, its angled roof capped with a weather vane in the shape of a Douglas fir. The family called this structure the atrium, and it served not only as an entrance, but as a visual anchor for the two wings. On the east, the first floor was taken up with a four-car garage; and on the west, the living room with its big windows overlooking a deck. The latter was a new addition since Conan's last visit six years ago. It began at the atrium, ran along the front of the living room, then widened and continued around the west wall. The shake roof was steep-pitched to slough off winter snow, the slopes punctuated by six gables, three above the living room, three above the garage, and no less than eight stone chimneys, one for every bedroom. Each bedroom was also furnished with a private bath, and Conan smiled, remembering Lise King's commentary: "All the comforts of a good hotel."

If there was some bitterness in that, it was because this lodge had originally been built as a retreat for the family, but as A. C.'s fortune grew it had become primarily a deductible business expense frequently occupied by businessmen, domestic and foreign, and by politicians. Albert Charles King was in a position to enrich any politician's war chest, and thus he could count many of them as friends.

But this weekend the lodge would again be a family retreat. Tomorrow, Saturday, October twenty-fifth, was A. C.'s birthday, a milestone he refused to celebrate except as the occasion for this reunion. For thirty-four years the King family had come to the lodge on the last weekend in October, and its male members—A. C. and his sons, Al, Mark, and Lucas—made the annual hike up King's Mountain, a minor peak chosen as the goal of that traditional trek simply because it was the highest point on A. C.'s domain.

Conan stopped in front of the atrium, noting that the garage doors were open, but it was empty. This didn't surprise him. He had purposely arrived two hours before one o'clock, when the rest of the family was due. Lise was already here. She spent six months of every year here in the inspirational presence of Mount Hood.

And Lise King, A. C.'s only daughter, was the reason Conan was here. The invitation from A. C. wasn't enough to draw him. He received a similar invitation every year. It was an inherited courtesy. A. C. and Conan's father, Henry Flagg, had been boyhood friends, growing up on ranches near Pendleton. Their friendship had survived A. C.'s departure from Eastern Oregon and even, in a sense, survived Henry Flagg's death, since A. C. continued to proffer Henry's son invitations to these family gatherings. Conan usually found reasons to decline, but this year A. C.'s invitation had been seconded by a note from Lise. The first part had been uncharacteristically chatty, which in itself sounded an alarm. Lise King didn't chat.

Then there was the final paragraph: "You'll find a great deal changed since Mom's death. Things fall apart—the center cannot hold. Well, our center is gone. Oh, Conan, please come." The *please* had been underlined. Twice.

Things fall apart . . .

Lise was asking for help.

Conan saw her red Toyota minivan parked next to a

blue pickup on the edge of the wide, asphalt turn-around. He frowned at the pickup, then realized it probably belonged to the couple from Zigzag who took care of the lodge. He couldn't remember their names.

Rasmussen. It came to him as he got out of his car and heard the chunk of an ax from beyond the northeast corner of the garage where Conan knew there was a woodshed with a door opening on the north into the outside work area, and another opening into the garage. A balding man with his shirt sleeves rolled up came around the corner, ax in hand, and walked toward him. Art Rasmussen. Art and Doris. Doris was no doubt busy in the kitchen.

Art offered a smile. "You're Conan Flagg, right?" Then before Conan could answer, "Lise said you'd be early. She's up to the studio."

Conan nodded. "Where should I park my car?"

"Might as well put it in the garage. Well, I gotta get back to work. I'm almost done splittin' the wood. I'll have two cords stacked for you folks before we go." With that assurance, he walked back the way he had come.

Conan parked the XK-E at the east end of the garage, which was clearly Art's domain, the plywood walls whitewashed, the concrete floor painted battleship gray. The east wall was divided by the open door into the woodshed from whence Conan heard Art whistling as he stacked his freshly split wood. On the left side of the door, gardening tools hung in an orderly collage; on the right was a worktable with tiers of tiny drawers at the back under a collage of carpentry tools.

In the center of the long south wall, a black-and-red, 10,000-watt emergency generator squatted. A wire ran up the wall behind it, then west along the ceiling, finally disappearing into a breaker box next to the door on the west wall. The generator was a reminder that warm, clear days like this could, in these mountains, give way to bitter cold, and the heat and light supplied by power lines could fail.

Conan patted his shirt pocket to be sure he had his cigarettes and started to leave the garage, but Art emerged from the woodshed door and stopped him with, "Say, Mr. Flagg, if you're goin' up to see Lise, wonder if you'd remind her Doris and me have to leave for Portland in a little while." He grimaced. "Doris has to see the dentist."

"I'm sorry to hear that. I'll tell Lise."

"And tell her I checked the generator and filled the gas cans. They're out here in the woodshed. Twenty-five gallons, altogether."

Art ducked back into the woodshed, but, before Conan had taken more than two steps, ducked out again. "Oh, and tell her Doris said she'll have the cold lunch fixed to lay out for the folks when they get here, and ever'thing's ready for the cookout this evenin'."

"We'll all be grateful for that."

"Right." Again Art disappeared into the woodshed, this time, apparently, for good.

As Conan left the garage, he paused to savor the view of Mount Hood. Its peak was seven miles away, as the eagle flew, yet in the lens of the clear air, it seemed closer. Not a cloud shadowed its vast slopes or softened the white glare of its snowfields. There was, he thought, the same awesome presence about this mountain that he felt in looking at the Pacific Ocean from his windows at home. Each view had inherent in it an element of risk.

He continued across the asphalt to the west end of the lodge then veered left across a lawn of mowed native grass and into a copse of alders, their leaves gone brown and dull, where a path led him up an easy slope.

The sun-loving alders were soon replaced by fir and spruce and a cool, moist silence. He knew where the path led, but when he saw a building through the trees to his left, he stopped. This wasn't the same building he remembered. The old studio had been little more than a log cabin. This new one was larger, its lines spare and clean, the north wall fronted with floor-to-ceiling windows.

He found the entrance on the south side, and the moment his feet hit the plank porch, an insistent barking erupted behind the door. This, too, was a new addition.

The door was open, the screen vibrating with the new addition's lunging sorties. The source of this brave and noisy show looked like a miniature collie, not even two feet tall at the shoulder. A Shetland sheepdog. He knew the breed because the owner of a ranch adjacent to the Ten-Mile had imported five of them when he decided to run sheep. The sheep business had not prospered, but various members of the Travers family had ended up with fine pets.

"Heather, it's okay! Come on in, Conan."

He came, extending the back of his hand for Heather to sniff—or bite, for all he knew. Lise King was standing at a drafting table, which was tilted at a slight angle, a white enamel palette on a smaller table to her right, with the north light and Mount Hood to her left.

Lise had once told him that as a child she had studied dance, but she had grown too tall too soon and had found another means of expression that consumed her. To Conan's eye, there was still a ghost of the dancer about her, even in worn Levi's, paint-smeared sweatshirt, and Birkenstocks. Her long hair was chocolate brown, tied at the nape of her neck with a blue scarf to keep it out of her way. Her face was plain and strong. Her mother's face, Conan realized as he saw her now in profile. Carla King had had the same candid profile, and the same gray eyes the color of a scrub jay's wing.

At the moment, Lise's gray eyes were focused with ferocious concentration on a three-inch-wide *hake* brush as she swept it across the painting on the table. Her focus didn't waver when she offered the vague assurance, "I'll be through in a minute."

Conan knelt to see if he could come to terms with Heather, relieved to find the sheltie willing to accept him in exchange for a good back rub. He worked his fingers through her thick, mahogany-hued coat, while she turned her long nose heavenward with an expression that could only be interpreted as bliss. At length she seemed satisfied and curled up under Lise's table.

He rose and looked around, finding himself in a large, cluttered room where living and working were inextricably mixed. A state-of-the-art woodstove crouched cold and ready in the center, while the east end was occupied with a bed and rudimentary kitchen. The remaining space was crowded with bookcases, paper cabinets, storage closets, and shelves filled with an undusted jumble of drawing pads, bouquets of brushes, tiny tubes of paint, dried leaves, rocks, seed heads, and an occasional animal skull.

And propped around the room at opportune spots were drawing boards on which were taped sheets of watercolor paper. Some had already made the magical transformation from flat, white surfaces to paintings; others were in various stages of transition. Lise seldom confined herself to recognizable subject matter, yet it was all recognizable on a deeper level, all born of the mountain and forest.

Conan crossed to a wicker chair near the stove, and, noting the clean ashtray on top of the stove, lit a cigarette, then settled back to study the extraordinary worlds caught in each rectangle, awed by the bold colors, the sheer courage in them, while the minute Lise had promised lengthened to twenty. But he wasn't impatient. He knew just enough about watercolor to understand its unforgiving nature. She couldn't stop until the paint was ready for her to stop. There was no going back with watercolor, no painting over or second thoughts.

He had finished his cigarette when at length she paused, squinted at the painting before her as she plunged the brush into a jar of water and stirred it with a hollow clanking. Then she shook the water out of the bristles and looked across at Conan, as if she had just remembered he was there.

"Thanks for coming, Conan."

"So far, it's been my pleasure. By the way, I have messages for you from Art Rasmussen."

She put the cover on her palette, laughing. "Yes, I know. He has two cords of wood split, the generator's in perfect working order, and Doris has enough food prepared to feed an army for a weekend. She's so embarrassed at having to leave early. Doesn't seem at all concerned that the reason she's leaving is to have a root canal."

Conan rose and went to one of the paintings propped against the windows. "Is this one for the Cassandra Gallery show?"

"All of them are. Would you like some coffee?"

"Yes, thanks." While she went to the kitchen area, he added, "You can consider this one sold."

Lise looked around at the painting. "Yes, that one worked. Okay, but you'll have to buy it through the gallery. Cass is having a hard enough time without my selling paintings sans commission."

"Considering the commissions you pay, I admire your loyalty."

She filled two hand-thrown, earth-hued mugs with coffee and handed him one, then kicked a big floor pillow near his chair and sank down onto it, folding her legs under her. "Cass keeps the commissions to forty percent, and when you run a gallery in Oregon, you need that. One of the greatest places in the world to paint, and one of the worst to sell paintings."

Conan returned to his chair, while Heather joined Lise on the pillow. He said, "Judging by your new surroundings, I'd say the sales are going well."

"Oh, Conan, I'd starve if I had to depend on sales. I'm a kept woman, really. When I graduated with an art major, Dad decided I'd need financial assistance. Of course, it helped that I was the lone girl-child. The boys never got a cent once Dad put them through college, unless it was a loan—fully documented and collateralized. But he figured it was okay to subsidize his girl-child, at least till I got married and had a man to take care of me. His words."

Conan tasted the coffee, not surprised to find it less than fresh. Lise wasn't famous for her coffee. "But that hasn't happened."

"And it won't." Her tone, which had been light and ironic, turned somber. "I guess he'll never understand that. To tell the truth, I have mixed feelings about the money, but I take it. In this line of work, you have to keep your priorities straight. Actually my new surroundings are a bequest from Mom. We were all surprised to find out how much she'd set aside and invested—all out of her household allowance. Can you imagine that? A grown woman having to live off an allowance? *Kids* get allowances. But it didn't seem to bother her. She understood the rules. And . . . she loved him."

"Carla King was an extraordinary woman." He leaned forward, resting his elbows on his knees. "Lise, do you want to tell me now why you asked me to come here?"

Her eyes flashed up to meet his, then she shrugged. "I was just seconding Dad's usual invitation when I wrote to you."

"You've never done that before. Lise, what's wrong? What are you afraid of?"

CHAPTER 2

Lise drew Heather into her lap, then gave Conan an oblique smile. "Are all PIs so perceptive? Yes, I know you're a private investigator even if you don't advertise it. It's sort of like having a Clark Kent in our midst."

Conan laughed as he reached for his cigarettes and lit one. "The mild-mannered bookshop proprietor who goes into a phone booth and emerges as a mild-mannered private eye? Lise, do you need a PI?"

"No. I just thought . . ." She frowned, then, "I guess what I was hoping for is a friendly outsider for this weekend."

"I suppose I fit that bill. Why do you need a friendly outsider?"

"To keep us on our good behavior. Conan, this family is close to disintegration. We need a time when we're all on our good behavior. If we can get through this weekend without falling apart, maybe that will lay a

13

foundation for the future. If we can't hold together now, well, when I think about that . . . yes, I'm afraid."

Conan studied her downcast face, and he realized for the first time that there was a new element in the paintings that filled the room: a stark bleakness underlying the rich color. He said, "Tell me about it."

"I'm not sure where to begin. With Mom's death, I suppose. She was the real center of this family, but I don't think any of us realized that, not even Dad. I guess he's too used to taking top billing just by sheer force of will, and Mom always let him think he was the star. Maybe in her mind he was. Oh . . ." Lise's shoulders slumped as her eyes flickered closed. "It was so hard, the dying. She had cancer, and it had already metastasized by the time it was diagnosed. It had never occurred to her to have any sort of regular physical. You only go to doctors when you're sick."

Conan sipped at his coffee. "Typical, Lise, of her generation and Eastern Oregon. Any rural culture, I suppose."

"Well, Mark finally talked her—and Dad, too—into getting a check-up and making Will Stewart their primary physician. Mark and Will have been friends since college, and Dad and Mom both liked him. He found the tumor. Of course, he's a GP, so he sent her to the oncologists. You've met Will, haven't you?"

"Yes, at your last gallery opening in Portland."

"Anyway, when Mom died, it hit Lucas hardest. Well, maybe not. Dad's so good at keeping a stopper on his emotions, it was hard to tell. Lucas *never* stoppered his feelings."

Her smile at that was fond and forgiving. Conan had met Lucas Jackson King both here at the lodge and at gallery openings, and he was aware of the soul-deep rapport between brother and sister. They were fraternal twins, and no doubt even if they didn't share as many genes as identical twins, there was a kinship that ordinary siblings couldn't share established in nine months together in the close embrace of the womb.

Conan asked, "Is Lucas coming today?"

Her breath caught. "No. Not today, not ever. Soon after Mom died, he moved his architectural firm to Los Angeles. Doing very well, he tells me. By phone. He never writes. In fact, he's taken to life in the California fast lane like a sunflower to the sun. He's branched out into contracting. He always had the artistic talent *and* a head for business."

"Is that why he opted for California's fast lane? Because of his head for business?"

"No. LJK Unlimited was grossing a million a year here. He said he went to L.A. looking for greener pastures, but I knew better. He wanted to get away from Dad. Even before Mom died, Lucas and Dad were going at it. Lucas kept saying Dad wasn't doing enough for her. He even accused Dad of wanting her out of the way. Well, that was insane. When she died, it broke Dad's heart. I think Lucas just wanted someone to blame for the pain, and for him, Dad was the obvious scapegoat."

Conan took time for a puff on his cigarette before asking, "Why?"

"Oh, because they never really got along. The trouble was, Lucas was always Mom's favorite. She tried not to show it, but it was obvious. When we were kids, I was a little jealous of him, and I know Al was a *lot* jealous. Al was ten years older and used to being the alpha. The sibling rivalry was vicious sometimes. Al and Lucas were always fighting about one thing or another." Then she laughed. "But Lucas was smart—even sneaky on occasion—and he always had Mom on his side. Of course, by the time Lucas was eight, Al was off to college."

"How did Mark fit into the hierarchy?"

"Right in the middle. The essential middle child. Al kept him in his place, and he couldn't compete for Mom's affection with Lucas. Damn, I wonder if all siblings go at each other so hard. And I was low person on the totem pole as far as all three boys were concerned. But if there was any sort of outside threat to their little sister, they closed ranks so fast, nobody could get past them. When I was a teenager, I didn't much appreciate that. They seemed to think every boy I dated was a threat. Conan, do you have brothers or sisters?"

Cumulus clouds were materializing in the sky now, casting shadows on the flanks of the mountain. "I had a younger brother. He died when I was thirteen. The same time my mother died."

Lise was silent for a moment, her gray eyes shadowed, reflecting her own grief. "I'm sorry."

"It was a bad winter. So Lucas departed for greener pastures after your mother died?"

"Yes, although he came up from L.A. occasionally for family gatherings, like Christmas and the Fourth of July. When he and Dad ended up in the same room, they were like two tomcats circling, but it wasn't till Dad remarried that the hissing and clawing really started."

Conan frowned after a memory. Something he'd read in a newspaper about A. C. King's second wife. The marriage itself hadn't been publicized. He asked, "When was that?"

"The marriage? Three years ago. Two years after Mom died." Lise rose and stretched, then turned to look out at the mountain. "Kimberly Kaiser. She was head of the wood products division's accounting department at

Ace Timber. Before that, she worked for Al's construction company. Well, it was still King and Ryder then. When Jerry Ryder had to retire, Al bought out his share of the partnership. Now it's just King Construction Company."

Conan waited, then had to ask, "What's she like?"

"Kim?" Lise turned to face him, hands pushing into the pockets of her Levi's. "She's my age. Thirty-six. Very attractive. Good bones."

"The usual May-December romance?"

Lise thought about that, then, "No, I don't think so. Kim's . . . hard to read, maybe, but I think she's made Dad happy."

"But not Lucas?"

"Oh, God, no. He thinks she's a gold-digging bimbo. Anyway, it was a quiet wedding, just the family and a few friends, but Lucas didn't show up till the reception." Lise seemed to be looking back into memory, finding something there that frightened her. "He unloaded everything, all the resentment, all the grief. And Dad fired back at him. They went at it at the top of their lungs, and finally Dad hit him. Floored him, literally. That's when Lucas said Dad would never see him again, and of course Dad said that was fine with him, and he could consider himself disinherited. Or words to that effect."

"Disinherited?" Conan blew out a contemplative stream of smoke. "Did A. C. go through with that?"

"No, but he would have if it weren't for Kim. Dad never was good at forgiving. It was Kim who convinced him he should hold off, and maybe Lucas would come around. Dad told me that. Later, I told Lucas that Kim had saved his slice of the estate, but he wasn't impressed. He's not very good at forgiving, either. Is your coffee cold?"

"It's fine. How did the rest of the family react to A. C.'s bride?"

"Well, no one seemed overjoyed." She leaned down to pick up her mug, tasted the coffee, and grimaced. "I'll make a new pot." She took his mug and crossed to the kitchen, and as she filled the coffeemaker's reservoir, added, "But Lucas was the only one who challenged it, although I think Al was just as upset. That's odd, too." She paused to count spoonfuls of coffee into the filter basket. "He seemed more broken up about Dad's remarrying than he did about Mom's death."

Conan didn't verbalize the possibility that Al King was concerned about *his* slice of the estate, which might have been diminished by the marriage. That uncharitable thought arose from Conan's initial impression of Al: a man who fancied himself a stud and valued power, but whose only real source of power was his father; a Vietnam veteran who emerged from that emotional crucible unscathed and convinced that it had been a just war. But he had served in the Air Force and seen nothing of the ground war. Besides, Al was, like his father, a staunch Republican who accepted the party's tenets as articles of faith.

But that assessment, Conan reminded himself, had been made years ago, and it didn't account for what had always seemed an anomaly in Al King's life: he had married a Vietnamese woman.

A. C. had earned the nickname Ace as a flyer in the Pacific theatre in World War II, and perhaps that was where he acquired his distaste for people of Asian ancestry. Not that he was any more tolerant of blacks, Hispanics, or anyone who didn't fit the WASP mold. Al's choice of a non-WASP wife must have been a major revolt against his father.

Lise laughed softly. "You never did care much for Al, did you?"

Conan looked around at her, then shrugged. "No. At least, I always found him hard to understand."

"Oh, I think you understand him. Actually I don't especially *like* him, but families are irrational entities. He's my brother. In spite of everything, I care about him, and I'd probably kill for him under the right circumstances." She smiled wryly. "Maybe it's instinctive. I'm driven to protect my genes in my siblings. Isn't that the latest theory? But, you know, I've never understood family murders. History is full of them. The newspapers are full of them. Yet it seems to me it would mean going against hard-wired instinct. It shouldn't be possible."

Conan stubbed out his cigarette. "Maybe not for a properly wired brain, but—"

Whatever he might have had to say about the wiring of brains was cut off by an explosion of barking as Heather leapt from the floor pillow and raced to the door.

Lise said, "That must be Art."

But the man who appeared at the screen was not Art Rasmussen. Lise stared at him, then ran to the door with an exultant shout.

"Lucas!"

CHAPTER 3

Lise flung the screen door open and herself into Lucas's arms, while Heather drowned their joyful greetings with increasingly ferocious barking. But when Lucas knelt to talk to the sheltie, he had her enthusiastically wagging her tail in a matter of seconds.

Conan waited by his chair, noting the uncanny resemblance between these fraternal twins. Lucas Jackson King even had his sister's grace, although his was the grace of an athlete, not a dancer. Tennis, perhaps. Whatever his sport, it kept him in the sun, and his tan made his gray eyes startling by contrast. He wore a casual linen suit, cut wide at the shoulders, over a brown turtleneck that was probably silk. His sun-streaked hair was long enough to fall forward across his forehead until he pushed it back, but cut close at the back and sides.

He was saying, "Well, you probably won't believe this, Lise, and I'm damned sure Dad won't, but I came to make my peace." Lise stared at him as he gave her his trademark crooked grin, then turned and offered Conan his hand. "Conan! How the hell are you?"

"Fine, Lucas. You look well." Then feeling himself the third that made a crowd here, he added, "Lise, I'd better go unload my luggage—"

"Hey, don't leave on my account," Lucas cut in. "You're staying for the weekend?" When Conan nodded, Lucas laughed. "Don't tell me you've come for the ascent of King's Mountain?"

"Well, that seems to be highlight of the weekend."

Lucas laughed again, shaking his head. "Weird, isn't it? Grown men playing king of the mountain on a foothill."

Lise took his arm and intoned with weighted irony, "Lucas, it isn't the height of the mountain, it's the excuse for male bonding." She included Conan in her wry smile. "I followed Dad and the boys once. I was eight years old, and I couldn't understand why Mom and I were never allowed on the hike. I thought there must be deep, dark secrets revealed at the top of King's Mountain."

"I remember that." Lucas hugged her affectionately. "We didn't even know you were around till it got dark."

"Of course not. I hid in the trees all day with only a package of Oreo cookies to sustain me. When you guys got to the top of the mountain, I was convinced I was going to see some mysterious ceremonies, but you just sat up there and ate lunch, which was one of the major disappointments of my childhood. Then when you came back to the campsite on Loblolly Creek, well, I was *sure* I'd see the arcane rituals then. Ha! All you did was incinerate wieners, while I was sitting in the dark freezing."

Lucas put in, "Oh, Conan, you should've seen her when she finally came out of the woods. Shivering, scared silly, eyes as big as saucers."

"I was not scared!" Lise objected, then laughed.

"Well, there's a lot of strange sounds out in the woods in a pitch-black night. I kept hearing bears. Of course, I don't know whether I was more scared of those invisible bears or of Dad when he found out I'd followed you."

Lucas nodded, his laughter fading to an introspective smile. "But Dad didn't get mad at you, did he?"

"No." She sighed. "He just took me on his lap and wrapped his jacket around me and held me till I stopped shivering. You know, that's the only time I remember Dad holding me like that. Usually it's just a quick hug. Even when Mom died . . ."

She stopped, looking at her brother with searching eyes, and Lucas said, "There were no arcane secrets revealed on those hikes, Lise, but there was . . . well, call it male bonding. I have a lot of good memories from King's Mountain."

"Is that why you came back now?"

"Yes. It seemed like a good time to try to make my peace with Dad." Then he turned on his quick laughter again. "Conan, I don't know whether Lise told you, but I've been, well, you might say *away*."

Conan nodded. "I understand you've set up shop in Los Angeles."

"Yes, but before I left Oregon, I said some things to Dad I shouldn't have. Never was good at holding things in, as Lise can tell you."

She said softly, "Oh, Lucas, I'm so glad you came back. If you can make your peace with Dad, maybe there's hope for Mark, too."

Lucas embraced his sister without questioning that. Nor did Conan question it, although Lise hadn't mentioned any dissension between Mark and A. C. But this wasn't the time to ask her about it.

Then Lucas looked at Lise, his hands resting on her

shoulders, his smile secretive, almost childlike. "Lise, I'm a changed man. You'll see. And now I have some-one I want you to meet."

"Is she the cause of this miraculous change?"

Lucas didn't ask how Lise knew this someone was a *she*. "Yes, she's the cause." Then he went to the door and out onto the porch.

Lise glanced at Conan with a smile that sent color to her cheeks. But a moment later the smile vanished. Lucas had returned with his someone, and Conan was absently aware that he, like Lise, was staring. He was looking at one of the most beautiful women he had ever seen.

Lucas said, "This is Demara Wilder," then grinned, obviously enjoying the silence this woman created.

Conan wondered if Lucas assumed the silence was one of consternation because Demara Wilder was black. If so, he misjudged his audience. That she was black was relevant only because her beauty was a product of her racial heritage. She was at least six feet tall, with long, lithe muscles forming subtle, sustained curves dis-played to advantage in a short skirt and halter of deep, cool red, with a voluminous black shirt of a filmy cot-ton draped around her shoulders. Her skin had the flaw-less texture of satin; her magnificent eyes gleamed night black under curved lids, and her hair was straight and short, combed forward in a cap that emphasized the fine shape of her head.

Lise blurted, "Have you ever modeled?"

Demara glanced at Lucas, laughed, and replied in a voice as satiny as her skin, "That's how I've made my living since I was five."

Lucas said, "I think Lise has a different kind of mod-eling in mind." Then to Lise, "If you ever read fashion magazines, you'd recognize Demara's face from *Vogue*, *Bazaar*, *Vanity Fair* . . . et cetera."

Demara shrugged. "Oh, Lucas, it's been a while since my face has been in any of those magazines."

"Their loss. Demara, this is my sister Lise." Lise offered her hand and a smile, then Lucas turned to Conan. "And this is Conan Flagg, bookshop owner and private investigator."

As Conan exchanged greetings with Demara, he wondered why Lucas had chosen to introduce him in that way.

Demara didn't comment, but looked around the studio with an air of indifferent curiosity. "Lucas says you're a really good artist, Lise."

Conan bristled at what seemed to be faint praise, but Lise apparently didn't notice it. She was studying Lucas with a distracted frown, and Conan guessed she was thinking past the aesthetic beauty of Lucas's *someone* and wondering what kind of reception Demara would get from A. C. King, who had never bothered to expunge from his vocabulary such words as *spic*, *hymie*, *wetback*, *Jap*, and *nigger*.

Lucas went to Lise and took both her hands. "Don't worry. He'll come around, Lise. He finally accepted Loanh, didn't he?"

"Only after she presented him with a male grandchild—who looks more like Al than Loanh."

"Lucky Charles," Lucas returned acidly. Then he made a show of checking his watch. "Well, it's twelve-thirty. If the traditional schedule still holds, Dad should be arriving soon. Demara . . ." He looked at her, his gray eyes warming. "Brace yourself."

But she only laughed. "Lucas, I can take care of myself."

Conan didn't doubt that.

CHAPTER 4

Lise and Lucas, deep in private conversation, walked ahead on the path to the lodge with Heather trailing them. Demara seemed content with Conan as an escort. He asked the stock questions, and she replied with stock answers. Yes, this was her first trip to *Oregawn*, as she pronounced it, but she'd heard they had year-round skiing here. No, she wasn't doing much modeling lately. When her career hit the twenty-year mark, she didn't mind easing up. She still did occasional assignments. She didn't mention any particular publications. Yes, she and Lucas had known each other a long time. Nearly a year. They met at a party at a friend's house in Malibu.

As Conan and Demara crossed the lawn to the deck at the west end of the lodge, she studied him with a dubious smile and asked, "Are you really a PI?"

"Well, I carry a license to that effect, but fortunately I don't have to depend on it for a living."

"Your bookshop must be a gold mine, then. That *is* your Jag in the garage, isn't it?"

"Yes, it is." Conan didn't comment on what kind of gold mine the crotchety old Holliday Beach Book Shop had proved to be. It was his pride and joy, as well as a source of figurative and literal headaches, but it had never produced enough gold to even pay for the upkeep of the XK-E.

They had reached the south end of the deck. Lucas and Lise were already at the far corner, Lucas apparently surveying the deck's construction with an expert eye.

Demara smiled up at the sun that pounded the cedar planking. "This is terrific! Warmest spot I've been for days." She went to one of the two lounge chairs, asked, "Think anybody'll mind?" as she disposed her lithe body like an odalisque on one of the chairs, and obviously didn't expect any objections.

Conan certainly had none. He walked on down the deck, passing the kitchen's bay window and the four French doors into the living room, all of them open. He noted that A. C. had retained the outdoor fireplace and grill and incorporated it into the west side of the deck. Near the fireplace a picnic table stood draped with a checkered tablecloth for the evening's cookout. He also noted as he reached the corner of the building that A. C.'s come-and-get-it bell was still there: a bronze bell, perhaps a foot in diameter, that had once rung-in the students at a one-room schoolhouse near Pendleton.

Lise and Lucas were leaning on the deck railing near the atrium when Conan caught up with them. The blue pickup was gone, which meant the Rasmussens had departed, Doris to meet her fate in a Portland dentist's chair. A. C. hadn't arrived yet.

As Conan approached, Lucas asked, "Where's Demara?"

"She's enjoying the sun on one of the lounge chairs."

"Complaining about the cold, I suppose. I told her to wear something warmer, but when you live in Southern California it's hard to understand there's a happy medium between bikinis and ski pants."

That was spoken in a tone of bemused tolerance that made Lise smile but didn't dispel the anxiety shadowing her eyes. Conan understood it. If Lucas was as infatuated with Demara Wilder as he seemed to be, that might create an insurmountable obstacle between him and his father.

Heather, who had been lying at Lise's feet, clambered upright, ears on full alert, but she didn't bark, only whined impatiently. Lise looked down the road and said with a resigned sigh, "Here they come."

A black car emerged from the alders at the curve of the road. Lucas resolutely took his stand a few feet from the front door at the top of the two steps that led down to the asphalt, while Lise moved to Conan's side, shaking her head. "I told him I'd talk to Dad first to sort of cushion the shock, but ... well, Lucas always was stubborn."

The car was, not surprisingly, a shining new Cadillac DeVille. A. C. King could easily afford a Rolls-Royce, but it was against his principles to buy any car that wasn't made in the U.S.A. No doubt the downsizing of American cars had put a crimp in his vehicular style, but the DeVille still made a suitable entrance, humming sedately across the asphalt. The tinted windows hid its occupants.

When the Cadillac stopped in front of the atrium, and the passenger door opened, Conan watched curiously as Kimberly Kaiser King got out. Attractive, Lise had said.

Good bones. That was manifestly true. She wore sunglasses but no hat, and her hair was white-wine blonde,
cut in a short, casual style. She looked every inch the
country gentlewoman, with her beige cords and sweater,
her leather-piped blazer of beige and pale blue plaid,
and her Ferragamo flats. She surveyed the deck, focused on Lucas King.

But he didn't seem to see her. He waited, immobile,
as his father got out of the car, slammed the door, and
glared at him with his hands resting in fists on top of
the car.

There was about Albert Charles King an elemental
quality, like a slab of granite, its surface weathered to
tan, but underneath, ice gray and impervious. His face
was webbed with creases, emphasized by the squint that
hid his eyes, set deep under bristling brows. His gray
hair still had a reddish cast, but it had receded until only
a wispy veil covered the top of his head. Yet there was
no slump in his wide shoulders, no stoop in his uncompromising posture. And nothing of the country gentle-
man about him. He wore Levi's, leather work boots,
and a red plaid shirt, and his freckled hands were those
of an old timber faller rather than a manicured CEO.

He strode to the deck steps, and it occurred to Conan
that Lucas had chosen the place to take his stand for the
subtle advantage of looking down at his father. But A.
C. didn't concede the advantage. He mounted to the
deck, forcing Lucas to back up. "What the hell are *you*
doing here?"

Lucas met his burning gaze unflinchingly. "Dad, I've
come to make my peace with you, to tell you . . . to tell
you I'm sorry."

Conan heard Lise's quick intake of breath as A. C.
dismissed that with a snorting laugh. "I told you, you

can't expect any help from me. The answer's the same. On the phone or in person."

Lucas looked puzzled, then produced his crooked smile. "That little problem has been taken care of, Dad. Before we left L.A., I got the bid to design and contract a thirty-million-dollar office complex."

Conan frowned at that exchange. Had Lucas phoned his father in hope of financial assistance? If so, he must have been truly desperate.

A. C. offered a grudging, "Well, I'm glad to hear it."

"Dad, I was out of my mind," Lucas said, thrusting his hands in his pockets. "I mean, when Mom was sick and . . . afterward. I just didn't know how to handle it. I loved Mom so damn much—"

"You think *I* didn't?"

"No, I don't think that," Lucas replied steadily. "Maybe I did then, because you . . . well, you didn't *show* it. But I understand now—"

"I didn't *show* it? You mean I didn't go around blubbering like a woman—"

"I mean because I didn't *understand* then. I do now, Dad. And another thing I understand: Mom wouldn't have minded your marrying again. She'd never have wanted you to be alone forever."

That assertion silenced the retort A. C. had ready, and Kim came up beside him, taking his arm while Lucas went on: "Dad I said things to you I'll regret the rest of my life. I can't take them back. All I can do is apologize." He turned to Kim, gave her a wistful smile. "I can't take back what I said to you, either, Kim, but I wish I could. If you can make Dad happy, I know that's what Mom would have wanted."

Conan had a clear view of Kim King's face, but the sunglasses masked her reaction. She started to speak, but A. C. cut her off with "Damn you, Lucas, you can't just waltz in here and—"

"A. C., just hush." Kim spoke in a matter-of-fact tone that reminded Conan of Carla King. "Your son has offered me a gracious apology, and I intend to accept it. I understand what grief can do. Lucas, thank you. I know it didn't come easy."

A. C. seemed, atypically, unsure of himself, but finally he cleared his throat and muttered, "Well, Lucas, I'm . . . glad you could make it for the reunion."

He offered his son no handshake, certainly no embrace, but perhaps that grudging welcome was of equal significance. Lise sighed gustily, and Heather, who had remained silent at her side, ran to A. C., as if she had just been freed from a leash.

The sheltie's exuberance broke the tension, and A. C. knelt to give her a rough rubbing, then embraced Lise with a brief hug, asking, "How's my girl?" For Conan, he had a vigorous handshake and a welcome. And an introduction to his new wife.

Kim took off her sunglasses, revealing eyes as blue as the mountain sky. As Conan made the expected responses, he was thinking that those eyes could be mesmerizing. For him, they were warmly polite, but behind that he saw a glittering amusement mixed with curiosity and a quality he couldn't define until the word *audacity* came to mind.

She said, "I'm delighted you could come, Conan."

It was at that almost jovial moment that A. C.'s gaze fixed on some point beyond Conan's head with an expression that shaded in a split second from surprise to contempt to suspicion. "Who the hell is *that*?"

That was Demara Wilder, walking toward them at a leisurely pace, as sensuous as a stalking leopard.

Lucas watched her with a smile bordering on the fatuous, while Kim glanced from Lucas to A. C., who asked irritably, "She come with you, Lucas? Well, she's a looker—for a nigger."

Lucas's head whipped around, his gray eyes fiercely cold, while Lise leaned close to her father and whispered, "Dad, I swear, if you use that word again, I'll never forgive you."

A. C. seemed puzzled. "Well, hell, Lise, that's what she *is*."

"Dad, for God's sake!"

If Demara heard this *sotto voce* exchange, she gave no indication, only taking Lucas's hand as he drew her close. He said, "This is a friend of mine. Demara Wilder. She was one of the models for a brochure LJK put out last year. Demara, this is my stepmother, Kim, and my father."

There was a prickly silence, then Kim smiled and said, "I'm glad to meet you, Demara."

Demara acknowledged that with a simple, "Thanks, Kim," then looked at A. C. with a challenging gaze that even he seemed to find intimidating, especially since she was tall enough to stand eye to eye with him. But he was spared the necessity of meeting her challenge by Heather's announcement of another arrival.

He turned away, squinted out at the road. "Somebody's coming."

Lise in particular seemed to welcome the distraction, but Conan was watching Demara, and what he read in her hooded eyes and flared nostrils was akin to disgust.

A. C. folded his sinewy arms and said, "Looks like Al and Luanne."

Al's wife's name was Loanh, but A. C. always called her Luanne, apparently finding her Vietnamese name too subtle for his tongue.

The approaching car was also a Cadillac, an inevita-

ble choice for Albert Charles King, *Junior*, but Al's was
a white convertible. It was also, Conan noted, at least
five years old. Al drove with more verve than his father,
wheeling past the small crowd gathered on the deck and
on into the garage. Within seconds, he came striding toward the deck, shouting over his shoulder, "Just leave
it. We'll get it later."

Al had clearly recognized his brother. He approached
at full steam with no hint of pleasurable anticipation in
the set of his jaw, and Conan realized how much a
clone of his father Al was becoming as he aged. They
had the same slablike physique, although Al obviously
spent more time in a gym; his blue polo shirt showed
off brawny arms and hinted at a muscular torso. His
hair was sandy blond, as A. C.'s had been in his youth,
but Al sported a mustache. He also sported aviator's
sunglasses, and no doubt felt he presented a macho image.

Conan sighed, wondering why uncharitable thoughts
came so easily with Al King.

Possibly because the peace—or perhaps it should be
characterized as a cease-fire—established between
Lucas and A. C. was a fragile thing, and it didn't seem
likely that Al would regret seeing it broken. His opening gambit was a caustic, "Jesus, Lucas, I was hoping
you'd keep one promise in your life when you said
you'd never come back."

Lucas only laughed at that. "Great to see you, too,
Al."

Perhaps Conan's role as friendly outsider finally had
some effect. A. C. glanced at him before he said, "Al,
we're all here for a nice weekend together, so just settle. Where's Lu—oh, there she is. Well, Luanne, you're
looking pretty as ever."

Loanh King had trailed Al at a circumspect distance,

and now she quickened her pace and called up a smile. "Thank you, A. C."

Loanh was, indeed, pretty as ever, showing little sign of aging in the last six years, although she must be at least forty now. Her blue-black hair, caught in a sleek swirl at the crown of her head, betrayed no hint of gray. She was scarcely over five feet tall with hands like a jade figurine. The same delicacy shaped her face, sloe-eyed and high-cheeked. She was dressed for a weekend in the country in twill slacks and a beige cableknit sweater, but the ensemble didn't become her. Silk and pearls would be more appropriate.

And clear eyes, Conan thought, would be more typical. She had been crying.

Al glared at Lucas, but he apparently decided to settle. Or perhaps he was simply distracted by Demara Wilder. One eyebrow shot up above his sunglasses as he asked bluntly, "Who's this?"

Lucas replied coolly, "*This* is a friend of mine. Demara, *this* is Al, my *older* brother. And, Al, you can just keep your hands to yourself."

"Don't worry, little brother, I never had a taste for dark m—"

"Well, I don't know why we're all standing around outside," Kim cut in briskly. "Come on, A. C., let's get our things upstairs. Lise, would you show Lucas and Demara to their room? They can have the one next to Conan's. Al, you and Loanh will be in the east room, as usual. . . ."

With that, Kim effectively got everyone moving and—what was no doubt more critical at the moment—separated.

CHAPTER 5

The garage was full, a problem Conan didn't concern himself about except to wonder if Mark and Tiff would get their noses out of joint at having to park outside. He got his duffel bag and parka out of his car and headed for the door on the west wall, passing a blatantly un-American, silver Mercedes convertible, then Al's white Cadillac convertible, and finally, nearest the door, A. C.'s black DeVille.

The door opened onto the atrium, which was to Conan's eye an architectural gem—an octagonal space twenty feet across, its oak floor glowing with a waxed patina. He entered on the east face of the octagon. The front door occupied the north face, while the two faces flanking it consisted of windows divided into beveled panes that fragmented the image of Mount Hood. On the west face, a wide archway opened into the living and dining room. The southeast face consisted of a wood-paneled wall that served to show off one of Lise's watercolors, an atypically realistic rendering of the mountain. On the south face a closet was nearly hidden in the paneling, and the remaining face was open to accommodate the stairway to the second floor. But what always fascinated Conan was the vaulted ceiling with its radiating pattern of massive, ponderosa-pine beams. It was like looking up into the interior of a huge umbrella. Hanging from its apex, thirty feet above the floor, a wrought-iron chandelier, suspended on a chain of hand-forged links, took up the octagonal theme.

There was about this room and the entire lodge an authenticity derived from the fact that almost everything in it was handmade. Unsung hands and minds were evident in every detail, from the carving of native plants on the front door to the framing of the arched doorway, to the wrought-iron light fixtures, doorknobs, and strap hinges. Even most of the furniture was handmade. These artisans had stamped their presence upon this building. It was their immortality.

"Oh, Conan, I didn't mean to leave you standing in the lobby. Come on, I'll show you to your room."

Conan looked up to see Lise on the stairway. He followed her upstairs to the hall that traversed the length of the building at right angles to the stairway, and her characterization of the lodge as a hotel was particularly apt here. The hall was wood paneled, as were all the rooms, the oak floor cushioned with runners of oriental carpeting. Light was provided by amber glass lamps in wrought-iron sconces next to each of the eight bedroom doors.

Lise led him through the door across the hall from the stairway into the same bedroom he had occupied six years ago. She made a show of opening the muslin curtains on the window on the opposite wall, patting the pillows on the bed on the left-hand wall, opening the bathroom door to the left of the bed, then crossing the room to check the wood box next to the small fireplace. Finally she returned to him, said, "I hope everything is satisfactory, sir," and held out her hand.

Conan laughed and made an ironic bow as he kissed her hand. "I'll call room service if I need anything." Then he sobered. "So far, it looks like there's hope for an armistice between A. C. and Lucas."

"So far." She sighed and pushed a straying strand of hair back from her face. "I'm not sure I believe it yet, but it's a start."

"Lise, why should *Mark* need to make his peace with A. C.?"

"Mark? Well, that's a long story. I'll tell you about it later. Right now I'd better get down to the kitchen to help Kim. We'll have a cookout on the deck for dinner, as usual, but Doris left cold snacks to tide everyone over."

Conan nodded as he dropped his duffel and parka on the bed. "I assume there'll be no formal recognition of A. C.'s birthday—as usual?"

"No. I thought he might relent this year, since it's sort of a special birthday. His seventieth. But I talked to Kim, and she said her advice was to cool it. Stay with the hallowed traditions."

"Well, it's *his* birthday. I'll be down in a few minutes if I can help."

"In the kitchen?" She gave a curt laugh. "Conan, that's *woman's* work." With that, she departed, closing the door behind her.

Conan looked around the room. It seemed more familiar than it should have from his memory of it six years ago, perhaps because it reminded him of his childhood room in the old house at the Ten-Mile Ranch where he grew up. It had the same beamed ceiling angling down to the outside wall, with the window set in a deep dormer. But his room had been smaller, and instead of a handwoven rug with a Haida raven motif, there had been a braided rug his grandmother had made from discarded scraps; instead of a queen-sized bed adorned with a green satin comforter, a narrow bed covered with a Star of Bethlehem quilt; and instead of an adjoining bath, generously furnished, a long trek downstairs to the one bathroom, and that had been considered a luxury after the years in which the Flaggs of two generations had braved dark and stormy—and often frigid—nights to reach the outdoor privy.

Perhaps the similarity was in that quality of handmadeness. The fireplace was faced with dark gray basalt, each block shaped and laid by hand. The bed, the small tables on either side, the desk to the left of the window, the chest of drawers on the right, the wardrobe to the right of the door, the armchair in front of the fireplace, were all crafted by hand.

But there was nothing in his childhood experiences to equate with the tensions that threatened this family. He remembered his last visit here and the easy camaraderie that had existed between the members of the family. He remembered Carla King, with her soft voice, her brown hair muted with silver, the lively intelligence in her gray eyes.

Our center is gone....

Conan went to the window, an old-fashioned sash window, turned the lock, and pulled the sash up. The air was warm, a taste of summer in it, yet with a dry tang that declared the true season. He looked out at young hemlocks with their tops gently bowed, shrubby salal at their feet, shiny leaves dull now, patched with brown and scarlet. The mossy ground was only three feet below the window; the lodge had been built into a hill so that the bedrooms at the back of the second story were at ground level. To the west, the hill sloped down, making a more precipitous drop from the windows in the next bedroom.

Conan leaned against the window frame, realizing that he was putting off going downstairs. Defusing familial tensions was not his forte. On the other hand, he believed fervently that anyone possessed of as much talent as Lise King should not have to suffer the anxieties to which lesser mortals were subject. He did not believe that art was necessarily a product of suffering, but rather that suffering was usually unavoidable, and some people managed to produce art in spite of it.

Holding on to that thought, he shut the window and left the room.

When he reached the atrium, he heard voices from the living room and saw Lise, Kim, and Loanh laying out the cold buffet on the dining table at the far end of the room by the French windows. The front door was open, and he went out onto the deck, where A. C. stood gazing at the mountain. He turned at the sound of Conan's footsteps.

"Conan! Damn, it's good to see you again. Been a long time." Then he added with a sigh, "Lot of water under the bridge."

Conan nodded. "Especially for you. I'll miss Carla."

"Yeah. We all do." He squinted toward the cloud-shadowed mountain. "Sorry you had to see that little set-to. I mean, with Lucas."

Conan said carefully, "It seems to have resolved itself."

"Maybe." He focused on the road and the vehicle emerging from the alders, a dust-beige Vanagon, advancing with a typical VW sputter. "That's Will!" Then he added by way of explanation, "Will Stewart. Friend of Mark's from their varsity football days at OSU."

"Yes, I've met Will. He's your doctor now, isn't he?"

"Yeah. He's hitched up with a real nice clinic in the West Hills. He was Carla's doctor, too. Really hurt him when nobody could help her." For all the craggy stoniness of A. C.'s features, they were remarkably expressive, and Conan watched the old grief renew its hold then dissipate in an avuncular smile as the Vanagon came to a stop.

The man who emerged in worn cords and sweatshirt was a year or so shy of forty and an inch or so shy of six feet, with a muscular body that suggested he could still play a passable game of football. He had typical Scots coloring: fair, freckled skin and pink cheeks that made him always look as if he'd just come in from the cold; unruly red hair and equally unruly eyebrows over eyes somewhere between gray and green.

He extended a broad hand as he mounted the steps to the deck. "A. C., you look great. Am I late? Had an emergency at the storefront."

"No schedule here, Will. Mark and Tiff haven't even arrived yet."

Will's hand went out to Conan. "Hey, it's great to see you again, Conan. How's everything at the coast?"

Conan restrained a gasp of pain as his hand was crushed in a vicelike but mercifully brief grip. "Fine, Will. You're still running the storefront clinic on Burnside?"

"Three days a week." Then casting a sidelong glance at A. C., he added, "Us knee-jerk liberals have to keep ourselves occupied."

A. C. laughed. "Yeah, you keep 'em healthy, so I can pay out my taxes on welfare to keep 'em in cheap wine."

If Will had any retort for that, he apparently forgot it.
Lise had just come out on the deck. His cheeks glowed
pinker, his smile turned into a longing grin, and Conan
sighed. This, at least, hadn't changed.

"Will!" Lise crossed to him, gave him a sisterly embrace. "Oh, Will, it's so good to see you. Mark didn't
tell me you were coming."

It was obvious that Will Stewart wished the embrace
had been less sisterly. "Well, I wasn't sure I *could*
come, and I may have to leave early. Got a patient due
to go into labor this weekend. Hello, Heather. How're
you doing, pretty girl?" He leaned down to pet the sheltie, whose tail-wagging greeting made it evident that
they'd met before.

Lise said, "I came out to announce that lunch is on
the dining room table. Serve yourselves anytime."

Will asked, "One of Doris's simple little buffets? Terrific. But I better unload my stuff first and get the van
out of the way."

"I'll help you," Lise volunteered.

He opened the side door of the VW. "Well, I've just
got the one bag. . . . Oh, there's this thing." He handed
her an attaché case equipped with a combination lock,
adding, "Just my emergency case and some of the medications I can't leave at the storefront."

As they started into the lodge, she said, "I'll put you
in one of the little bedrooms at the front. Oh, by the
way, Lucas is here. . . ."

When Lise and Will were gone, A. C. said, "I keep
hoping those two will finally get together. Will's a good
man. Make a fine husband for Lise, but she can't seem
to come down to earth enough to see it."

Conan wouldn't have ventured a comment on that
under any circumstances, and he was relieved that he
didn't have to. The distraction was provided by Lucas

and Demara, approaching arm in arm along the deck.
They had changed clothing, Lucas into Levi's and a
chamois shirt, Demara into white stirrup pants and an
outsized white sweater with a tantalizing V-neck.

Lucas was undoubtedly aware of the cool look A. C.
sent Demara, but he only slipped his arm around her
waist and smiled. "This deck is a great idea, Dad.
Should've done it years ago. Who built it?"

"Al contracted it a couple of years ago. Did a damn
good job, too."

"Nobody can fault Al's building, Dad."

A. C. raised an eyebrow, then frowned as he looked
toward the road. "Well, finally. Here comes Mark."

Lucas asked, "Are they bringing the girls?"

"No. Didn't want to take 'em out of school. They're
at Saint Anne's, you know. At least . . . Diana and
Nancy are." Then he turned his squint on the gray Lincoln Continental careening up the road.

Before it jerked to a stop in front of the Vanagon,
Will and the rest of the family had gathered on the
deck. A. C. stood next to Kim with his hand resting on
her shoulder. Lise and Loanh were talking together
about Loanh's daughter, Carla Thuan, and Oregon State
University's art department. Al hung back by the door,
muscular arms crossed, head cocked to one side. The
shaded aviator's glasses gave him the expressionless an-
onymity of a Secret Service agent.

Tiff was driving, and the reason for that was evident
as soon as Mark opened the passenger door: His right
foot was encased in a navy blue walking shoe with
Velcro straps latticing a Fiberglas cast. Conan leaned toward Lise to ask, "What happened to Mark's foot?"

"Didn't I tell you? He broke his ankle a week or so
ago. Said he fell off his deck. Something like that."

Conan nodded, then restrained a smile as he watched

Tiffany Rose Dalhousie King, small and erratically vivacious, her green eye shadow matching the unlikely green of her eyes, emerge from the car talking, a condition that seemed permanent. It came out as a stream of sound as haphazard as her ensemble of heliotrope harem pants and a pink shirt big enough for three of her, on top of which she wore a sort of vest brocaded in yellow and orange flowers and adorned with foot-long fringes. Her forehead was bound with a purple scarf, and above it her red-gold hair erupted in a permed frizz.

" . . . *totally* forgot they're working on the Markham Bridge, you know, and we had to make a *huge* detour. Oh, Loanh, allergies? I have an aloe eye poultice that'll just do *wonders*. Hi, Lise, did we drag you away from your work? Oh, isn't it a *gorgeous* day. I mean just *smell* that air! Will, why don't you help Mark with those *silly* crutches? Hi, Dad, Kim . . . *Lucas*?"

That shut off the verbal stream. She stood openmouthed, while Mark, securely mounted on his crutches, grinned and swung toward Lucas, who met him half way. "Lucas, you son of a gun, you made it!"

They embraced, and Lucas asked, "Mark, what'd you do to your foot? Didn't fall off your golf cart, did you?"

Mark seemed uncomfortable with that, mumbling, "Hell, it was the hot tub that got me. Lucas, it's so good to have you back."

Al King remained by the door and said with unfeigned disgust, "Mark, you damned fool."

Mark gave him a glance in which anger overlaid pain, but he ignored the remark. There were other greetings, and Tiff resumed chattering. Conan found himself again amazed at the contrast between wife and husband. Mark was so ordinary in appearance. A little shorter than his father and brothers, his hair somewhere between Al's sandy blond and Lucas's brown; a little beefier than either of them, with a softness beginning to expand his waist. There was a softness about his face, too, which Conan privately characterized as a typical Republican subcutaneous layer.

Conan also noted that although Mark had smiles and greetings for Will, Lise, Loanh, and even, guardedly, for Kim, he barely glanced at his father. A. C. had to force an acknowledgment of his presence with, "Well, Mark, how's the ankle?"

"Not bad." Then he focused his attention on Demara while Lucas introduced her. Mark was polite enough, but Conan could see a moment's distaste in his eyes, an impervious wall going up.

Tiff went through a gamut from shock to suspicion on being formally introduced to Demara, who didn't conceal a wry smile as she said, "Terrific outfit, Tiff. I love the flower-child look."

Lise was obviously trying to change the subject when she asked, "Tiff, how are Diana and Nancy?"

"Oh, they're just doing *beautifully*, Lise. I mean, Nancy's showing a *real* talent for art, you know— must've gotten that from *you*, of course—and Di's on the gymnastics team? Oh, she's *so* graceful and supple. I mean, I just wish one could hold *on* to that—must've been the yoga. You know, I started the girls with yoga when they were just *tiny*, and—"

Mark cut in quietly, but almost defiantly, "And Karen's fine, too, in case anyone's interested. She'll be home for Christmas."

There was a sudden silence, and all eyes focused on A. C. He stood motionless, staring at Mark. Conan knew a raw nerve had been hit, but it made no sense. All he remembered of Karen was that she was Mark and Tiff's oldest daughter. She must be thirteen or fourteen by now.

Kim put on a smile and said, "I'm sure Tiff and Mark would like to freshen up and get unpacked, then we can all have some lunch." She took A. C.'s arm, and although it obviously required quite a little pressure to move him, finally he departed with her into the lodge.

She's good, Conan thought. She might even be the only real hope of maintaining the armistice.

CHAPTER 6

The afternoon passed far more pleasantly than Conan had expected. Perhaps his presence—and Will Stewart's—had the effect desired of friendly outsiders, and the Kings were on their good behavior. Or perhaps it was simply that during the afternoon the individual members of the family were free to avoid each other.

At four o'clock, Conan decided he could safely leave the job of friendly outsider to Will for a while and indulged himself in a solitary walk down the road the quarter mile to the highway, then to the King's Creek Bridge, and back along the boulder-strewn stream, where he tarried as long as his conscience would allow, absorbing the peaceful sounds of birds and squirrels and rushing water. When finally he returned to the lodge, he found Lucas, Demara, Lise, and Will engaged in a Frisbee toss on the lawn, with Heather pursuing the yellow disk at every throw and commandeering it when a player failed to catch it, which added a new element to the game. Heather was not a retriever. It was not in her genes to willingly return the prize, once captured, and she had to be caught before the game could proceed—not an easy task, since as a herd dog, broken-field running *was* in her genes.

There was no wind and only a scattering of cumulus clouds that offered little respite from the sun. In the high, thin air, every breath felt hot, an impression intensified by the white smoke curling up from the stone chimney of the grill. When Conan reached the deck, A. C. was presiding over the grill, adding briquettes from a twenty-pound sack, and sporting a denim apron with red letters proclaiming him CHEF DU JOUR. Conan wondered why a man who considered cooking and anything associated with it "woman's work"—and thus to be avoided at all costs by any red-blooded, American male—was content to assume the role of cook as long as it was done outdoors.

Al, still looking like a Secret Service agent with his shaded aviator's glasses and trim mustache, perched on the railing near A. C., perhaps ready to lend assistance in this exclusively male endeavor, although he seemed primarily focused on the can of beer in his hand. Loanh was absent from the scene, but soon after Conan's arrival she came out through one of the open French doors with a tray of condiments for the table. Kim followed with silverware and napkins.

A. C. called to Loanh, "What do you hear from Charles?"

"He made the dean's honor roll last quarter," she replied proudly. "He must be a chip off his grandfather's shoulder."

"Oh, no," A. C. replied with a laugh. "That boy's smarter than his old granddad. I never did make it to college."

Kim smiled at Conan and asked, "Would you like something to drink? We have various soft drinks, coffee, tea, three brands of beer, white and red wine, or anything you'd like from the bar."

"The tea sounds wonderful, Kim, but I can get it."

"The pitcher and ice bucket are in on the dining table."

Conan went inside to avail himself of the tea, which was too pale for his taste, but at least it was wet. With the glass in hand, he leaned against the frame of one of the French doors and surveyed the deck. Mark was at the northwest corner of the building leaning on one crutch while he unfurled the blue awning that provided the only shade. Tiff occupied one of the folding chairs by the southernmost door, and she looked like a multicolored mushroom under the enormous brim of her straw hat. At her side was a square bag decorated with bright patches, beads, and fringes; in her lap was a tangle of colored threads, which she seemed to be trying to sort out with an oversized, plastic needle. On the TV table beside her was a tall glass whose contents were even paler than this tea, and Conan remembered that Tiff always began her private happy hour at any hour that suited her.

"Conan, are you sure you would not like a beer?"

He turned, a little startled, as Loanh came out of the living room carrying a tray laden with sweating cans.

"No, thank you, Loanh."

She nodded and went past him to intercept Mark as he finished securing the awning rope. Mark shook his head when she offered him a beer, but his polite smile faded as she leaned close to whisper to him. His gaze flicked toward the grill, he nodded, then Loanh hurriedly moved away to offer libations to A. C. and her husband. A. C. took a can with a smile and hearty thanks, but Al took his with no hint of either. Loanh hurried back through the French doors and on into the kitchen.

Something was very wrong, Conan thought, between Al and Loanh. Six years ago they hadn't exactly been lovebirds, but there had been an air of comfortable affection between them. Now there seemed to be nothing but constrained animosity.

As Conan was considering this, Mark swung past him and went into the living room. Conan didn't move, but it took only a quick glance inside to see that Mark's purpose was a conference with Loanh in the corner by the kitchen door. The exchange was short, and when Mark returned to the deck, his soft face was noticeably pale. He slumped into a chair next to his wife, who launched into a monologue on the deleterious effects of UVB radiation, while Mark nodded absently.

Conan crossed to the grill to offer his assistance, but A. C. turned him down with a laugh. "I've got everything under control here. You coming along on the climb up King's Mountain tomorrow?"

"Well, I brought my hiking boots."

"Good! Damn, it'll be just like old times. You and the boys." He sent Mark an irritable frown. "Except for Mark. Even when he was a kid, he was always sick or had something broke. Wonder if Will plans on coming. That really would be like old times. You and Will are the only people we've ever asked on the hike. Well, except for your dad. Al, maybe you better check the gear. It's in the storeroom upstairs."

Al took a long swig of beer, muttered, "I know where it is, Dad, for Christ's sake," then strode into the lodge.

A. C. watched him, eyes narrowed. "Don't know what kind of burr Al's got under his saddle today."

Conan left A. C. to tend his coals and sat down in a

chair near Mark and Tiff. A few minutes later, the Frisbee tossers came to the deck, panting and searching for refreshment. Heather trotted from one person to another, as if checking to make sure she had everyone accounted for. In the process, she crossed in front of Kim as she came out of the living room with a tray of candlesticks with glass chimneys.

"Damn!" Kim barely managed to keep herself and the tray upright. "Lise, *please*—keep this dog out of the way."

Lise's cheeks reddened, but before she could get a word out, Lucas turned on his crooked smile as he relieved Kim of the tray. "I'll take that, Kim. Heather's just not used to having so many people around."

"Yes, I know," Kim replied, managing a smile. "And I guess I'm just not used to having animals underfoot."

Lise called Heather and said coolly, "We'll get out of your way, Kim. Will, come on up to the studio, and I'll give you that preview."

That incident hinted at the tensions under the surface, but as the afternoon progressed it was the only such revelatory incident, and when Lise and Will returned a short time later, she was obviously ready to play the game again.

The game might be called Peace in the Family, and all the members seemed willing to play, even Al. At least Al was willing to remain, on the whole, silent. The players' success at the game was achieved mainly by carefully avoiding any personal subject. There was some discussion of politics in which Will, seconded by Conan, served as devil's advocate in this predominantly conservative group. There was also some discussion of the old-growth forest controversy, with Mark expanding on the court cases brought by "preservationists" that as head of Ace Timber's legal department he was forced to

deal with, and even there a light tone was maintained.
Lucas described his new project in Los Angeles, com-
paring notes with Al on the technical problems of blast-
ing out a hole big enough for a three-story, underground
parking structure. Al seemed ready enough to offer his
expertise, although he was reticent about his own on-
going projects.

Conan watched Lise, who seemed always to be smiling, and sometimes it was genuine. It was usually Lucas
who elicited that kind of smile. Otherwise her smiles
had a distinct fragility about them.

Lucas's smiles were frequent, often turning into
laughter. It all seemed relaxed and easy, but Conan
sensed method behind the smiles. He regarded Lucas
with grudging admiration as he worked this crowd.
Lucas knew these people, knew what worked for them,
even his father. A. C.'s attitude of wary doubt gradually
shifted to wary hope. He told Conan once, "Never
thought I'd see it—all my boys together again. Hell,
who says you can't teach a young dog old tricks?"

But not everyone was convinced. Al seemed to be
constantly watching Lucas, usually over the top of a can
of beer, as if waiting for his brother to make a mistake.
Kim was a gracious and solicitous hostess, but Conan
had the feeling that she knew exactly where Lucas was
and exactly what he was doing at any given moment.

And Conan overheard Mark say to Tiff, "Lucas always could charm the bark off a tree. Or the money out
of an old man's pocket."

Tiff, wielding her needle with an abandon no doubt
inspired by her fourth Scotch and soda, laughed and
said, "Oh, sweetie, now *don't* you worry about *Lucas.*"

Conan didn't find out what she meant by that assurance. At that moment, Kim brought out a platter of
inch-thick, T-bone steaks ready for the grill. While the

KING OF THE MOUNTAIN

other guests expressed amazed anticipation, Tiff said, "Dad, don't cook one of those for *me*, I mean, the *cholesterol*, you know, not to mention the *calories*, and besides, I really *have* decided I just *can't* in good conscience eat *any* sort of meat, you know."

A. C. began forking the steaks onto the grill, and the sizzling scent was ambrosial. "Well, Tiff, I wouldn't think of corrupting your body or your conscience. There'll be plenty of salad."

Demara Wilder seemed always at Lucas's side, with his hand in hers or his arm around her. She seldom spoke, but she watched, and her sensuous mouth was ever on the edge of a cynical smile. Yet it was clear that Lucas occupied her attention at a more basic level, as she did his. There was between them something that suggested they occupied a private pocket of space/time, and everything going on around them was only peripheral to their intense physical awareness of each other.

"Pheromones," Will commented as he pulled up a chair and sat down next to Conan.

Conan laughed. "Undoubtedly."

"Even Al seems susceptible." Al was sitting on one of the lounge chairs, one hand as always occupied with a can of beer, a faint smirk stretching one side of his mouth as he watched Demara. Will added wearily, "But Al is always susceptible, unfortunately."

Conan didn't comment on that. Al King's susceptibility to attractive women was no secret, but Conan guessed that in Demara's case it was highly ambivalent and that Al was more preoccupied with his prodigal brother than his attractive escort.

At five o'clock, with the cool shadows of the firs on the banks of King's Creek reaching across the lawn, A. C. went to the bronze bell, grabbed the rope attached to the clapper, and shook it vigorously. The clear tones echoed in the ebbing afternoon as he shouted, "Come and get it!" Then he returned to the grill, and Kim passed out plates, while A. C. deposited a sizzling slab of beef on each one, filling requests for rare, medium, and well-done from various positions on the grill.

Finally A. C. took his place at what he apparently considered the head of the table—the south end nearest the grill—while Lucas seated himself at the opposite end, and the other family members arranged themselves along the two sides of the table. Conan ended up on the east side between Demara and Loanh.

It was a hearty and simple meal, the steaks augmented with baked potatoes, hot rolls, green salad, and a Tualatin pinot noir for those who didn't opt for beer. Tiff served herself a plateful of green salad, sans salt or dressing. Conan surmised she was not only concerned with her health and the welfare of animals, but was on another of her diets. She weighed, he guessed, little more than a hundred pounds, and it was obvious that her optimum weight was perhaps twenty pounds more, but she fought constantly to maintain her fashionable emaciation, despite the fact that now that she had reached her fourth decade, the effect of this hard-won slimness was simply scrawniness.

The chill in the mountain air whetted appetites, and the business of eating and drinking seemed to require everyone's full attention. The table was made festive with the lighted candles in their glass chimneys, but there was little conversation, except when A. C. again brought up the subject of tomorrow's hike up King's Mountain.

"Al, did you check the gear like I asked you?"

"It's all there and ready to go, Dad. Art saw to that, probably."

"Will, how about you? City life make you too soft for a little hike?"

Will laughed at that. "Life in my part of the city has made me damned fast on my feet, A. C. But I can't make the hike tomorrow. Jayleen's due any minute now. I'll have to drive out to find a phone to check on her tomorrow morning."

"Jayleen? Patient of yours?"

"Yes. First pregnancy. She's a little nervous."

Tiff gave that a high-pitched laugh. "Well, she *should* be nervous. Oh, if I'd *known* what I was getting into when *I* got pregnant, but you know, you just *forget* all the agony once you have that little mite of new *life* in your arms, and you feel—"

"How about you, Lucas?" A. C. asked, cutting Tiff off as if he hadn't even noticed she was speaking. He probably hadn't.

Lucas looked down the length of the table at his father with a warm smile and said quietly, "Dad, I wouldn't miss it."

A. C. nodded, and it seemed he wanted to respond, but instead cleared his throat and turned to Mark, who was staring at his plate, his knife gripped hard in his right hand. A. C. said irritably, "Well, Mark won't be going, that's for damn sure. Conan? You still game?"

"Of course. I need the exercise."

Al sliced a bleeding gash in his steak. "Conan, you know, you don't really have to go. You could just stay here and relax. Spend some time with Lise. Besides, it's sort of a *family* tradition. . . ."

The reference to Conan's spending time with Lise had Will sitting bolt upright, but Conan was focused on Al. Perhaps he was trying to be diplomatic, yet the emphasis on *family* was obvious. Conan might have taken the hint, but A. C. glared at his son and said curtly,

"Conan is Henry Flagg's boy, and that makes him family. I invited him to come on the hike, so if he wants to, he damn well *can*." And with that, the subject was dropped, obviously settled in A. C.'s mind.

By the time the meal was finished, it was after six o'clock. The only light in the sky was a pale, golden pink glow behind the hills to the west, and the chill in the air was reaching the point of discomfort. A. C. sighed with repletion as he rose. "Well, gentlemen, we'll just let the womenfolk tend to the cleaning up while we go inside for a brandy."

It was said with a straight face, but Kim laughed. "It's a good thing the *men*folk around here are so much all thumbs in the kitchen that I'd go out of my mind having any of you there. Well, *ladies*, let's get at it." She rose and reached for the empty tray on the side table and handed it to Tiff. "Why don't you collect the glasses, Tiff?"

She stared at the tray. "Oh, Kim, I just *can't* have anything at *all* to do with detergents, you know— they're just *disastrous* for my skin."

Kim had both hands full of plates as she headed for the French doors. "We have a dishwasher, Tiff."

The other "womenfolk," including Demara, set to work with apparent willingness. Conan decided that any offer of assistance he might make would only muddy the waters, and with the other "menfolk" retreated to the living room.

The room materialized out of the twilight as A. C. switched on the lamps on the end tables. It was an impressive space, at least thirty-five feet long. It was in fact three rooms in one. Just inside the French doors was the dining area with its long, oak table under another octagonal, wrought-iron chandelier; then the living room in the center, divided by its furnishings into two conversational groupings—two couches, each flanked with end tables and arm chairs—one facing the fireplace on the south wall, the other facing the windows that ran the length of the north wall; and in the southeast corner, the bar with its burl counter and three barstools. On the wall behind the bar, a glass case displayed A. C.'s collection of vintage firearms.

Like the rest of the lodge, the living room was a showcase of craftsmanship, including the magnificent grandfather clock to the left of the fireplace. The color scheme was determined by the muted ochre of the beamed ceiling and paneled walls, and by the dark gray basalt of the fireplace. The couches and chairs were upholstered in gray leather, the drapes made of gray wool, with Haida raven symbols woven in threads of ochre, black, and red. The walls seemed oddly barren, with neither bookshelves nor paintings. The only painting in the lodge, as far as Conan knew, was Lise's watercolor of Mount Hood in the atrium.

Once the women had carried all the dishes through the swinging door to the right of the fireplace, Al closed the French doors. A. C. went to the bar and flicked on the overhead light spotlighting the armory behind glass, and Will and Conan busied themselves building a fire. Lucas watched all this activity from one of the armchairs. When Mark made his way to the couch, sank into the cushions, and laid the crutches beside him, Lucas asked, "That ankle hurting you, Mark?"

Mark sent him an oddly exasperated look. "No, not anymore."

Finally, with the fire burning well, Conan sat down on the couch, and Heather leapt up beside him and settled with her head on his thigh. He smiled and stroked her head, glancing toward the bar, where Al perched on one of the bar stools. A. C. served the promised brandy, then sank down in the other armchair and began the ritual of lighting his pipe. Conan took out his cigarettes, a little surprised to see that Lucas also smoked. Mores, in fact, which was also Conan's current brand. He wondered who smoked the Marlboros. An open pack was on the end table next to A. C.'s pipe paraphernalia.

For a time A. C. led a desultory conversation on such scintillating—and safe—subjects as the weather, especially the El Niño effect in the Pacific that had resulted in a six-year drought in the Northwest that was devastating forests as well as farm lands. From the kitchen came the sounds of voices, occasional laughter, and the murmur of the dishwasher. The conversation in the living room was lagging into uneasy silence, when the clock's Westminster chimes rang out seven o'clock. Lucas came to his feet and said, "Come on, Dad, let's put on some of your records, and when the ladies are done in the kitchen, we'll get down to some serious dancing."

The idea appealed to A. C., who responded with a self-conscious "Right on!" It had no appeal to Al and Mark, but Will got into the spirit, and while A. C. and Lucas went to the stereo on the angled wall between the entryway and the bar to look over the records, Will and Conan rolled up the rug between the couches to make a small dance floor.

"Take the 'A' Train" was the first selection, and the lively beat wrought a magical transformation. After a few bars, the kitchen door opened and Kim led the women out. Laughing, her blue eyes sparkling, she reached for A. C.'s hand, said, "This is more *like* it!" and the two of them took to the dance floor.

Lucas and Demara joined them, and a few minutes later, Will and Lise. Mark shifted to stand with his back to the fire so he could watch, while Tiff sat on the wide hearth ledge, clapping her hands to the rhythm. Only Al was unmoved by the music, and he remained glued to his bar stool, with a can of beer seemingly glued to his hand. Loanh went behind the bar to mix herself a gin and tonic. Al watched her silently, but she left the bar without even glancing at her husband, and crossed to Conan, who was standing by the fireplace. She brought forth an uncertain smile and asked, "Would you like to dance, Conan?"

"I'd be delighted." He led her out onto the makeshift dance floor, which was crowded now with four couples on it. Under the influence of the music and the laughter around her, Loanh seemed to relax. So exquisite, Conan thought, so slight and pliant in his arms, following his lead with graceful precision, and when she smiled, he understood why Air Force Captain Al King had been so captivated that he brought an Oriental bride home to his father. Conan could imagine her in the traditional silk *ao dai* looking like a princess out of an exotic fairy tale.

But many years had passed since the dashing captain had swept this princess off her feet and carried her away to his homeland. Conan wondered why this fairy tale seemed to have no happy ending.

A. C.'s collection of records was probably priceless, but to him it was simply the music he loved, the music of his youth. Glenn Miller, Tommy and Jimmy Dorsey, Les Brown, Duke Ellington, Woody Herman, Harry James, Benny Goodman, Count Basie, Artie Shaw—the 78 rpm records slapped down on the turntable, one after another. The volume was high, and the sound had a rasping edge, but it had a salutary effect on this tension-riddled group.

It precluded all but the most minimal conversation, for one thing, and since Kim set the pattern of constantly changing partners after the first record, it created a constantly changing mix that left little time for anything but the most innocuous small talk. And the rhythms were so compelling, they demanded physical exertion that siphoned off much of the tension.

But the exertion had the disadvantage of increasing everyone's thirst, and the bar was perhaps *too* well stocked. Conan danced more than once with Tiff, and every time it became increasingly difficult to lead her, and her high-pitched laughter verged on the hysterical. Even Lise got happily tipsy as the evening wore on. Once she hugged Conan as they danced and said, "Oh, isn't it wonderful? Everybody together and having a wonderful time. I remember Mom taught us kids how to dance with this music, and I loved it even if it *was* passé even then."

Kim was quite sober, he found, but she did in fact seem to be enjoying herself. Nor was Demara at all tipsy, despite the quantity of Scotch she consumed. She even carried her glass with her when she danced with Conan. She kept glancing at A. C. with that sensuous, cynical smile, but all she said about him was, "The old man's showing a lot of life yet."

It was Loanh in whom the unresolved tension was most evident, and Conan was surprised to see how much alcohol she was putting down. She was quickly passing the point of tipsiness.

It was after eight when A. C. called a short intermission while he sorted through more records. Conan crossed to the French doors to open one of them. Lucas joined him, apparently for the cool, fresh air, and said, almost as if it were a confidence, "It's great to see Dad having such a good time, isn't it?"

Conan agreed, then waited. Lucas had more to say, and finally he got to it. "You know, Conan, I hardly ever agree with Al, but you don't really need to feel obligated to tag along on the hike tomorrow. I mean, it's not *your* tradition, after all. It's Dad's."

He didn't add that it was a *family* tradition, but again the hint was obvious. Conan said, "I know, Lucas, but it's your dad who invited me."

The music started again with "Begin the Beguine," and Lucas saw Demara approaching. He shrugged, and the two of them whirled out onto the dance floor.

Kim and Will joined them, and Conan avoided Tiff's eye like a busy waiter as he headed for the bar in search of something to slake his thirst, but Lise intercepted him. "Dance with me, Conan."

"Always my pleasure, Lise." He guided her to the floor, opting for a slow step despite the quickness of the recorded rhythm. The edge was off Lise's tipsiness, he noticed, and off her happiness. "What is it, Lise?"

"Was Lucas asking you not to go on the hike tomorrow?"

"Yes, as a matter of fact."

"Are you going?"

"Do you want me to?"

She nodded soberly. "Yes. I'm worried, Conan. About Al, really. I don't know what's eating at him, but I know he's not glad to see Lucas home or to see Dad welcoming him."

She spoke so quietly, Conan had to lean close to hear her. He saw Will looking over Kim's shoulder at them with an expression of hurt defeat. Conan realized he needed to have a long talk with Will, but now he asked Lise, "Is whatever's bothering Al something new?"

"No. He's been . . . erratic since Dad's marriage, and I know he's having a hard time financially. But tonight he seems to be on the edge of something. Maybe it's Lucas. I don't know."

"But you want a friendly outsider on King's Mountain tomorrow?"

She laughed. "I'd be very grateful, Conan."

"I'll be there." He saw that Kim and Will had left the dance floor. Will was leaning over the back of the couch to pet Heather, who seemed bored with the human activities and had settled down for a nap. Conan said, "I'm going to get something to drink, Lise. Why don't you finish this dance with Will?"

Perhaps she recognized his matchmaking motive, but she took his suggestion. A. C. was behind the bar when Conan reached it, an empty ice bucket on the counter before him. But he was focused on Al, and neither of them noticed Conan's approach. Despite the volume of the music, Conan heard A. C. say, "You've had three extensions already, Al. Hell, all I'm asking for is the interest."

"Goddamn it, I'm your *son*! Doesn't that mean anything to you?"

"It's a business transaction, and you knew it when—" A. C. stopped; he had just seen Conan. He put on a smile, asked, "Well, what can I do for you, Conan? We're out of ice until—oh, here comes Kim."

Kim brought four trays of ice cubes, and when she had emptied them into the ice bucket, A. C. poured Conan the ice and soda he asked for, put the bucket in the small refrigerator, then came out from behind the bar and for a while stood with his arm around Kim, watching the dancers. Conan saw Loanh make her way to the bar, a little unsteadily, and pour more gin into the tonic left in her glass.

Al stared at her, a muscle twitching in his jaw. Finally, as she left the bar, he demanded, "You're a few past your limit, aren't you?"

She mumbled, "I been pas' my limit a long, long time, Al."

The record ended, and in the silence before the next one hit the turntable, A. C.'s voice was audible as he said to Kim, "Wonder if Lucas plans on marrying that nigger girl."

Neither Demara nor Lucas apparently heard that, but everyone near A. C. did, and to Conan's amazement, it was Loanh who took exception to it. The music came on again with "Lady Be Good" as she strode to within a foot of him and glared up at him defiantly. "So, would that be sush a tradegy, Dad? Your oldest son married a *gook*. And that makes your only gran'son half a gook—"

"You bitch!" Al shoved Conan aside and grabbed Loanh's arm so hard she gasped in pain, jerked her around to face him.

A. C., who had been only surprised, not angry, at Loanh's outburst, said, "Damn it, Al, there's no call to—"

"She's going to apologize!" Al insisted, shaking Loanh like a doll. She cried out, and Al found himself being pried off her by both A. C. and Conan. Al bellowed, "Let go of me!" and pulled free, repeated, "She's going to *apologize*!"

A. C. snapped, "You idiot, just shut up!"

"She's my wife, and she's got no right to—"

"*Please!*" Loanh pressed her hands to her forehead, eyes squeezed shut. "*Yes*, I will apologize. Oh, Dad, I am sorry, it was never you . . ." And she began to weep so piteously that A. C. was left open-mouthed.

Lise took her in her arms. "Come on, Loanh, let's go upstairs."

Loanh nodded mutely as Lise led her away. Al stood with his feet apart, hands in fists at his side. He looked around, and it seemed that his angry gaze rested longer on Kim than anyone else, then he stalked to the French doors and out into the darkness.

Kim put on a smile and said to A. C., "Well, maybe he's got it out of his system now. A. C., are you going to dance with me, or are you just going to stand there like a lump?"

A. C. was still frowning, but after a moment he laughed and led her onto the dance floor. Demara and Lucas stayed to finish the song, but no one else did. The party was, for all intents and purposes, over.

At least, Conan thought, he wouldn't have to try to move Tiff around the dance floor again tonight. She was slumped on the couch next to Heather, snoring gently. Heather was looking around anxiously, and Will went over to her, offered her a reassuring rub, then offered Mark his services in getting Tiff upstairs.

Mark sat hunched on the hearth. He nodded as he came to his feet and was ready to walk away without his crutches, then he stared blankly at his encased foot. Conan helped him onto the crutches, and steadied him as they followed Will and Tiff. Mark had a hard time with the stairs, but finally they reached the second floor and the bedroom west of Conan's. The walk had sobered Tiff enough for her to thank Will and assure him she could take care of Mark. The glance Will sent Conan hinted that he doubted that, but considered it none of his business. He and Conan retreated, closing the door behind them.

As they reached the head of the stairs, Lise came out of Loanh and Al's room. Conan stopped and said, "I'll be down in a minute, Will."

Will correctly interpreted that to mean that Conan wanted to talk to Lise privately. Will could not, unfortunately, interpret *why* he wanted to talk to her, and again Conan saw that look of hurt defeat just before Will hurried down the stairs.

When Lise reached him, Conan asked, "How's Loanh?"

"Well, she's calmed down. Conan, I've *never* seen her drunk. I mean, she hardly drinks at all."

"Did she tell you what was bothering her?"

"She just kept apologizing for what she said to Dad. Actually, they've gotten along very well, once Dad got over the shock of Al coming home with an Oriental war bride. Besides, Mom loved her like a daughter, so Dad *had* to come around. Anyway, Loanh said it wasn't Dad she was mad at. Then she said something really odd." Lise closed her eyes to clarify the memory. "She said, 'For me, for my people, family is everything. Without family, one might as well be dead.'"

"Maybe she's afraid her family is on the verge of dissolution."

Lise started down the stairs. "The way Al's acting, it is."

By the time they reached the living room, the music had stopped, and A. C. was putting away the records, while Will and Lucas were restoring the rug, and Demara and Kim were cleaning up glasses and ashtrays. The fire had burned down to coals.

Heather trotted to Lise to give her an anxious greeting, and Lise knelt and ruffled her fur. "Hi, sweetheart. Yes, you've been a really good girl tonight. Come on, we'd better go home." She rose as the grandfather clock marked the hour. "Well, it's only nine. Maybe I'll get some work done tonight."

Will offered, "I'll walk you up to the studio, Lise."

She smiled but shook her head. "Thanks, but you don't need to, Will. I know that path by heart. Besides, I've got my trusty guard dog."

Will nodded, looking crestfallen, and watched her make her exit through the French doors. Then he looked at Conan almost accusingly, quickly made his excuses to A. C. and Kim, and headed upstairs.

Conan sighed, wondering how he had been put in the position of competitor for Lise's favors. He wondered, too, where Al was, but decided not to ask. He said his good nights and went up to his room.

He wouldn't sleep soon, he knew, but at least there was the quiet of solitude, and a good book to keep him company. He could only hope he would get to sleep before his usual two A.M.

For the hikers, the day would begin at five.

CHAPTER 7

On the occasions when Conan Flagg was forced by circumstances to rise to greet the dawn, he was usually so surprised to find that early mornings offered such a cornucopia of beauty that he wondered why he didn't rise early more often. On the other hand, he knew he was getting too old to tolerate many nights of four hours or less sleep.

Besides, it was pitch-dark when he woke, and the electric wall heater in his bathroom didn't have time to take more than the edge off the chill. But the kitchen was warm, and Kim was awake to prepare a hearty breakfast that reminded Conan of the ranch breakfasts his mother had cooked for the buckaroos and hay crews at the Ten-Mile: bacon, eggs, hashbrowns, and biscuits. Of course, a true ranch breakfast might include steak, gravy, and even a pie or two.

Kim's white-wine-blonde hair was tousled, her sky blue eyes less than bright, and Conan wondered if the domestic role she had assumed might be wearing thin. A. C.'s early morning cheer was relentless. Lucas was equally cheerful, but Al, who was obviously suffering a world-class hangover, didn't even make an attempt at cheer. He ate sparingly and in silence, putting down cup after cup of black coffee.

After breakfast, the campers—happy and otherwise— carted the camping gear downstairs from the storage room and stowed it in the four backpacks. Kim had prepared their lunch by then, and finally, at seven o'clock, the expedition set forth and marched west across the lawn toward the palisade of trees shielding King's Creek.

It was at that point that Conan became aware of the beauty of the early morning. The sun hadn't yet topped the hills east of the lodge, and the lawn was misted with dew, every blade of grass beaded with crystal drops; the sky was deep blue, streaked with pink cirrus clouds, and Mount Hood hung in the mists, its highest slopes already bathed in the coralline light of the rising sun.

A staked NO HUNTING sign marked the beginning of the trail. Inevitably, A. C. took the lead. Lucas followed, then Al, hanging back out of range of conversation, and finally Conan. The chill air was perfumed with resins and rich earth as the trail curved south, following King's Creek downstream. Conan heard the rush of water behind a screen of vine maples displaying their small, perfect, gold and scarlet leaves; from above came the *tchk* of squirrels, pipings of chickadees, and raucous shouts of jays. He settled into an easy stride, relishing the reassuring sturdiness of his hiking boots, the rustle of his hooded, down parka with its Gore-Tex shell, even the weight of the backpack.

All too soon, the tall silver firs and hemlock gave way to a clear-cut where young Douglas firs crowded like Christmas trees, a monoculture waiting to grow into pulp for paper or, if left to grow long enough, into two-by-fours. Or waiting for a mutating insect, bacteria, or virus to devise a means to overcome the species' natural defenses and destroy all of the trees. Whichever came first.

Conan followed the trail through this tree farm for perhaps half a mile before he caught up with A. C. and his sons. They had stopped on the footbridge that crossed King's Creek. The bridge consisted of a couple of planks laid on a fallen log, with a pole railing on one side. The creek was only four feet wide at this dry end of a dry season.

A. C. turned, a finger to his lips, and as Conan cautiously approached, he saw why they had stopped. Downstream a hundred yards, a doe and her two fawns, both nearly grown, their coats the same gray-brown as their mother's, were drinking, constantly flicking their huge ears. The light wind was from the south, so they didn't catch the human scent. The doe might be suspicious, but as long as the humans remained still and quiet, she apparently considered herself safe.

A. C., speaking in a whisper, offered a further explanation. "It's past deer hunting season. They know. If this was deer season, you'd never even see them. Now it's just the elk that have to worry." Then abruptly, he waved his arms, shouted, "Shoo! Get outta here!" and the deer flashed instantly away into the forest.

Lucas asked, "Why did you do that, Dad?"

"Don't want 'em getting too tame. You don't ever want to let a deer think men are friends."

Al gave that a curt laugh. "Dad, I never thought I'd see the day when you gave a damn what a deer thought." He turned and strode up the trail on the other side of the creek. A. C.'s lips compressed, but he didn't speak, and after a moment Lucas started after Al.

Conan followed A. C. and, noting another NO HUNTING sign, asked, "A. C., did you have the area posted last time I was here?"

"No. I just got tired of those city yahoos swarming all over my land shooting at anything that moves. Most of those guys sit behind a desk in Portland all year. Come hunting season, they get a rifle and a case of beer, and they think they're hunters." He paused to give Conan a dubious squint. "You don't like any kind of hunting, do you?"

"You know I don't."

"Yeah, I remember ol' Henry giving you a hard time about that when you were still a kid. Said you were a good tracker and a good shooter, but—"

"—a lousy killer," Conan finished for him. "I've never changed my mind about that part. Have you?"

A. C. shrugged uneasily. "Haven't done any hunting since Carla died. Seemed like after spending so much time watching her die, I just didn't have the stomach for watching anything else die." Then before Conan could make any response, A. C. struck out up the trail.

The trail moved gradually away from King's Creek, and Conan began to feel the steady upward tendency. His body had adjusted itself over the years to absolute sea level, and it needed more than one day to adjust to the rigors of functioning at over four thousand feet.

The Christmas tree farm gave way to an older manmade forest of Douglas firs, most about forty feet tall. The shade they cast was dense and cool, but sunlight slanted through in hazy shafts, patching trunks and undergrowth with mottled shadows. On the few occasions when the trail was straight for any length of time, Conan could see A. C. ahead, then Al, then Lucas taking the lead, none close enough to each other to carry on a conversation. At intervals of about a quarter mile, A. C. had posted more NO HUNTING signs. Sometimes Conan caught glimpses of Mount Hood through the trees, radiantly clear now that the morning mists had dissipated. It was after eight-thirty when the trail made a wide turn to the southeast and entered old-growth forest.

The sensation was much like hearing the lush chords of Sibelius for the first time. *The Swan of Tuonela,* perhaps. The lords of this forest were a mix of fir, cedar, and hemlock, their trunks like columns of rough stone, three to five feet in diameter. Only a green-gold shimmer of light escaped the canopy above to fall on the undergrowth of bunchberry, with its small, white blossoms centered in huge leaves; wild lily of the valley flaunting fronds of berries like red jasper beads; and red huckleberry with its tiny scarlet berries. The earth was sienna brown, dotted with mushrooms and fungi ranging from fleshy white umbrellas to wiry lavender stalks to ochre ledges that clung to the tree trunks and the flanks of fallen giants.

It was the kind of forest Conan had often heard A. C. dismiss as trash forest because of the wind-downed trees rotting into nurse logs and the mix of noncommercial species. His recommendation was simple: clear-cut it and start fresh with Doug fir.

In the past, Conan had discussed the wisdom of that alternative with A. C., who always enjoyed a good argument, even if it never occurred to him that he might change his mind. A. C. grew up at a time when the forests of Oregon still seemed infinite, and he refused to believe that in his lifetime those forests had been decimated, leaving the man-made monocultures and only a few remnants of true forest.

The trail wound through the old growth for over a mile, its upward incline constant, and Conan was content to lag well behind the others. Then abruptly he was in second growth again and, after another half mile of climbing, came out onto a fresh clear-cut that occupied the top of a rounded knoll. The stumps were still black from the slash burn, the controlled fire that left the razed earth bare for Douglas fir seedlings. Some of the seedlings, less than a foot in height, were green and thriving. Others had died, probably browsed by deer. There was no sign of deciduous shrub growth, and Conan wondered what kind of herbicide spray Ace Timber was using.

A. C. and his sons were waiting in the center of the clear-cut, and as Conan approached, A. C. pointed northeast. "Conan, if your eyes are sharp enough, you can see the lodge down there."

Conan picked out the highway, the access road, and the gray box of the lodge with its angled roof. It was so small he doubted he could have identified it if he hadn't known what it was. Nearly four miles as the crow flies, A. C. said. Five miles by trail. Conan looked beyond it to the incredible mass of Mount Hood, its snowfields blinding in the mid-morning sunlight.

"And there—" A. C. turned and pointed south toward a hill marked by a bare, basalt cap. "—there's King's Mountain."

Conan nodded and didn't bother to remind A. C. that this wasn't his first hike to the hill he called a mountain. A. C. enjoyed his rituals, and pointing out their beginning point and destination at this halfway mark was one of them, although six years ago Conan had had to find the landmarks through the trunks of the trees growing on this knoll.

With Lucas and Al falling in behind him, A. C. continued across the clear-cut, where the trail had been only recently restored, red-brown as dried blood slashed across the gray of burned earth. It entered another stretch of old-growth forest, still climbing, and finally, after another quarter mile, the hikers reached the camp site.

It was surrounded by old growth, and Conan found it ironic that A. C. had never logged around this place that was so meaningful to him. It was a flat, open area, about fifty feet across, covered with reddish pumice. A circle of stones served as a fire pit, with chain-sawed logs arranged around it as seats. Nearby was a pile of split wood left, no doubt, by Art Rasmussen. To the west, a forested slope dropped into a ravine thirty feet deep where Loblolly Creek chattered in the shadows. To the east, the prow of a ridge capped with columnar basalt loomed a hundred feet above them. Below the basalt palisade was a barren talus slope made up of rocks eroded from the basalt, ranging from pebbles to man-sized boulders. Miniature falls of gravel intermittently whispered down to join the ragged skirt of debris at its foot.

This slope, to Conan's eye, had not achieved its angle of repose. But of course he'd had the same thought six years ago. For that matter, he'd had the same thought the first time he camped here when he was fourteen years old. He said nothing. A. C. would only assure him that the slope had never given way in all these years, which he assumed meant it would never give way in the future.

A. C., Lucas, and Al gathered by the fire pit and divested themselves of their backpacks. Conan joined them, sighing as he eased the weight off his shoulders, then he twisted the top on his water bottle for a long draught. A. C. pulled a stainless-steel thermos out of his pack. "Find your cups, and we'll have a coffee break," he said.

It took awhile for them to unpack their collapsible cups. A. C. filled them, stopping abruptly when he reached Conan's. It was a Sierra Club cup, which he had brought along precisely for the reaction it got from A. C.: a snort of disgust and a mocking threat to throw Conan and his cup off the top of King's Mountain when they reached it. But A. C. filled the offending cup now, and everyone chose a log to sit down on.

While Conan savored the first taste of coffee, Lucas leaned over to peer at the gear Al had dumped out of his pack, then asked with a conspiratorial grin, "Al, is that what I think it is?"

Al looked down at the two six-packs of Heineken and conceded, "Well, I figured it might—"

"You carried all that beer up here?" A. C. cut in. "Goddamn it, Al, don't you get enough beer at home—or out of my icebox?"

Al had been close to smiling, but at that his jaw went tight, and despite the shaded glasses, Conan could almost see the shutters slamming shut behind his eyes.

Lucas said, "Hey, Dad, lighten up. A couple of beers'll taste like heaven by the time we get down from the mountain. *Cold* beer. Al, let's put this in the creek. Best refrigerator around."

But Al was already on his feet. "*I'll* take care of 'em," he muttered as he grabbed both six-packs and set off for the creek.

Lucas grimaced as he took a swallow of coffee. He said nothing, but A. C. was on the defensive. "Hell, Lucas, you haven't seen Al for—what? Two years? He's turning into a lush, and I thought just for this one day of the year, he could stay sober."

Lucas looked at Conan, perhaps calling his father's

attention to the friendly outsider in their midst. "Okay, Dad, but if we do our share on the Heineken, I don't figure Al can get too drunk on what's left."

Nothing more was said about the beer. Al came up from the creek, and they finished their coffee in silence, then A. C. rose. "Well, let's get the lunch into one backpack, and I'll carry it." He looked up at the sky, hazy with cirrus clouds, then took off his parka. "Don't figure I'll need that. Getting downright warm."

Conan pulled off his parka, too; the wool sweater was more than sufficient now, and the sun at this altitude called for the cloth hat and sunglasses he'd carried in his pocket. They left the camping gear stacked around the fire pit, then resumed their journey. A. C. again took the lead as they headed south toward King's Mountain.

The second leg of the trek was harder than the first, with the trail constantly winding around ridges, down into ravines and up again, and taking a tortuous course up the rugged flanks of King's Mountain, and in the next couple of hours, Conan began to think that perhaps this *was* more of a mountain than a hill after all. Still, the exertion in this setting was a physical and sensory pleasure.

He had checked his watch when they left the campsite. It had been ten-twenty. It was twelve-forty when they finally reached the top of King's Mountain, where the rocky surface and savage winter winds discouraged all but the toughest growth: a few twisted white pines and the dried seed heads of stunted plants finding a precarious existence in clefts of rock painted with orange and green lichen.

The view was magnificent. A. C. stood looking north as if surveying his domain. In fact, his domain occupied only a small part of this view. Conan gazed at Mount Hood, the sleeping volcano. At its feet, he could discern the fine line of the highway, but it asked too much of his eyes to find the lodge. He turned to the south and saw the next pearl in the strand, Mount Jefferson, hazed in distance. In the southwest, a bank of clouds stretched pale tendrils toward the zenith.

They sat down on a boulder and ate lunch—thick roast beef sandwiches on sourdough bread, potato chips, and crisp Jonagold apples—and every mouthful was made ambrosial by exertion and altitude. Afterward Lucas wandered to the edge of the caprock, found a flat spot, and stretched out to absorb the sun, arms folded behind his head. Al wandered off in a different direction apparently to study the view of Mount Jefferson.

A. C. began filling his pipe, while Conan lit a cigarette. The silence in this place was primordial, broken only by bird calls and the hum of insects. There had been little conversation during lunch, which had satisfied Conan because he cherished this quiet, but he knew the Kings hadn't been restrained by a respect for wilderness silence.

At length, his pipe lit, A. C. puffed out a cloud of smoke whose scent reminded Conan vaguely of juniper. A. C. said, "Well, I guess a man has to face up to it sooner or later. The good old days are dead."

Conan studied his granitic face, finding there a weary regret. "A. C., the good old days are always dead by the time you get around to recognizing them as such."

A. C. gave that a rumbling laugh. "Like they say, all you can count on is that things change." He puffed at his pipe, lips opening and closing around the stem. "Guess I should be happy with what I've got."

"Like having Lucas back?"

"Yeah. You know, I really think he meant it when he apologized."

Still, there was doubt underlying that affirmation.

Conan ventured, "Well, maybe it's worth taking a chance on believing him."

"Maybe. But it bothers me, having to take a *chance* on believing my own son. Hell, I did everything I knew how to bring my boys up right, but look at 'em. Sometimes I think . . ." He hesitated, and Conan wondered if he would go on. He did, finally. "Sometimes I think they're all just waiting for me to die. The money— that's all they want from me. Look at Al. Can't hold his business together, drinking too damn much and getting mean about it. And Mark. Staying on with the company, staying on with me, even if he hates my guts. Just waiting. Lucas? I want more than anything in the world to trust him, but I'm still not sure about him. Damn it, I didn't raise my boys to end up this way."

Conan felt uneasy with those confidences, but he understood that this was part of being a friendly outsider. He was a safe receptacle for such revelations. He inhaled on his cigarette, watched the smoke dissipate. "A. C., they're not boys anymore."

A. C. looked at him sharply, then laughed. "Well, you never had kids. They're always your boys—or your girl—no matter how old they get. But you've got a point. Maybe it's too late to worry about what I did wrong, but I'm not dead yet, not by a long shot, so I have to keep on trying to do what's right by my kids, and I don't know what it is."

Conan thought a moment, then, "No, I didn't have kids, A. C., but I remember something my dad told me when *I* was a kid. About breaking broncs, actually. He said you can make a horse your partner or your slave, and a horse that's a slave isn't worth the powder to blow it up. But if you want your horse to be a partner, you've got to let it know when it does things right, not just when it does wrong. Any good horse will figure out

what to do when it knows what's right." In fact, Henry
Flagg might have espoused that Skinnerian philosophy,
but he had never verbalized it. Still, Conan thought the
moral might sit better with A. C. if it was put in the
mouth of his childhood friend.

Perhaps it did. A. C. didn't comment on it, but obviously he gave it some thought.

At length, he looked at his watch. "It's nearly two.
High time to head back to camp." He called to Lucas
and Al, then stowed the detritus of the lunch in his
backpack. Before they set off down the mountain,
Conan looked again to the southwest. The bank of
clouds was closer and darker, the blue faded in the rest
of the sky, the sun circled with a glowing ring bright
with the rainbow fragments of sun dogs.

The descent from King's Mountain was a great deal
easier than the ascent, but it was after four when they
reached the Loblolly Creek campsite. Conan wondered
if tensions might be exacerbated by the chores necessary to setting up camp. It was the kind of work that required cooperation in close proximity. But undoubtedly
these chores had also over the years become rituals, and
they were accomplished with easy precision, Lucas and
Al working amicably together to set up the two bright
blue dome tents, A. C. splitting kindling with a hand ax
and starting a fire, while Conan helped out where he
could, spreading out bedrolls in the tiny tents, bringing
water up from the creek. Before the chores were finished, there was a degree of camaraderie among the
Kings, and when Al retrieved the beer from the creek,
A. C. welcomed a cold can. Conan usually didn't enjoy
beer, but here in this setting after a long day's hike, it
seemed exactly what he was thirsty for.

A. C. set up a folding grate over the fire, started coffee brewing in a battered aluminum pot, and again as-

sumed the role of chef du jour. The menu consisted of freeze-dried beef stew, served with slabs of skillet-toasted, sourdough bread, and for dessert, Doris Rasmussen's dense, rich brownies. By the time the meal was consumed, darkness had fallen, and a cold wind blew out of the southwest. They were all wearing their parkas before they finished cleaning up after the meal.

"Don't worry about it," A. C. assured Conan when he asked about the noticeable drop in temperature. "Hell, Conan, the nights are always cold in the mountains this time of year."

With the cooking gear stowed away, the fire replenished so that it's whispering, hectic light closed out everything else, they sat on the logs, finishing the beer and exchanging memories. It was A. C. who steered the conversation in that direction, reminiscing about Al when he made the varsity football team at Oregon State University, and Lucas when he set a record in the hundred-meter dash, about Al when he got his captain's bars, and Lucas's first commission after he went out on his own and established LJK Design, about the birth of Al's first child. His son. A. C.'s grandson.

It was, Conan realized, entirely purposeful on A. C.'s part. He was remembering times when he was proudest of his sons, even if he never actually managed the words: *I'm proud of you.*

But perhaps one day he would. At least now the reminiscences and the fire drew them together with quiet laughter and affection. Even Al seemed to let go of his frustration and resentment.

Male bonding, no doubt, Conan thought. Lise would be happy to know that it still worked on the trail to King's Mountain.

CHAPTER 8

When Lucas and Al suggested that Conan sleep in
A. C.'s tent, they had an ulterior motive, but Conan
didn't discover it until an hour after he had crawled into
the tiny, nylon igloo with A. C.

A. C. King snored.

Not only did he snore, he whiffled, brayed, trumpeted
like a bull elk, at a decibel level that billowed the dome
of the tent. This wasn't ordinary snoring that could be
dismissed as white noise. This was a veritable symphony in an alien musical scale, repeatedly rising from
whispering wheezes to a crescendo of rattling snorts,
percussioned by honks and grunts and sounds much like
muttered words.

That Conan didn't expect this aural phenomenon was
due to the fact that on previous treks up King's Mountain, he had never slept in the same tent with A. C. That
he didn't become aware of it tonight for an hour was
due to weariness earned by physical exertion at a high

altitude. It had been seven o'clock when he crawled into his sleeping bag, and against all his expectations, he fell asleep almost before he got it zipped up. But now his brain had apparently reopened for business and accepted input from his senses. What his senses put in was the raucous serenade from the sleeping bag only two feet away.

Conan lay in his own Quallofil cocoon, muscles tightening by increments with the annoyed resentment that snorers inspire in the wakeful, and with the unease of incipient claustrophobia.

And something else: cold.

His nose felt like a chunk of ice attached to his face, and even in the confines of this high tech, insulated body bag, his feet and hands were turning numb. He realized then that it wasn't A. C.'s spectacular snoring that billowed the dome of the tent. It was the wind.

Finally, driven by anxious curiosity, a yen for a cigarette, and a desire to put some space between himself and A. C.'s symphony, Conan unzipped his sleeping bag and felt for his boots. By the time he got them laced, he could feel gooseflesh pebbling his skin under his Levi's and wool sweater. He pulled on his parka and wool gloves, made sure his flashlight and cigarettes were in his pockets, then wormed his way through the tent's opening into the night.

To his dark-accustomed eyes, the sky seemed eerily light, the diffuse light of a waxing moon behind an opaque layer of clouds. The wind had not only quickened, it had turned frigid. He pulled up the hood of his parka as a gust tossed a rain of fir needles into his face.

He managed to get a cigarette lit and took a long drag while he looked up at the black silhouettes of cedars and hemlocks swaying in an ominous dance. He could still hear snoring from A. C.'s tent. Lucas and Al slept more quietly, but at least one of them had inherited their father's undoubtedly deviated septum.

There was a smell about this wind, something pungent and electric that generated a prickle of fear at the back of Conan's mind. He didn't know this country well, didn't know how to read the signs, but if he were on the Ten-Mile, he would regard this rising wind and sudden drop in temperature as warnings.

But he was in a bowl here, encompassed by trees and the talus slope looming over the camp, and he couldn't see enough sky. If memory served him, it was no more than a quarter mile to the clear-cut that had this morning provided such a fine view. Perhaps from that vantage point he could find some stars to tell him how extensive the cloud cover was. He almost laughed, reminded of his father's acerbic dismissal of the forests of western Oregon: "Hell, a man can't see a damn thing for all the *trees*."

Conan flipped the cigarette into the fire pit, then started down the trail. The diffuse light was just sufficient for him to stay on the trail without resorting to the flashlight. He wanted to hold on to his night vision, even though it meant stumbling occasionally over exposed roots. The distance seemed longer than he remembered, but finally he emerged from the trees onto the bare knoll.

The wind here caught his breath, and now the sky was perceptibly darker, featureless, not a star anywhere. To the northeast, against the velvet black of forest, he saw a yellow light. The lodge. As he watched, a smaller light appeared beyond the lodge, moving west. A car on the highway. The light seemed to slow then wink out.

He turned, looked up toward the camp. He could barely discern the black contour of the talus slope above the trees. Something colder than wind touched his

cheek, a sprinkle of moisture. It felt like the fine drop-
lets of a coastal mist.

But not here, not at this elevation, not at this temperature.

He jerked the flashlight from his pocket, turned it on.
He had come looking for stars, and in a sense he had
found them. The snowflakes caught in the beam looked
uncannily like a shower of falling stars.

The panic he felt was born of memories of blizzards
he had survived in his youth, one in particular that had
cost the lives of his mother and brother.

But the panic ebbed as he took a deep, cold breath.
At least he could be grateful for A. C.'s deviated septum. He pushed up his left sleeve, squinting at the
glowing numbers on his watch. Eight o'clock. They had
warning now and time to hike back to the lodge
before—

It came from the direction of the camp, a sundering
blast that hammered at his eardrums, incited his heart to
frenzied pounding. Then a cracking rumbling that
seemed to go on forever yet ended with singular abrupt-
ness, a gust of wind that staggered him.

Conan stood stunned, seeing nothing but darkness,
hearing nothing but the ringing in his ears. On some
level, he understood exactly what had happened, but his
mind balked at acceptance.

Then he broke into a run across the clear-cut and
back into the forest, the beam of the flashlight glancing
in quick arcs on the ghostly shafts of tree trunks. Panting with dread more than exertion, he sprinted toward
what he knew was a catastrophe.

Dust. The starflakes in the beam were obliterated in a
pall of dust. But he didn't stop. Not until he stumbled—
literally—into a barrier of broken rock. He sprawled on

the sharp-edged rubble, coughing, eyes stinging with the dust, fine grains gritting between his teeth.

"*A. C.! Al! Lucas!*"

And why was he shouting their names into the wind?

The camp was buried under tons of rock, and A. C. King and two of his sons were beyond hearing anything.

Conan couldn't have untangled the emotions that forced from his throat a long, desolate cry. Grief? Yes, even though he hadn't known the victims intimately. Frustration, certainly. Terror when it came to him that *he* should have been in one of the tents smashed under this rock slide. And finally rage.

This was not an accident.

Yes, that talus slope had been on the verge of a slide for years, but the explosion that triggered this avalanche could not in any way be regarded as a natural phenomenon.

He got to his feet, found the flashlight, and backtracked a short distance, then climbed to the crest of the ridge, detouring around trees and clumps of underbrush uprooted and wedged aside. When he reached the top of the slide, he cast the beam downward.

It was as if the slope had been scooped out with a huge spoon. A rubble of boulders was mounded halfway up the raw concavity and had spilled down the ravine toward Loblolly Creek. It had probably dammed the creek. Methodically, he crisscrossed the area near the edge of the slide, teeth chattering with cold as he bent over the seeking beam of the flashlight, but it revealed no traces of dynamite wrappings or fuse, and the ground was too rocky for footprints. He found a crumpled, empty Marlboro pack and put it in his pocket, knowing full well that it might have been here for months.

So intent was his mental focus that it was some time before it came through to him that he was finding nothing else because the ground was covered with snow, that the icy flakes were no longer showering stars, but dense waves riding the moaning wind.

He felt a resurgence of panic. He wasn't equipped for this. He had set off this morning dressed for a brisk autumn day in the mountains, not for a blizzard.

He had to get back to the lodge.

And tell the people waiting there that their father, brothers, husbands, and friends were buried under that tumulus of fallen rock? That they had been murdered?

Oh, Lise, this family needed more than a friendly outsider.

A rush of wind rocked him, so intolerably cold that it forced a groan from him. The lodge. He had to reach the lodge.

He made his way back down to the trail, then switched off the flashlight, but the eerie glow in the sky was gone, and he was blind without the light. Five miles to the lodge; an hour minimum, probably more in this storm. He wondered how fresh the batteries were. If they died before he reached the lodge, it was likely he would, too. He wouldn't survive the night in a mountain blizzard if he got lost.

At least it was downhill most of the way. He aimed the flashlight beam along the trail, and began jogging toward the clear-cut, setting a pace he hoped he could maintain for five miles. He counted his steps, one count every time his right foot hit ground. On the beach at home, that meant six feet for every count. One. Two. Three. Four . . .

His count had reached two hundred when he came to the clear-cut. Halfway across it, he stopped, feeling the brunt of the wind. From the southwest. Had to keep it at his back to hold a northeast heading.

Where was the trail? In the forest behind him, the trail had been a discernible aisle cut through trees and underbrush, but here the accumulating snow obliterated the line between trail and bared ground. Couldn't see where it entered the forest beyond the clear-cut.

A sign. He remembered seeing one at the edge of the clear-cut—one of the multitude A. C. put up to post the woods against hunters. The beam sliced through white veils, trembled with his shivering.

And struck the sign. Unreadable with the snow adhering to it, but the rectangular shape was enough. He ran toward it, followed the open lane of the trail into the trees, then slowed to reestablish his jogging pace. One. Two. Three. Four. Five. Six . . .

He focused on the count because it provided something to occupy his mind besides fear. In this context, fear would be lethal if it escalated into panic. So he counted his monotonous, ceaseless footfalls.

By the time he reached four hundred, he was in old growth. He remembered this stretch of forest, remembered how richly beautiful it had been this morning, filled with spun-gold light. Now it was steeped in bone-deep cold, and the towering pillars of trees groaned as they swayed in the wind. Hard to see the trail here. Not enough underbrush. He jogged on, the snowy beam jerking back and forth. The falling snow wasn't as thick here with the forest canopy to catch it, yet the ground was white, snow heavy on the arched fronds of ferns, weighing them down. Down. Downhill all the way.

His count reached a thousand, and his legs were beginning to ache. Wasn't enough oxygen at this altitude, not when the cold sapped his energy, when the wind kept sucking the air out of his lungs.

But he couldn't stop. The fear. An invisible shadow, pursuing him, driving him on, footfalls thudding as he counted them. Sometimes he felt like Alice and the Red Queen. *It takes all the running you can do, to keep in the same place.* No measure of distance in this fog of snow. He might have traversed half a mile or two or none; he couldn't tell. All he knew was that he couldn't stop.

A startled cry. His own. He stumbled, crashed against the white earth, and lay shivering, head pillowed in snow. Wheezing. Just like A. C. *Must've deviated my septum,* and he began to laugh. Or perhaps he was trying to weep.

Someone should weep for Albert Charles King, seventy years old, and just now beginning to learn what questions to ask about his life. Might've found some answers, too. Stubborn enough to keep looking. Always kept the wind at his back.

Conan abruptly raised his head, shook the snow away. Can't go to sleep. Sleep and death were synonymous here. Get up! Now!

Flashlight. Where's the damn flashlight?

He saw it ahead, casting its beam into the snow. Was it dimmer? He crawled to it, grasped it with aching fingers, staggered to his feet.

The trail. He threw the beam around him. He'd lost the trail again.

There. A snow-pasted rectangle on a stake. Another NO HUNTING sign. He had wandered at least fifty feet off the trail. He fixed the light on the sign until he reached it, then goaded his recalcitrant muscles into a swaying jog, starting the count anew. One. Two. Three. Four. Five. The snow crunched under his boots like pieces of Styrofoam rubbing together.

His feet had grown inexplicably heavy, the ground

treacherous with roots and rocks hidden in the snow that constantly tripped him up. The cold burned his hands, his face, his feet; ached in his trembling muscles, and the air was like a slush of ice in his chest.

But he kept going. The fear wouldn't let him stop.

One hundred ninety. One hundred ten . . .

No, that was wrong. Start all over. One. Two. Three. Fourteen. Fifteen. Sixteen. Sixty-one . . .

He was out of the old growth now, but he couldn't remember when he left it. Might have been hours ago. These Douglas firs had been seeded no more than twenty years ago, and the trail's clear aisle was easy to follow. Fourteen. Fifty. Fifty-one. Had to keep moving. If he stopped for an instant, the shivering took over. And the fear.

The flashlight *was* dimmer. Couldn't deny that now. He could only go on forcing his legs to pick up his feet, move them forward, again and again and again. . . .

But his teeth were frozen. If he wasn't careful the chattering would crack them. He laughed, remembering that old buckaroo at the Ten-Mile Ranch. Harlan? Hanson? Hampton. That was it. Called him Hamp for short. Never would wear his false teeth when he was riding in the winter. Said if he came down too hard on 'em, they'd break to smithereens. Kept 'em in his shirt pocket, and ever'time he rode in over Cayuse Ridge, where you could first catch sight of the ranch house, he'd take his teeth out of his pocket and pop 'em in.

Long way up to the top of Cayuse. Didn't remember it being so long, but he didn't usually walk it. Couldn't manage more than putting one foot in front of the other, pulling himself up with branches, sliding a step back for every step forward with the snow up to his knees.

Why wouldn't Hamp wait for him? He knew better

than to leave him here, the boss's only boy. Henry Flagg'd eat ol' Hamp alive if anything happened to . . .

Finally. Ground leveled out, and that meant he'd reached the top of the ridge. The ranch house would be down below.

Nothing. Blackness thick with roiling snow. And with an inward jar that paralyzed him, Conan understood where he was.

No. He understood with terrifying clarity that he *didn't* know where he was, that he had wandered off the trail again, and he had no idea how to find it. The flashlight had faded to yellow, reaching no more than a few feet into the whirling snow fog.

He turned it off, stood shivering in the dark, gasping for breath, mouth open, lips cracked and numb. Think. Think or you're dead.

Might be dead anyway, but not for lack of trying.

The wind. It was at his right, and it was like leaning into a wall of ice. He turned, put his back to it. Downhill all the way. That's all he could do now. Head downhill.

He switched on the flashlight as he started down the other side of the ridge with long, sliding steps. Too steep, too fast. Feet couldn't keep up with the slope, and suddenly he was rolling, plunging, shouting hoarsely all the way until he splashed into rushing water a foot deep.

He thrashed out of the water as if it were bubbling acid, knelt on the bank, muscles cramped and twitching. He could feel his soaked Levi's and gloves already beginning to freeze. The parka was waterproof, but water had poured up the sleeves, under the collar. The boots—he couldn't tell whether the water had gotten into his boots. Couldn't feel his feet, even when he got himself upright.

He started to strip off the wet gloves, then shook his head. Wet or not, they were better than bare, wet flesh. He thrust his hands into his pockets. That unanticipated dip might be the death of him.

But the creek . . .

He heard himself laughing. The creek could be the life of him.

King's Creek. Yes, it had to be. He couldn't be too far from the footbridge, and if he found that, he would have found the trail.

The flashlight! Where was the flashlight?

Not in his pocket. Dropped it when he tumbled down the hill into the creek. Oh, God, not in the creek.

No. A gleam of pale, yellow light twenty feet up the slope. He slogged toward it, panting, picked it up. Pulled his sleeve down over his wet glove, then stumbled back toward the creek and set off upstream along the bank, pushing through the snow-burdened vine maples.

Every few yards, he traded hands with the flashlight, keeping his free hand in his pocket. Sometimes that exchange ended in his dropping the flashlight, stopping to pick it up. Never going to make it with both hands intact. Don't need two hands, anyway. One was plenty.

Eventually a pallid, horizontal line caught in the light. It took him a while to understand that it was the railing of the footbridge, sleeved with snow. He shambled forward, and it was a moment of exalting triumph when he reached the bridge, leaned on the railing with the waters of King's Creek rushing beneath his feet.

He had found the trail. How far to the lodge now? He tried to remember, but whatever his clouded memory turned up meant nothing. Half a mile? How many steps was that on freezing feet: Half an hour? He had left time behind him somewhere. The bell was tolling for

him. He didn't have to send to ask. Sweet, gentle tolling, so faint it was drowned in the troughs of the waves
of wind.

But he wasn't ready to give up yet. Perhaps he would
be if he had reached the point where surrendering
would stop the pain. Not yet.

He turned the fading beam on the trail that curved to
the left from the bridge. He followed the light. An open
aisle bordered by flocked Christmas trees. Too early.
He'd already had ten catalogues advertising Christmas
gifts. Wasn't even Halloween, and they were starting on
Christmas, ringing a bell in the last night.

He tried to revive his jogging pace. Tried and failed.
No way he could keep up the jogging. Lucky to maintain a lurching walk. The drifting snow dragged at his
feet like white 'dobe. All he could do was plead with
his body for one more step. One more. One more.

Listen! The bell. He stopped and pushed his hood
back to hear the distant tolling. A. C.'s come-and-get-it
bell, the bronze bell that hung on the deck at the lodge.
No human hand rang it now. The tolling was too erratic.
The wind rang the bell tonight, but it still called him.
Called him to the closest thing to life he could imagine
at this moment.

But if he could hear the bell, why couldn't he see the
lights of the ranch house? His mother always left lights
in every window downstairs if anyone was out at night.

He pulled the hood up, got his legs moving again.
Had to keep going, had to listen to the bell. Come and
get it, son. . . .

She'd have a cup of hot tea ready for him. Some
tangy, bitter concoction meant to give him strength. An-
nie Whitefeather had been separated from her genetic
family and the surviving remnants of her cultural heritage as an infant, so where had she learned to brew all

those herbal medications? Tribal memory. So she said, and always laughed softly, black eyes shimmering with light.

Another sign. Snowy rectangle with no words, but it told him he was still on the trail. The flashlight was fading fast. Let it rest. Turn it off and let it rest. That was Henry Flagg's first response to failed mechanisms. Let it rest, then try it again. Still fading. If resting didn't help, try a good swift kick. Or falling down. Falling down in knee-deep snow, that'd fix it. But then you have to find the damnfool thing.

Hell, how's a man supposed to find a light buried in the dark? Feel around on hands and knees. Only trouble was, his hands had turned to stone, petrified, and a man damn sure can't feel nothin' with his hands petrified.

But this time his right hand knocked against the flashlight. Hold on to it. Both hands, that's fine. A golden circle of light. Didn't even have to kick it.

Now get back on your feet. Listen. That bell's still tolling for you. Stand up and listen!

Right. Move, get moving. Good. Downhill from here on out. Sometimes he hardly had to touch his feet to the ground. Was the bell closer? Had to be. He was still heading downhill. Probably. The flashlight made the driving snow look like pellets of pure gold. Kept coming at him, all that gold, and he couldn't catch a grain of it.

No more Christmas trees. Someone must've taken them down. New Year's Day already. Missed Christmas. Nothing around him except swirling snow, golden snow, all closed in this little glass sphere. Turn the brass key and the bell rings; tip the sphere and the snow keeps coming. But the little snowman inside the sphere has fallen over. Let it rest. Just let him rest awhile.

No! Have to pick him up. A good swift kick, but he probably couldn't feel it.

He'd fallen again, lost the flashlight again, and when he levered himself to his knees, felt through the snow with his hands of stone, he couldn't find it. Snow was too deep out here in the open. If he didn't stand up, it would bury him.

He listened to the mourning toll of the bell, gazed into blackness. Keep the wind to your back. But he couldn't even feel it now. He turned his head, leaned into the wall of ice.

And saw the light.

Golden gleam, suspended in a film of snow. He reached for it, but his hands closed on nothing. How had the flashlight got so far away?

How had it got to be so many, and every one so square?

His eyes came into focus, and perhaps it was the sudden adrenaline rush that brought his mind into focus, too.

The light came from the windows of the lodge. He had nearly stumbled past it. No more than fifty yards away. He staggered to his feet, shuffled stiff-legged through the mire of snow.

Help . . .

Couldn't make sound of the word. He tried again, got out a rasping whisper. Had to make someone inside the lodge hear, because his legs weren't working anymore. He slumped to his knees.

"Help . . ."

No one in the lodge could hear that. Try something else. Any ranch hand who couldn't whistle through his teeth loud enough for the cow dogs to hear him half a mile away wasn't worth his salt.

But he'd never tried whistling when he couldn't feel his lips.

Try. Deep breath, take a deep breath. . . .

What came out sounded like a variation on the theme of wind.

Again. Deep breath, and give it whatever you've got left. Better. Yes, better, but the sound seemed trapped in his head.

Again. Start high, drop a note or so, end with an upward fillip. . . .

And he heard a new sound, a sound sharp and crisp enough to cut through the wind.

Heather's audacious, high-pitched bark. He pulled in another breath, forced out another whistle. Poor excuse for a whistle, but Heather could hear what the humans in the lodge could not.

A new rectangle of light. The front door opening, and Heather hurtled into the darkness, bounded toward him, barking a challenge. She hadn't recognized him by those pitiful whistlings, only heard a sound outside the house that might be a threat. It occurred to him that such bravery should never be taken for granted. She was a small creature racing out into an opaque, frigid storm, through snow up to her shoulders, to face she knew not what.

Yet face it she did, and find him she did, and she led the way. Two figures shuffled toward him, shouting, the white beams of their flashlights blurred with snow.

CHAPTER 9

Lise and Will. Conan recognized their voices. They supported him, one on each side, wading through the snow toward the lodge, and Lise kept asking him what had happened. Conan shook his head. He could only answer that once, and the others were waiting in the lodge.

Will asked him how long he'd been out in the storm.

He muttered through numb lips, "Don' know. What time's it?"

"About ten."

It took him a while to remember what time it had been when he last looked at his watch, and by then they had reached the deck. The front door was open, and there in a haze of light he saw Mark, Tiff, Kim, Loanh, Demara. Wives and lovers, brother and son.

"Two hours," he said. It didn't make much sense.

Lise asked, "But where's Dad? And Lucas and Al?"

He shook his head. Again.

The light in the atrium was blinding. He heard the
door close behind him, heard the rattle of voices around
him, felt the blurred, questioning faces pressing toward
him. Will said firmly, "Be quiet, everybody! Give him
a chance."

Conan said hoarsely, "There was a rock slide. The
camp . . . it buried the camp." His eyes were adjusting
to the light, and he could see their faces now, and in
every one was the same stunned bewilderment.

Demara whispered, *"Lucas . . ."* Kim pressed a hand
to her mouth, blue eyes wide. Tiff, repeating the single
syllable *oh*, put her arms around Loanh, but Loanh
seemed oblivious to her embrace, staring at Conan with
no hint of comprehension. Mark blinked and frowned as
if he'd been presented with a riddle he couldn't find an
answer for.

But Lise—she stood directly in front of Conan, so
pale she seemed on the edge of fainting. "You mean
they were—were *buried* in the rock slide? *All* of them?
But *you're* here! How did *you* get out alive!"

"I wasn't—I went out to look for . . ." *To look for
stars.* That didn't make sense, either. Not now.

Her hands convulsed into fists, pounding at his chest,
her face warped in despairing rage. *"You're* here! Why
are *you* here? Why? Why? *Why?*"

Conan understood her pain, but it overwhelmed him
now. He sagged against Will, shaking uncontrollably
and closer to weeping than he had been for years.

"Mark!" Will's voice, sharp and peremptory. "Take
care of her. Damn it, I've got a case of hypothermia
here. Somebody give me a hand. Conan? Just hold on."

Will headed him toward the stairs. Someone was supporting him on the left. Demara. As they moved up the
steps, Will snapped orders. "Loanh, get my medical
case from my room—looks like an attaché case. Kim,

I'll need all the heat I can get in his room. Turn on the heater in the bathroom and get a fire going in the fireplace. Tiff, run some warm water in his tub. Not hot, just—"

"Approximately one hundred degrees," she said with surprising steadiness as she hurried past them up the stairs.

"Right. Demara, you had any first-aid training?"

"No, but I'm strong, and I've never run into anything that shocked me."

By the time they reached Conan's room, every light was on, Tiff was in the bathroom filling the tub, Kim at the fireplace lighting a fire, and Loanh hurrying in with Will's medical case. He sent her out again for extra blankets, and Kim departed with her, then Will sat Conan down on the bed and opened the case. Tiff came out of the bathroom, said, "I need a thermometer, Will."

"You'll have one in just a minute. Demara, start unlacing his boots—carefully. Might have some frostbite." He slipped a sterile cap on a digital thermometer, and thrust it into Conan's mouth, then felt his damp Levi's and gloves, muttered, "Hell, Conan, what'd you do? Take a swim?" He hurriedly removed Conan's parka, pulled his sweater and T-shirt up, pressed a stethoscope against his chest, and listened for a few seconds, then when the thermometer beeped, took it, frowning at the reading. "Ninety-four point seven. Well, at least that classifies you as mild, so I don't have to worry about fibrillation so much. That's what usually kills severe hypothermics. Tiff! You can use this thermometer." When she bustled out of the bathroom to get it, he asked, "By the way, how'd you know about the water temperature?"

"Oh, hypothermia treatment is in the first-aid curric-

ulum we offer at Trinity." And she bustled away, her
pink robe fluttering behind her.

Demara finished unlacing Conan's boots. "You want
these off?"

Will took a pair of scissors from his case and began
cutting away Conan's right glove. "No, let me do that,
Demara. People with frozen feet have been known to
take off their toes with their boots."

Conan groaned, and Demara hissed, "Jesus, Will!"

"That's my best bedside manner. Don't worry, Conan,
I doubt you were out long enough for that kind of frostbite." He removed the glove and examined Conan's
hand. The skin had a fish-belly pallor, and the heat in
the room was already arousing a burning ache. Will began cutting away the other glove. "Next time, wear mittens."

Conan cleared his throat, a little surprised to find he
could speak clearly now, except for the shivering that
wouldn't stop. "I'll remember that next time I get
caught in a blizzard. Is there a radio in the house?"

"Yes, but we couldn't pick up anything except static
tonight. The power's out, by the way. We're running on
the generator now. Oh, thanks, Kim." That as Kim
brought in an armful of blankets.

She left the blankets on the bed and headed for the
door. "If you don't need me for a while, I'm going to
get some warm clothes out of A. C.'s trunk. We may all
need an extra layer or so before this is over."

Will nodded without looking up from the task of slipping Conan's boots off, then his socks. "Good boots.
Toes don't look too bad. Okay, let's get the rest of your
clothes off. Tiff, how's the water?"

"A hundred one point two," she called.

"Close enough. Conan, don't try to help. Just relax."

He nodded, surrendering himself to being undressed

like a child. He was too spent and shaky to do more, and certainly beyond modesty when Will and Demara had stripped him of his wet, icy clothing. Will wrapped a blanket around him, then checked his blood pressure. The constriction of the cuff on his arm made his fingers ache. Will didn't comment on the reading, but delved into his medical case and came up with a syringe, which he filled from a rubber-capped vial.

Conan asked, "What's that?"

Will plunged the needle into Conan's left deltoid with a lack of finesse that made him flinch. "Demerol. You'll thank me when you start thawing out. If you're wondering about the rush, quick thawing is the latest thing. Okay, Demara, let's get him into the bathroom."

It was only a few steps, but Conan surrendered to their assistance in this, too. Will sent Tiff out, and Conan surrendered to being helped into a sitting position on the side of the tub, turning, and having his feet eased into the water. He stiffened with the pain that made his feet feel as if they had been submerged in molten lead. Demara and Will lowered him into the tub, while he gasped like a porpoise, and Will murmured, "Just lean back ... that's right ... you're doing fine. ..."

The messages Conan's nerves were sending made him doubt that, especially when Will said, "You've got to get your hands in the water, Conan," and forced his hands down into the molten liquid.

The pain was pure and white, and he couldn't contain a muffled cry, while Will kept promising, "The Demerol will kick in soon."

Conan doubted that, too, but he wasn't sorry to be proven wrong, even though it seemed to take an inordinately long time. Gradually the pain retreated to a bearable level, and the water began to seem warm and comforting, rather than scalding and excruciating. Finally he closed his eyes, letting the tension ease out of his fatigued muscles, surrendering again, only vaguely aware of Will periodically checking his pulse and temperature, or adding water to maintain the ideal hundred degrees, or occasionally offering a glass of lukewarm water.

The only problem with this comforting submersion was that it left his mind free. Free to remember Lise's despairing *why*? Free to remember Albert Charles King and his sons around a campfire by Loblolly Creek in the tentative first stages of reconciliation. Free to remember that stunning explosion, the rumble of tons of rock smashing down on the two tents. Free to imagine being in one of those tents, waking a split second before the boulders—

No!

"Conan? What's wrong?"

He had spoken the denial aloud. He murmured, "Nothing, Will."

Don't imagine, he admonished himself. Think.

But that wasn't easy now, between his exhaustion, the Demerol, and the warm water. His mind was nowhere near sleep even under their influence. He just couldn't think coherently.

Still, one thought was trenchantly clear: He was dealing with premeditated murder designed and committed by one of the people who had Friday evening shared a meal with the victims. One of the family.

Timing and the locale were vital to these murders, and who would know that A. C. and his sons always camped at exactly the same place on this particular weekend? Who would know about the unstable talus slope looming over that campsite? Only someone who had made the trek. No one outside the family except Will and Conan.

Will's voice derailed his train of thought. "Okay, Conan, temp's almost normal, and you've got a nice, rosy glow on your toes and fingers. I don't think they'll even blister. Of course, they'll never let you forget what you did to them for the rest of your life."

Conan opened his eyes, wondering how long he had been steeping in this enervating warmth. At least half an hour, he guessed. Demara was still here, studying him with an oddly dispassionate gaze.

He again surrendered to Will and Demara's ministrations, while they got him out of the tub, dried him, and clothed him in flannel pajamas that he guessed were A. C.'s. He hadn't owned a comparable set since he left Eastern Oregon. Will also provided a pair of lambskin scuffs. Conan leaned heavily on him during the short walk to his bed, easing his weight onto his feet. Kim was standing by the fireplace, a brittle tautness in her face, but she remained silent until he was in bed and under the covers, his aching hands at his sides under the sheets.

Then she came to the foot of the bed and said flatly, "Conan, I'm sorry, but the rest of us have to deal with this tonight. I mean, *begin* to deal with it. We have to know what happened."

He considered how much to tell her, finally said, "All I know is I woke up about eight and realized it had turned cold, and the wind had come up. I walked to a clear-cut about a quarter of a mile away, thinking I could get a good look at the sky, and that's when I heard the rumble. I ran back to camp, but . . ." He didn't try to finish that.

Kim only nodded. It was Demara who asked, "But

wasn't there any warning? I mean, rocks don't just fall off mountains. Do they?"

Will said, "In that particular spot they do. I'm no geologist, but even I could tell that slope was unstable. Always made me nervous, the times I went on the hike. Now, let's get out of here and let Conan sleep. Thanks for the help, Demara. You'd make a damn good nurse."

She smiled briefly and headed for the door, leaving it open behind her. Kim started to follow, then paused. "Will, we can't leave the generator on all night. I brought up a kerosene lamp—there on the side table." She turned to Conan and after a moment said, "I'm sorry for what you've been through, Conan, and glad you lived through it."

"Thanks, Kim."

When she was gone, Will lit the lamp, frowning as he adjusted the wick. The warm, oily smell was oddly reassuring. "Conan, Lise didn't really mean what she said about—well, you know."

"Yes, I know. She was hurting, Will, and maybe you'd better go see how she's faring—and the others, too."

"Right. Damn, I just can't believe it yet." He shook his head and ran a hand distractedly through his red hair. Then he looked around, found his medical case open on the floor by the bedside table. "Better take this with me. Anything I can get for you, Conan?"

He replied lightly, "A cigarette and a good stiff drink."

"No way. Nicotine and alcohol are definitely contraindicated for hypothermic patients. I'll check on you later, but just remember, my room is kitty-corner across the hall. Holler if you need me."

Will turned out the ceiling light and closed the door behind him, and only now did Conan become fully conscious of a sound that had been a subliminal awareness before: an unrelenting, muffled roar. The wind. Outside, a magnificent, indifferent, and terrifying beast commanded the night and laid siege to the lodge.

And perhaps another kind of beast lived within its walls.

CHAPTER 10

Conan's body cried out for sleep, but his mind denied him that. He lay listening to the tumult of the wind in a warm cocoon of blankets in a room filled with dim, golden light from the kerosene lamp and the fire.

And he thought about murder.

It was the callous audacity of these murders that kept him awake in spite of weariness and Demerol. Someone had been willing to kill four people, at least one of them—Conan Flagg—an unintended victim. Conan hadn't been expected on the hike, but the killer didn't regard his unanticipated presence as reason enough to abort the plan.

Who was the *intended* victim?

A. C.? That conclusion offered the most obvious motivation: money. At the top of King's Mountain, A. C. had admitted his fear that his sons were just waiting for him to die. For his money.

Conan flinched, realizing that A. C. had been alive to speak those words no more than twelve hours ago.

At least Conan could be sure A. C. had in fact been a victim, intended or not. A. C. was in his tent when Conan left the camp; that snoring was unmistakable. He couldn't have escaped the rock slide unless he departed the camp immediately after Conan. In that case, Conan would have seen him or a flashlight on the trail, unless he struck off across country. Why would A. C. take such an irrational course? To make it seem he had died in the rock slide?

Conan accepted the possibility that a person might go to great lengths to stage his own death for any number of reasons. But not A. C. King, who, in spite of uneasy relationships with his sons, was so manifestly satisfied with his life. And one thing Conan was sure of: if A. C. staged his own death, he would not kill his sons in the process.

But what about Lucas or Al? Had either of them some compelling reason to make it seem he had died?

Conan was sure that the second tent had been occupied before he left camp. Again, he had heard snoring. But who was in the tent? Both Lucas and Al? Or only one of them?

A distant banging startled him, tightened every muscle. He lay still, breathing deeply. The wind had blown something loose; an eaves trough, probably. Now it thudded incessantly like a funeral drum.

Lucas might have been an unintended victim; no one expected him for this year's reunion hike, either. On the other hand, he might have come here solely for the purpose of murdering his father and staging his own death. From what Lise had said, Lucas's hatred for A. C. ran deep, which might be motive enough for murder. Then there was the obvious motive of money. A. C. had not, as he once threatened, disinherited Lucas, and he knew it. Lise had told him. He was still in line for a share of A. C.'s estate, which, rumor had it, ran into the tens of millions.

There was also that "little problem" Lucas had mentioned. He told A. C. that it was taken care of with a contract to design and build a thirty-million-dollar office complex, which suggested the problem had been financial and not at all little. And A. C. had apparently earlier turned Lucas down when he asked for help in solving that problem.

So, had the problem actually been solved?

Conan thought irritably that if he could only get to a phone, he could call his friend Charlie Duncan in San Francisco and have him send an operative to Los Angeles to discover the nature of Lucas King's problem and determine whether it had in fact been solved.

But A. C. had refused to install a telephone in his mountain retreat, and the cellular phone in Conan's car—or those in any of the other cars—was well out of range of any antennas. The nearest pay phone was ten miles away at Government Camp, and until this storm ended, it might as well be a thousand miles.

But if a share of his father's estate was part of Lucas's motive, his own faked death wouldn't help him, although it might solve the little problem in L.A. To escape that problem, Lucas might choose to "die" and make a fresh start elsewhere with a new identity, but a dead Lucas couldn't collect his share of A. C.'s estate. Not unless . . .

Demara Wilder. If Demara and Lucas were married, it was conceivable, depending on the provisions of A. C.'s will, that as Lucas's wife and heir *she* could collect his share of the estate and, after a reasonable interval, rendezvous with him, probably in a foreign country that did not have an extradition treaty with the United States.

But would Lucas trust Demara with his fortune and future?

Possibly. He had seemed hopelessly infatuated with her.

And would Lucas be willing to kill his brother incidental to killing his father? Again, possibly. With Al dead, Lucas's share of the estate would be that much bigger.

Whatever Lucas's motive, he had opportunity. He might have planted the explosives days earlier, then made his dramatic appearance as the prodigal son yesterday, taken the hike, but left the camp in the hour after the four of them retired and before Conan wakened. The explosives might have been detonated with a timer or with a radio signal. Lucas could have been miles away at the time of the explosion.

Conan frowned at the waning fire. Already the air in the room had a dry chill, and the wind seemed to have increased in ferocity. The distant banging continued relentlessly.

He closed his eyes, consciously relaxing his muscles.

One of the problems with this scenario was transportation. A supposedly dead Lucas couldn't simply hike back to the lodge for his Mercedes. He *could* hike to the highway, but would he plan on hitching a ride from there, where he could be picked up or seen by a local who might recognize him? The King family was well known in the area.

Or he might have left another car parked on or near the highway. Demara could have driven one of the cars up from California, or they might have rented one along the way.

Or he might have another accomplice to provide

transportation. And would that accomplice also provide the expertise to engineer the rock slide? That was another problem with this scenario: Lucas was an architect and contractor, and had no doubt worked on building sites where explosives were used, but would he be expert enough to design the explosion that triggered the rock slide? If not, he would need to find someone who *was* sufficiently expert, and that person might also provide him transportation. For a price.

Yes. Conan sat up, staring into the flickering firelight.

A memory plucked at his sleeve. When he had walked to the clear-cut to search for stars, he saw the light from the lodge *and* another light, which he assumed to be a car on the highway. It had slowed and stopped not far west of the lodge. At least, the light had disappeared.

With a sigh, he sank back into the pillows. The light might have disappeared because the car went around a curve or behind some trees.

He reminded himself that Lucas was only one suspect.

There was Al King to consider.

The intended victim for Al would be A. C. Al would have known that Mark couldn't go on the hike, but he couldn't have known before Friday night that Lucas and Conan would be at the camp site. And Al had twice on Friday hinted broadly that Conan needn't go.

But so had Lucas. Did that imply prior knowledge on the part of either of them?

As Conan considered those hints—or warnings?—he became aware of voices in the hall that he couldn't identify over the rush of wind. Probably the family settling in for the night. He heard doors closing. At least Tiff and Mark wouldn't be alone. He thought of Demara, Kim, and Loanh all facing empty rooms, empty cold beds. And Lise? Where was she sleeping tonight? Certainly not in the studio. Probably one of the small bedrooms at the east end of the hall. She would have Heather with her, and such unquestioning comfort could be vital.

A light tap on the door, then before Conan could respond, it opened. Will Stewart came in carrying a candle in a wrought-iron holder. He asked, "Why aren't you asleep yet?" then put the candle down on the bedside table and pressed two fingers to Conan's throat, reading his pulse. "How're you feeling?"

"Probably better than I think I am. What about the others?"

Will sighed, looked over at the fireplace, then crossed to it and began adding wood as he answered. "Well, Lise has herself under control now. Put everything on hold, I guess. Kim and Demara never lost control, and I'm sure Kim doesn't intend to till the storm lets up, and we can get through to the real world. Loanh—she seems to have everything bottled up. I'm worried about her." With the fire sending out fresh streamers of flame, he returned to the bedside. "I'm worried about Mark, too. He's into denial. Says maybe you just imagined the slide, or maybe A. C. and the guys got out somehow."

Conan nodded. "We all need comforting delusions occasionally."

"Yeah. Well, what can I do for you? Need a Demerol booster?"

"No, but you can prop me up a little. I hate lying flat on my back."

Will rearranged the pillows against the headboard, and when Conan got himself repositioned, said, "Conan, I'll set my alarm and check on you at three, but, damn it, yell if you feel any weird symptoms."

"All right, Will. By the way, what time is it? My watch got lost in the shuffle somewhere."

"It's about twelve-thirty. Your watch is in the bathroom." He went into the bathroom, and when he returned, laid Conan's watch within reach on the table. "Just leave it there. I don't want anything constricting any of your extremities. You want the lamp out?"

"No, leave it on. Will, did anyone tell you how handy it is to have a doctor in the house?"

He laughed as he went to the door. "You're just lucky Jayleen hadn't gone into labor when I went down to Government Camp to phone this morning."

After Will shut the door, Conan watched the fire. Its rhythmic currents seemed synchronized with the roaring gusts of wind.

Murder. He had to think about it, understand it.

Al King. Was Al in fact a viable suspect?

Certainly as viable as Lucas. Motive: money. Both Lise and A. C. had said that Al's construction business was faring badly, and beyond that Conan was sure Al's exchange with A. C. at the bar Friday night indicated that he owed his father a substantial sum of money, and A. C. was demanding payment. At least the interest, he had said.

Would A. C. foreclose on his own son?

Probably. As he put it, it was a business transaction. And Lise had said that A. C.'s sons never got a cent from their father after he put them through college, unless it was in the form of a loan—fully documented and collateralized.

What would Al put up for collateral? If it were a large loan, probably his major assets, which would be King Construction Company's heavy equipment and possibly its extant building contracts.

Conan frowned, distracted by faint sounds in the hall.

Footsteps, perhaps? Voices? Or only the creaking of stressed timbers?

If Al had murdered A. C. and staged his own death, his modus operandi would be essentially the same as Lucas's. Al was just as likely to have access to explosives, although Conan had the impression that he was a manager more than a hands-on builder. Still, Al would be as likely to have access to an expert accomplice.

But Al's heir was Loanh. Would he trust her as his accomplice? Their relationship had seemed exceptionally shaky. And what was that Loanh had said to Lise about family? *Without family, one might as well be dead.* Did Loanh think she would have to give up her family—the Kings and her children, presumably, since she had left her own family in Vietnam when she married—to carry out her part in Al's scheme?

But if Lucas or Al were still alive, one problem either would have to face was that the authorities would not be satisfied that the Kings, father and sons, were in fact dead without excavating their bodies.

Conan winced as he considered the magnitude of that task in light of the remoteness of the location and the difficulty of access for the kind of heavy machinery necessary to moving so many tons of rock. He tried not to think of what might remain of those bodies. But none of the victims could be pronounced legally dead—and A. C.'s will could not be probated—until all three bodies were found.

At least that would be the case if the police had reason to think the rock slide was *not* an accident, an act of God. But Conan knew it was technically possible to create an explosion that would destroy all evidence of its origins. If the rock slide *did* seem an act of God, would the authorities demand the unearthing of the bodies? That decision would be up to the State Medical Examiner, Dan Reuben, a man Conan knew to be scrupulously honest but inherently sympathetic. Would Dan be willing to accept appearances for the sake of the grieving family?

"Damn." A tapping at the door. He was sitting up, so preoccupied had he been with his thoughts, and his arms and shoulders were chilled. The tapping repeated itself.

"Come in!"

Tiff King, in an unlikely assortment of flannel pajamas and wool sweaters under a pink satin robe, entered with a candlestick in one hand, a coffee mug, nested in a paper napkin, in the other. The candlelight haloed her frizzed hair, glowed in the steam rising from the mug, and she seemed such an unlikely apparition, he almost laughed.

"Oh, you're 'wake," she said in a stage whisper. "*Thought* I saw a light unner the door. Oh, dear, you rilly *must* stay unner the covers, y'know, *specially* after what you've been *through*, oh, and I shoulda brought some vidamin *E*. Take some or rub it on." She put the mug on the side table and made a fumbling attempt at tucking him in. The scent of Scotch blended unpleasantly with her floral perfume.

He said, "That's fine, Tiff. What's that? The mug?"

"Mm? Oh!" With a bright smile she picked it up and offered it to him like a seeress about to begin an incantation. "I almos' *forgot*. I mean, *Will* says you oughta have this, y'know, to help you *sleep*."

"What is it?"

"Hot toddy." She sniffed at it. "*Plenny* of lemon juice, y'know, for vidamin C."

"And bourbon?"

"Well, *yes*, thas what makes you *sleep*. Here, I'll hold

it for you." She thrust the mug under his nose, nearly spilling its contents.

Conan drew back. "Tiff, just leave it on the table."

She put the mug down and said amicably, "Don't let it get cold. Oh, I *gotta* get back to Mark. Oh, poor love, he's just *so* dishraught, y'know, and who can *blame* him. I mean, he's an *orphan* now, and a . . . a whaddayacallit when your brother dies?" She had begun wandering toward the door as she spoke, but she paused, looked fixedly at Conan. "Omigod, it musta been *awful*, being there—I mean, with all those *rocks* crashing down and . . . oh, what was it *like*, Conan?"

He said firmly, "Go to bed, Tiff."

"Okay." She turned and ambled out the door, closing it behind her.

And Conan let his pent breath out slowly while he stared at the steaming mug only an arm's length away.

What was it like?

Perhaps the question she meant to ask was: what do you *know*?

Before Tiff's arrival, he had, vaguely, recognized the implications in his position as sole witness to the murders. He knew the rock slide had been preceded by an explosion, that it could not be considered an act of God, and his testimony would guarantee that Dan Reuben wouldn't sign the death certificate necessary to probating A. C.'s will without a thorough investigation and the disinterment of the bodies.

Conan had to this point spoken only of the rock slide and refrained from mentioning the explosion because he felt these survivors had enough to handle without being told that the deaths were murders, but now he understood the unconscious or at least unrecognized reason for his reticence: Anyone capable of casually sacrificing one or more incidental victims to achieve the murder of the intended victim would not balk at killing a witness who could turn an act of God into an act of murder.

But apparently that person wasn't convinced by Conan's reticence.

Will Stewart had not recommended a hot toddy laced with whiskey for a hypothermia patient, not even a mild case.

CHAPTER 11

Conan sat on the side of the bed, shivering, his hands and feet aching with the cold, but he couldn't seem to decide what to do or even catch his breath. He had started to get out of bed to find a weapon, and finally realized there was little available to him in this room. His gun was in his car, but was it worth the risk of going after it? Or was it such a risk? Where the hell did he think he'd be safe?

He stared at the mug. Tiff. Tiffany Rose Dalhousie King. Daughter of a professor at the Stanford School of Law. Would-be flower child turned middle-aged. Borderline alcoholic.

And murderer?

His first inclination was to laugh. On the other hand, Tiff was not as air-brained as she seemed. And if she were a killer, she would probably be a partner in crime with Mark.

Motive?

Did the obvious motive of money apply to Mark and/or Tiff? Tiff's penchant for spending money extravagantly was no secret, but Mark always seemed peculiarly lacking in ambition, content to serve his father's empire as head of its legal department.

Yet Lise had hinted that Mark needed to make peace with A. C. A long story, she had said—one Conan knew he must hear.

He knew he must also find out more about Mark's broken ankle. According to Lise, Mark broke the ankle on his deck, yet Friday afternoon Mark told Lucas that he'd fallen in his hot tub. Even if the injury was genuine, Mark had an accomplice with two good ankles in Tiff.

Means?

That was problematical. Conan doubted either of them had any knowledge of explosives, although dynamite was sometimes used in timber operations, and Mark would have access to information or—like Al or Lucas—could probably find an expert accomplice willing to engineer the rock slide for a price. And if the explosion had been detonated by radio, then either Tiff or Mark might have done it without ever leaving the lodge. There was nothing between the camp site and the lodge to stop a radio signal.

Conan heard his teeth chattering and grimaced. He couldn't just sit here in his borrowed flannel pajamas in a room that was getting colder by the second as the fire burned down.

A poker. He looked over at the fireplace and saw the tool set. But would he be physically capable of defending himself with it? Would his aching hands fail him?

His shoulders sagged, and again he almost laughed. For God's sake, call Will. He was probably the only person in this house Conan was sure he could trust. So call him.

Then Conan's muscles snapped taut. The door was opening. Someone stood there, a shadow in the shadows. The lamplight didn't reach far enough to define the figure.

He was on the verge of shouting for Will, when he recognized his visitor. Rather, he recognized Heather, who nonchalantly trotted into the room.

Lise asked, "Conan, what are you doing out of *bed*?"

And could he trust Lise King any more than the other potential killers within these walls?

She hurried to the bed, put her arms around his shoulders. "You're shivering. What's wrong? Oh, Heather! Get down!"

Heather had leapt up on the foot of the bed and settled in, and Conan smiled, realizing he had found a weapon. At least, an ally. "Let her stay, Lise. And maybe you'd better tuck me in."

Lise helped him back into his warm cocoon and stood watching him. Her eyes were puffy with old tears, but there seemed to be no threat of new tears. She was uncannily calm, as if she were armored in steel control that would break her before it could be broken.

She said, "I came hoping you weren't asleep. I didn't want to wait any longer to tell you I'm sorry for what I said to you when you told us about . . ." She faltered, then: "It was unforgivable."

Conan lightly touched his hand to her arm. "No, Lise, it wasn't. It was only a natural response to pain and shock."

She almost took his hand in hers, then remembered, frowning down at his fingers, swollen and marked with the rosy glow Will Stewart had found so satisfying.

"God, I hope this blizzard is over soon. It's as if we'd been sucked into some sort of white hole."

"It's an early storm. Maybe it won't last long. Lise, I'd like to ask a favor of you."

"Sure. I owe you at least one."

"You owe me nothing, but this is a large favor, and I'll owe you if you grant it. May I keep Heather with me tonight?"

That was clearly not what she had expected. She looked down at Heather, and the lamplight caught in Lise's eyes, revealing something close to fear, something that rattled at her steel control.

"Why, Conan?"

"I can't explain. Not yet."

She waited a moment longer, then took a deep breath. "If Heather's willing, I am. She likes you. Like at first sight, and that's unusual for her." Lise went to the end of the bed and stroked Heather's tawny back while she explained the new sleeping arrangements. Then she said, "I'd better leave so you can sleep, Conan. Good night."

"Good night, Lise. Thanks."

She paused to give Heather a hand signal and a firm "Stay!" when the sheltie started to leave with her, then departed. Heather gazed at the closed door, puzzled, then stretched out at Conan's left side. He extricated his hand from the covers and ran his palm across her head.

"Well, Heather, I'm counting on you."

He turned to look at the mug. Lise apparently hadn't even noticed it. He wondered what it contained besides the usual hot water, lemon juice, sugar, and whiskey. Possibly dissolved sleeping pills or tranquilizers, something the killer would have available, something that would leave Conan vulnerable to an attack in the night. A pillow over the face, perhaps. Something inconspicu-

ous that might be blamed on the aftereffects of hypothermia. Heart failure due to fibrillation.

What the killer didn't know was that drugging him
was hardly necessary now. He was suddenly so overwhelmed by exhaustion that not even the thought of
murder—past or potential—could keep him awake.

Perhaps his mind surrendered at last to his body's
needs because he now had an ally, a guard whose acute
hearing had already saved his life once tonight.

CHAPTER 12

It was an aural cannonade and Conan came out of a deep sleep quivering like a struck drumhead. All he was sure of at that moment was that Heather was barking insistently, and someone was standing in the open doorway.

Again, a shadow in the shadows. A mask, something covering the face? Possibly.

Then Heather launched herself at the shadow figure, and it retreated. The door slammed. Heather kept barking, scratching manically at the door.

Conan found himself on his feet, swearing angrily because he knew he could not identify that shadow figure. The light had been too dim, his glimpse too brief, his mind too befuddled with sleep.

"Heather! It's all right, sweetheart." He sagged down onto the bed while Heather came to him. "Yes, you're a first-rate guard dog."

She wagged her tail, but a moment later began bark-

118

ing again, this time at Will Stewart as he lunged into the room.

"What the hell? Heather?" The sheltie went to him, sniffed suspiciously at his pajama legs. "Conan, what happened?"

"I guess Heather heard something banging in the wind." And in fact the eaves trough, or whatever it was, still thudded incessantly.

Will had no chance to comment on that explanation. The hall was full of voices and flashlight beams. Heather had apparently wakened everyone, and they began crowding into the room: Lise first, to take Heather in hand; then Mark on one crutch with Tiff at his side; then Kim and Demara. They were a motley crew in nightclothes augmented with sweaters, thick socks, and in Demara's case, a blanket, all shouting questions at once. Only Loanh had not been drawn by Heather's alarm.

Will held up a hand for silence. "Heather was just barking at something banging in the wind. Sorry, no Sasquatch at the window."

That garnered nervous laughs, and everyone began moving toward the door. Conan said loudly enough for any of them to hear, "Will, thanks for sending the toddy. It put me right to sleep." The mug was still on the table, and he only hoped that in the dim light no one could see that it was full.

"What? Here—get this on." Will helped Conan into his robe as he asked irritably, "*What* toddy?"

"The one Tiff brought me. She said you prescribed it."

Will frowned at Tiff. "I didn't prescribe any damn such thing."

She stuttered a moment, then insisted, "But you

must've, I mean, *Demara* gave it to me, you know, and she *told* me you—"

"I did *not* give it to you!" Demara snapped.

"Oh, yes, you *did*! Right outside in the hall. You *said*—"

"You must've been drunk, Tiff."

Conan whispered to Will, "Get them out of here. Except Lise."

Will nodded and began herding people out of the room. The argument between Tiff and Demara continued into the hall, but he closed the door on it. Lise, kneeling beside Heather, gave Will a startled look when he demanded of Conan, "Damn it, what's going *on* here?"

A good question, Conan thought, noting that his hands were still shaking. "Will, if you'll get the fire going again, I'll explain a few things to both of you." He slipped his feet into the lambskin scuffs and made his way carefully to the armchair to the left of the fireplace.

Will began reviving the fire, grumbling, "Why can't you do your explaining from bed like a good patient?"

"Because I can't think lying down."

Lise brought the straight chair from the desk and sat facing him, her hands pushed into the sleeves of her wool robe. "Conan, Heather wasn't barking at anything banging in the wind, was she?"

"No. She was barking at the person who opened my door."

Will placed a last wedge of wood on the fire, and while the flames leapt and hissed, he fixed Conan with a piercing eye. "Who was it?"

"I don't know, but I'm sure that he—or she—didn't intend for me to live through the night." Will and Lise stared at him, but before either of them could speak,

Conan asked, "Will, do you have some sort of specimen bottle in your medical case? And maybe a plastic bag?"

"I, uh, yes, I think so. What do you need them for?"

Conan pointed to the mug by his bed. "The toddy. The one you didn't prescribe."

Will looked at the mug suspiciously. "You said Tiff brought it to you? Maybe she just took it on herself to fix it for you."

Lise put in, "But she said Demara gave it to her."

"And Demara denied it," Conan noted, shrugging. "There's no way to get at the truth of that now. Will, I don't know what's in that toddy. Maybe just the usual ingredients, but if we ever get out of this white hole, I'd like to have it analyzed."

Will nodded, then strode out of the room, and in the silence he left behind, Heather sat down at Lise's feet, pressed her forehead against her knee in search of reassurance.

Conan said, "I owe that lovely lady my life—again."

Lise smiled as she reached down to pet the sheltie, and Conan found himself again amazed at her calm, knowing it was deceptive. The hand with which she stroked Heather trembled.

When Will returned with his case, he was wearing another sweater and a heavy robe. "Looks like everybody's gone back to bed. Okay, Conan, I assume you want the contents in the speci—"

"Don't touch the mug. Use the napkin."

"Oh. Fingerprints. Right." He carefully poured the liquid into a specimen bottle, handling the mug with the napkin. Just as Tiff had.

Lise said, "You might find my fingerprints on it or Kim's or Loanh's. We all helped take things out of the dishwasher tonight."

Will asked, "You want the mug in the plastic bag?"

"Yes. Initial and date both of them and lock them in your case."

"Okay. Damn!" Will began rummaging through his case, tossing bandages, stethoscope, and other paraphernalia out on the bed.

Conan asked, "What's wrong?"

"Something's missing. I have to maintain records of the drugs I use for the DEA, and I always keep everything in its place so I can see at a glance if anything's missing. It was just a bottle of Nitrostat tablets, but I haven't—"

"Nitrostat?" Conan felt a lurching sensation of vertigo as he asked, "What is it, nitroglycerine?"

"Yes. Sublingual tabs. Oh, no. Conan, you don't think . . ."

"That the toddy was laced with nitroglycerine? Yes, I think it's possible." And an overdose of nitroglycerine could be as deadly as cyanide, that much he knew. "Will, what if I simply turned up dead next time you checked on me? I mean, if the mug was missing, and you knew nothing about it. Wouldn't you think that maybe the hypothermia was worse than you realized, that maybe it triggered some latent defect in my nervous system and resulted in fibrillation?"

Will frowned as he put the bottle and mug in the case and snapped it shut, gave the combination lock a turn, then came over to the fireplace. "I suppose I might've chalked it up to heart failure, if I didn't have any reason to think it might be anything else."

"Maybe that's why my shadow visitor dropped in— not to do the deed, but simply to retrieve the mug. The evidence."

"Oh, dear God . . ." Lise moaned the words, eyes squeezed shut.

Will knelt beside her, his hands, which could be so sure and strong, hovering about her timidly. "Lise . . . ?"

She took a deep breath and faced Conan, so intent on him that she entirely ignored Will, who rose and turned to the fire, displaying fleetingly that look of hurt defeat.

She said, "Conan, if anything had happened to you . . ."

Will sighed, and Conan asked, more brusquely than he intended, "Who had access to your medical case this evening, Will?"

"Who *didn't* have access to it? Everybody was in and out of this room while it was in here—open on the bed. Except Lise and Mark."

"But who would know to pick Nitrostat?" That garnered blank looks, and Conan mentally filed that with the other unanswered questions waiting in the back of his mind. "Anyway, I think both of you realize that I haven't been entirely truthful about the rock slide. The truth is that it was not an accident. It was triggered by an explosion produced by dynamite or some other explosive."

Conan could have anticipated their reactions. Will aghast, frustrated, enraged. Lise frightened, ambushed by new grief, then finally, like Will, enraged. The rage was cold and channeled, and Conan was relieved. She could use it to keep the fear and grief at bay.

"Then it was murder," she said huskily. "Who, Conan? Who in God's name would . . ." She made fists of her hands, tangibly holding on to her self-control. "Demara!"

That took Conan off guard. "What makes you say that?"

Lise's rage waned, and she shrugged. "Maybe because she's the only outsider here, and I'd rather not believe it's one of the family. Well, I guess you don't consider Will and me suspects, or you wouldn't be telling us all this."

"True. Will isn't a suspect because if he wanted to dispose of an inconvenient witness, he had ample opportunity tonight while he was treating me."

"What?" Will scowled as if he'd received a mordant insult.

"Oh, Will, I was at your mercy. You gave me an injection and told me it was Demerol, but I had to take that on faith. It could've been cyanide, for all I knew. The point is, I wouldn't be alive if you wanted me dead. As for you, Lise, well, I admit I found it difficult to take you seriously as a suspect, but Heather absolved you."

"Heather? Because I was willing to leave her with you?"

"No. Because she barked at the intruder at the door. She wouldn't have barked at you. Unlike Sherlock Holmes, my clue was provided by the dog that *did* bark in the night."

Lise smiled, but it didn't last. "Then if Will and I aren't suspects, what can we do as your faithful Watsons?"

"First, say nothing about this to anyone. I might find it necessary to tell them the truth eventually, but not yet. Other than that . . ." He laughed bitterly. "I'll have to try to play Sherlock, which may prove difficult with no access to information from any source outside the lodge. So I'll start with you. I need to know where everyone was at around eight o'clock. That's when the explosion occurred, and it could have been detonated by a radio signal from here in the lodge."

Lise flinched, then nodded. "Around eight? I'm not sure I can remember exactly—"

"Start before eight. Whenever you remember noticing the time."

"Well, I remember it was seven-thirty when Kim and Loanh and I left the kitchen. The clock struck the half hour then. I've always loved the Westminster chimes, so I tend to notice them."

"Where were you then, Will?"

"I think Mark and I were standing in front of the fireplace talking. Yes, and Tiff was in her usual chair by the fire tending to her knitting."

Lise raised an eyebrow. "Crocheting, Will. She told me that thing she's working on is a wall hanging. 'Essence of Wildness,' she calls it. Yesterday she was out collecting cones and seed heads for it."

"Whatever. Wasn't Demara on the couch reading a magazine?"

"Yes, I think so. And it was about then that Kim suggested the pinochle game. That's when I went outside with Heather, wasn't it?"

"Right."

She turned to face Conan. "And that's when I first realized a storm was coming up. We'd been talking in the kitchen, and with the dishwasher running, I didn't hear the wind. But when I went outside . . ." She paused. "It was beginning to snow, and there was something about the wind that was frightening."

Conan nodded. "What was happening inside, Will?"

"Kim and I set up the card table. When Lise came in, she said something about the storm, but we had no idea how bad it was going to get, so we started playing. That was about a quarter till eight."

"Who was playing?"

"Lise and I and Mark and Kim. Tiff opted to stick to her knitting—crocheting—and her Scotch rocks. Where was Loanh, Lise?"

"She'd brought a book downstairs earlier, and she said something about reading for a while, but I think she went up to get a sweater about then. Wait. Yes, Demara went upstairs for a sweater first. She'd been lounging around in a silk blouse, as if this was California."

Conan asked, "When did either of them come back downstairs?"

"Not until after the power went out," Lise replied. "That was about five till eight. The come-and-get-it bell started ringing in the wind, and Mark turned on the radio, the portable Dad keeps . . . kept on the mantel, but he couldn't get anything except static and country western music we could barely hear on one station. He said maybe they'd have some news in five minutes on the hour. And that's when the power went out. Things got a little confused after that."

Conan leaned forward. "Just go through it step by step."

Will began, "Well, Kim said she was going to the pantry. That's where they keep extra flashlights and candles and the kerosene lamps. Mark volunteered to go outside and check the power lines into the house to make sure there weren't any live wires on the ground. And Lise and I went out to the garage to get the generator going."

"What was Tiff doing?"

Will looked at Lise, then shrugged. "As far as I know, she stayed in that chair the whole time."

Lise agreed. "When Will and I got back to the living room, she was just sitting there looking terrified and babbling about premonitions."

"How long did it take you and Will to get the generator going?"

"From the time the power went out? Maybe fifteen

minutes. It's been so long since Dad showed me how to use the thing, I had to check the instruction book."

"So it was about ten minutes after eight when you returned to the living room?"

"Probably."

"What about Mark? When did he come back inside?"

Will answered, "Right after Lise and I left the garage. He came in the front door at the same time Loanh and Demara came downstairs."

Lise added, "He said the power outage must be somewhere up the line, since the wires into the lodge were fine. He checked the outside thermometer, too. It was already close to zero."

"Everybody gathered in the living room then," Will said, taking up the narrative, "trying to figure out what to do about A. C. and the rest of you guys. Demara was in a panic. She wanted to drive out for help—in that Mercedes, for God's sake. Well, by then the wind was blowing a gale, and the snow was coming thick and heavy. Anybody'd be nuts to try driving without chains or four-wheel drive, and even if we could've reached the ranger station, what could they do? There was no way anybody could get to the camp. Besides, we figured when the weather turned bad, A. C. would've broken camp and headed for home."

That created an aching silence, and Conan let it stand. He considered this schedule and realized that, except for Lise and Will, at eight o'clock, everyone in the lodge was alone with access to windows or doors—and in Mark's case, he was outside.

At length, Conan said, "Tomorrow I'll see if I can gather more information. And try to stay alive, with your help—and Heather's."

Lise looked down at Heather. "She's yours for the duration."

Will said, "I'll bunk in here at night so you can get some sleep."

"I'm afraid that would be a little obvious. Heather is obvious enough. Of course, my shadow visitor already knows that *I* know what really happened at Loblolly Creek. But none of the others know, and I won't burden them with the truth until I have to. There's something you can do for me now, Will. My keys are on the chest there. Would you get something out of my car for me?" He waited until Will had the keys in hand. "It's in the glove box. That small, silver key opens it."

"What is it I'm looking for?"

"A gun."

Lise took a quick breath, but didn't speak. Will nodded and headed for the door. "Good idea," he said.

When the door closed behind Will, Conan studied Lise a moment, then said, "I'm afraid I'll find it necessary to ask a lot of questions that you'll consider impertinent, if not irrelevant."

"Like what?"

"Like why Mark needed to make peace with A. C."

Her pale eyes widened. "Mark? Conan, you can't think—" She stopped herself, then, "Okay, it may not be impertinent, but I hope to God it *is* irrelevant. Do you remember Karen? Mark's oldest girl?"

"Vaguely."

"Well, she was only nine when you last saw her. She's fifteen now and looks twenty, and she's trying to be a Madonna clone. Of course, it's a wonder all three of those girls aren't hopelessly spoiled. Tiff liked the *idea* of motherhood, but she just wasn't willing or able to accept the responsibilities or the dirty diapers and now puberty in the age of hard drugs. Demara was right about the flower-child look. That's exactly what Tiff always wanted to be, a flower *child*."

"Is Mark better at dealing with puberty in the age of hard drugs?"

Lise shook her head ruefully. "Poor Mark, he hasn't the foggiest idea what's going on. He dotes on those girls. His pretty little angels. That's what he calls them. The only intelligent thing he ever did for them was to hire Elizabeth Camp as a nanny. That woman was a saint. Of course, Karen called her a fascist. Elizabeth retired two years ago, and Mark enrolled the girls at St. Anne's."

"That's a Catholic school, isn't it?"

"Yes, which might seem an odd choice for such staunch Episcopalians, but it's also a *girls'* school. I don't think that crimped Karen's style much, though. Conan, she was into coke, and she wasn't above shop-lifting or stealing from Tiff and Mark to support her habit—and impress the gang she was running with."

The door opened, and Will Stewart came in. Lise frowned as he took a semiautomatic out of the pocket of his robe.

Conan said, "Just leave it in the drawer by the bed, Will. Thanks."

Will put the gun in the drawer out of sight then crossed to the fireplace, and Lise leaned forward, hands spread to the flames. "Will, I was telling Conan about Karen." Then to Conan, "Will knows about it. He was at the Fourth of July picnic this summer."

At Conan's nod, she went on, reluctantly, perhaps, but resolutely. "It was just another family gathering. Another hallowed tradition. It was at Dad's house in Portland, and all the family was there. Except Lucas. Anyway, Dad happened to go into one of the upstairs bedrooms, and he found Karen doing a line of coke. That's what he said, and I never saw any reason to doubt him."

She looked up at Will, who added bleakly, "Karen wasn't a heavy user, but I've seen enough substance abusers to know the signs. Even before that, I tried to warn Mark, but he never believed me."

Lise went on, "When Dad caught Karen with the coke, his first reaction was to slap her and give her hell. But Karen isn't easily cowed, and she's smart in a wily sort of way. She started screaming. That got everybody up to the bedroom in short order, and she claimed Dad had tried to rape her. It was almost funny, really. Whatever his failings as a father, Dad is . . . was never a molester. I was the only girl child, after all, and if he'd had any tendencies in that direction, I'd have been the target. I wasn't. Ever. There was never anything to even hint that he was capable of such a thing. But I guess Karen thought the accusation would distract everyone from the coke."

Conan raised an eyebrow. "Did she expect anyone to believe her?"

"Yes," Lise answered wearily. "Mark. And she was right. He practically exploded. He believed every word, and no one could talk him out of it, not then, not since. Dad was all for calling the police. He said he wanted the police to give both of them lie detector tests. Well, Karen's had a few run-ins with cops, and I don't think she was anxious for another. She almost backed down, but Mark didn't. It was Kim who came up with a compromise. If Tiff and Mark sent Karen to a drug rehab center, Dad would pay for it. And if she stuck with the treatment and behaved herself, Dad wouldn't call in the police. So Karen's getting rehabilitated, and the rest of us are trying to go on like nothing happened. Even Mark. He never believed in rocking the boat, anyway, and he's done no rocking since, although he wasn't exactly friendly to Dad. He just . . . I don't know. It's as if he's just been marking time."

Conan asked absently, thinking of the words A. C. had spoken on King's Mountain, "Just waiting?"

"Yes."

Conan turned to Will. "Tell me about Mark's broken ankle."

Will began working at the fire, avoiding Conan's eye. "What's to tell?" A silence held until he finished stoking the fire, then he straightened and frowned down at Conan. "Damn it, you look like hell, and it's nearly three. Come on, I'm putting you back in bed."

Lise rose. "He's right, Conan. You need some rest. We all do."

Conan didn't dispute that. It was true, and he knew that both of them had answered all the questions they were going to for now. He submitted to being put to bed, thanked Lise again when she got Heather settled beside him.

When at length Will and Lise departed, Conan lay in his cocoon of blankets, and again, despite his weariness, despite the security afforded by his erstwhile guard dog, his mind refused him sleep. He was intensely aware of every ache and pain, of the seeping cold as the fire burned down, and always of the sounds of the storm battering the old building, even of the moment when the loosened eaves trough ripped away, and its dull thudding was silenced.

He considered the fragile strands his mind cast out, enmeshing in a web of suspicion all the prisoners of the storm—except for Lise and Will.

Al and Lucas. Rather, Al *or* Lucas, since one of them was certainly dead. Mark and Tiff. Even Demara, whom he had come to think of as a secret member of the family, although he had no evidence that she and Lucas were married.

At this point, he had no evidence that any of them were guilty of murder, and by the same token, no evidence that any of them were innocent, at least of conspiring to murder.

Loanh. Why hadn't she joined the rush to his room after the shadow visitor opened his door and Heather sounded the alarm?

Yes, Loanh might be Al's accomplice, but on the other hand she might be the mastermind and Al her intended victim. Had she been willing to sacrifice A. C.—and Lucas and Conan, when they appeared unexpectedly—to rid herself of Al? Of course, if a share of A. C.'s estate was part of her motivation, A. C. was not an incidental victim.

Al and Loanh's marriage was obviously on shaky ground, and Conan wondered if Al had threatened a divorce, wondered where that would leave Loanh financially and in terms of the family she said was so important to her, wondered about the brief conference with Mark Friday afternoon that left him looking so worried.

It wasn't likely that Loanh would know anything about explosives, which simply meant that if she were guilty, she'd had to find a willing expert as an accomplice. But like everyone at the lodge at the time of the explosion—again, except for Will and Lise—Loanh could have detonated the explosion by radio.

It was even possible that Loanh had prepared the questionable toddy and asked Tiff to deliver it to Conan. Tiff and Loanh were friends, and Tiff would have carried out that task if Loanh asked it of her, especially since she seemed to be a few drinks past second thoughts. When confronted by Will, perhaps Tiff had pointed an accusing finger at Demara, the outsider, to avoid implicating her friend.

Conan watched the flickering amber shadows on the ceiling and turned his suspicious thoughts on the one person who would be the most obvious suspect if A. C. was the intended victim and his estate the motive: Kimberly Kaiser King. She wouldn't be the first woman to marry a rich man twice her age, then hurry his demise so she wouldn't be burdened with an aging husband while she enjoyed the prime of her life with his money. She had worked for King and Ryder Construction for years and might know something about explosives, or at least know who to seek out as an expert accomplice. And she, too, could have signaled the explosion by radio without ever leaving the lodge.

But would Tiff have delivered the suspect toddy for Kim and lied for her afterward?

Did the toddy have anything to do with anything? Possibly it was exactly what it seemed: bourbon, lemon juice, sugar, and water.

But what about the missing Nitrostat?

Conan irritably pushed the covers aside and sat up, then opened the drawer under the side table, noting the flashlight that was standard equipment at this exclusive hotel. But it was the gun that held his attention. He took it out of the drawer, handling it gingerly. His fingers were not only rosy, but as sensitive as if the nerves had been laid bare, and any pressure, even the sensation of icy metal, was painful.

A friend with the Oregon State Police had recommended this weapon to him: a 9 mm Ruger P-85, dull black down to the heavy plastic grips. Its magazine held fifteen cartridges, and it was loaded. It always was. Conan felt a grudging respect for the uncompromising precision of its engineering. It was an instrument designed exceedingly well for one purpose: killing people.

And he resented the realization that before this damnable blizzard ended, he might be forced to use this instrument for the purpose for which it had been designed.

CHAPTER 13

Awan light was seeping through the muslin curtains when Conan felt Heather leap off the bed. No barking this time.

"Good morning."

It was Will Stewart who stood by the bed, offering that greeting. Conan blinked his eyes into focus. For a moment, he thought he was at home and the dull roar outside was the breaking waves of the Pacific.

But only for a moment. He sat up, recognizing the savage undercurrent in the sound. The storm had not abated.

"Will. What time is it?"

"About eight-thirty. How're you feeling?"

Conan flexed his hands and shrugged. "I'm all right."

Apparently Will wasn't willing to accept his word for that. He had his medical case with him and insisted on taking Conan's temperature and blood pressure, and listening to his heart. Then he examined Conan's feet and

135

hands. Conan waited patiently, noting that Will had built a fire. Still, the room was far from warm.

Finally Will put his equipment away. "Lookin' good," he said almost cheerfully. "No blistering. Some of the skin might get crusty and slough off in a few days, and your fingers and toes are going to be sore, but nothing a little ibuprofen can't control. I'll leave a bottle. You can take up to four tablets at a time. You get any sleep?"

"Probably as much as anyone else. Did you try the radio this morning?"

"Mark did. Still nothing but static and country western."

"Is everyone else up and about?"

"Yes. In the kitchen. Except Loanh. I checked on her a while ago, and she's still in bed."

"Sleeping?"

"No. She says she's just not ready to talk to anybody yet." He frowned, pushing his fingers through his unkempt red hair. "Okay, if you're going to rise and shine, I'll give you a hand."

Conan was grateful for Will's helping hand, since his own hands made even simple morning ablutions difficult. And grateful for electric razors. He was also grateful for Will's assistance in getting dressed, although Will insisted on enough extra layers to make him feel like Charlie Brown in winter, including two sweaters topped by one of A. C.'s red plaid Pendleton shirts and two pairs of soft wool socks between his tender feet and the scuffs.

Before he left the room, Conan went to the window and pushed aside the curtain. He could see nothing; the inside of the glass was filmed with ice. But the sound was there: a sustained, panting rumble.

As he made his way downstairs—carefully, with Will

dawdling at his side—Conan was conscious of the lodge as an isolated bastion in some frigid, pulsing plane of existence that didn't make sense in the world he accepted as real. He heard the hum of the generator from the garage, but it was overwhelmed by the wind. In the atrium, a wan light filtered through the multiple panes on either side of the door, panes opaque with ice. The living room was in cavernous twilight, the heavy drapes drawn across all the windows, even the French doors, a small fire burning in the fireplace amid gray ashes. The grandfather clock chimed its stately preamble and tally of the hour. Nine o'clock. The sonorous sounds seemed to die too soon, as if there were no echo in this room. He couldn't hear the come-and-get-it bell. Apparently someone had muffled the clapper to stop its incessant clanging in the wind.

Light emanated from the kitchen. The swinging door had been propped open, and Heather lay sphinxlike just outside. Conan leaned down to pet her before he went in. She was inclined to follow him, but Lise, who was coming out of the pantry in the corner to his left, said firmly, "No, Heather. Stay!" That was no doubt in deference to Kim.

The kitchen was as chilly as the rest of the lodge, yet it had a comfortable, rustic ambiance, despite the shining new refrigerator and range on the lefthand wall, the microwave, blender, and other high-tech accouterments on the tile counter, the stainless-steel sink on the far wall. The beamed ceiling and oak floor pertained here as they did throughout the lodge, and the cabinets were decorated with wrought-iron strap hinges. The big bay window on the west wall, curtained in muslin with a scalloped edge embroidered in blue, surrounded a nook lined with banquette seats upholstered in pale blue leather, enclosing three sides of an oak table.

Mark occupied one of the two ladder-back chairs on the kitchen side, while Tiff, looking like a refugee from a war zone, bundled in mismatched layers of clothing, a purple scarf confining her ebullient hair, sat on the banquette at the far end of the table. Kim, similarly bundled, but with a better eye for blending colors and textures, worked at a chopping board near the range. Farther down the counter, Lise was buttering slices of bread. Demara stood at the door that opened onto the deck, and she seemed prepared to depart at any moment. She was wearing a black parka, with someone's brown wool pants stuffed into maroon suede boots too stylish to be borrowed, as was the small, matching purse hanging from a narrow strap over one shoulder. She had pushed aside the curtain on the door's window and was staring out, although Conan doubted she could see anything.

No one had been speaking, but when he came into the kitchen the silence seemed to intensify as everyone turned to look at him. He felt as if he were, by his very existence here, a confirmation of tragedy.

And for someone, he was a liability not yet dealt with.

Will sat down at the north end of the table, while Conan chose the other ladder-back chair. Lise asked, "Would you two like some coffee?" They both nodded.

Mark studied Conan dubiously. "I guess you're okay."

Conan didn't try to answer that.

Tiff only glanced at Conan, then said to Will, "I'm so *worried* about Loanh. I mean, this just isn't *like* her, she's so much *stronger* than she seems, you know. I mean, she *usually* is. . . ."

Kim turned, and there was no hint of redness or puffiness about her extraordinary blue eyes, no hint that she had yet wept. There was instead a tightness in her features that made Conan wonder if she was capable of speaking. She was, and her voice was steady. "I'm microwaving scrambled eggs for anyone who's hungry."

Will held up his hand. "Sounds great, Kim."

And Conan realized he was ravenous. "Sounds great to me, too. Thanks, Kim."

"Me, too," Mark put in, avoiding his wife's disapproving gaze.

There were no other takers. Kim began breaking eggs into a bowl. "There'll be no toast. The toaster takes too much electricity."

Lise brought coffee for Will and Conan, then returned to her buttering, and into the silence accumulating in the room, Demara asked, "For God's sake, how long is this going to *last*?"

"Only God knows, Demara," Kim replied. "I remember a blizzard in The Dalles when I was a kid that lasted four days."

There was no satin, only harsh panic in Demara's voice as she repeated, "Four days! Jesus, I can't believe it. I can't believe you don't have a *phone* in this place. We can't even call anybody for help."

Lise said, "Demara, even if we *could* call for help, no one could reach us. Look, we have food and heat and shelter. We'll be fine."

"But Lucas and the others . . ." She glared at the door and its opaque window. "What are we supposed to do about *them*?"

Mark said flatly, "What *can* we do? They're dead."

That from Mark was evidently such a reversal that everyone stared at him, amazed. Apparently, Conan thought, Mark had passed the stage of denial.

Tiff took her husband's hand but, mercifully, remained silent. For a while, the only sound was the rasp of a whisk against the bowl as Kim whipped the eggs, then, after she poured them into a glass skillet, the bleat of the microwave as she set the timer. But Tiff seemed incapable of remaining silent for any length of time. She sighed gustily, said into her coffee mug, "I suppose the police, or whoever, will want to . . . to exhume the bodies."

Will spluttered as he choked on his coffee. "Tiff, that's a hell of a thing to bring up now."

"Oh. Yes, I suppose . . . well, I was just, you know, thinking out *loud*, and I'm sorry if . . . but the body *is* only a vessel for the soul, you know, at least that's the way *I* think about it, and—"

"Darling, it's all right," Mark said gently. "Maybe the bodies *are* only vessels, and I'd like to see Dad and Al and Lucas stay where they are, undisturbed. I think Dad would've liked the idea of being laid to rest on his mountain." Tears formed in his vague, hazel eyes, escaping to course down his soft cheeks.

Demara went to the pump thermos on the counter by the sink, filled a mug with coffee, then carried it to the table, and Will slid around the banquette to make room for her. She said, "The police won't let him rest, Mark. Not any of them. I remember what happened to . . . a friend of mine a few years ago. Max Steinberg. He was a sweet man, a prince. Anyway, his son and daughter-in-law were killed when their Cessna went down in the Sierras. The air rescue people said the wreckage was scattered all over the side of a canyon. There was no way anybody could've survived, and Maxie said just to leave them there in peace." She paused to sip her coffee, then went on bitterly, "But they wouldn't do that. They had to send a search team in, and two people on the team got hurt before they reached the plane. But they brought the bodies out—what was left of them.

Poor Maxie. He'd had a heart condition for years, and the strain was too much. He died of a heart attack before his son was buried."

Lise brought the buttered bread, silverware, and paper napkins to the table, offering no comment on Demara's story. Conan saw her compressed lips and knew her steel self-control was being sorely tested.

"But that's *awful*," Tiff said as she took a piece of bread and began nibbling at it. "I mean, shouldn't the *family* have the final say on whether—you know, on the final *resting* place?"

"I suppose," Mark said absently, "the insurance company wouldn't pay on any life policies if there was no proof of death."

Demara shrugged. "That's what they told Maxie."

"Well, life insurance isn't an issue where A. C. is concerned," Kim said irritably. The microwave signaled for her attention, and as she spooned the eggs onto three plates, she added, "He didn't have any life insurance. Didn't believe in it."

Mark said, "I wonder if Al had life insurance. Probably did, since he has . . . had dependents. I don't suppose Lucas did, though."

He seemed to expect Demara to answer that implied query, and she stared at him, a cigarette between her fingers. She took time to light it with an elegant gold lighter, sent out a puff of smoke, and said, "How should I know whether Lucas had life insurance? Why would we ever talk about that kind of thing?"

"No, I guess you wouldn't. Nobody ever expects . . . oh, thanks, Kim." This as Kim placed before him a plate of steaming scrambled eggs filled with mushrooms and topped with melted cheese and parsley.

Lise served Conan and Will, and Conan reached for his fork, wincing when he inadvertently hit the edge of the table with his fingers. The sensation was much like an electric shock. It took a while to figure out that he could hold the fork against his palm with the lower part of his thumb. It was awkard, but functional.

With a moue of distaste, Tiff watched Mark dig in to his breakfast. "Oh, Mark, really, you *know* you shouldn't be eating *eggs*."

He ignored that, and for a time he and Will and Conan devoted themselves to the unhealthy but delectable repast. Kim went to the counter for a pack of Marlboros and sat on the banquette next to Demara, while Lise busied herself cleaning up the dishes.

But Mark hadn't lost his train of thought. "I'll have to talk to Woody Lavery. He's an estate attorney. Golfing buddy. Seems to me that if Dad's next of kin insist, the medical examiner would accept the deaths without trying to ... exhume them. I mean, that'd be hellaciously expensive, and since there's no possibility of foul play ..."

He was looking directly at Conan with that. But Conan didn't have a chance to respond. Kim said, "Mark, there may or may not be insurance involved, but there is damned sure an estate. Rather a sizable one. A. C.'s remains won't be left in peace, and you know it."

Mark frowned uncomfortably, and Conan tried to think of a tactful way to frame his question, but to his relief Will bluntly asked it for him: "*How* sizable, Kim?"

"The total is around forty million, but only half of it can be considered liquid." She apparently realized the others were staring at her and added defensively, "I was A. C.'s personal accountant. He liked to keep things in the family."

As Conan awkwardly spread blueberry jam on a

piece of bread, he said casually, "I hope he made a will."

"Of course he did," Kim said. "Mark drew it up. A. C. kept that in the family, too, even if Mark isn't an estate lawyer."

Mark wiped his mouth with a napkin then explained pedantically, "It was a simple will, so I thought I could handle it. Dad just wanted his assets divided equally between his wife and his children or their heirs."

From the sink came the crash of a breaking dish, a muffled cry, and Lise turned, demanded, "What's *wrong* with you people? How can you talk about life insurance and estates and *exhuming* crushed bodies as if they belonged to people none of you had ever known?"

In the stunned hush that answered that question, Heather whined uncertainly and circled in the doorway. Lise loosed a shuddering sigh and strode toward her. "I'd better let Heather outside."

After a moment of confusion, Lise's departure triggered a sudden exodus. Kim caught up with her in the living room, tentatively touched her arm. "Lise, I'm sorry. Look, everyone has their own way of coping."

Lise nodded and continued to the atrium, where she opened the closet by the staircase and got out a rope leash, while Will hovered mutely near her. Conan ambled toward the door, watching as Demara started up the stairs. Tiff was right behind her, explaining to anyone who happened to be listening that she was going up to check on Loanh.

"I'm turning off the generator," Kim announced. "We'll have to ration the gasoline. We have about twenty gallons left now, but we don't know how long we'll be stuck here. That means no electricity for heating. Or cooking, except for the microwave and the coffee maker. How's the wood supply, Will?"

"So far, we've gone through maybe half a cord. That leaves us a cord and a half, so I guess we better be careful with that, too."

"*Very* careful. Lise, would you hand me that tan parka? Yes, that's the one. Thanks." When she shrugged into the parka, she opened the door to the garage. "I'll get some wood while I'm out here."

Will said, "I'll come help you in a minute." But she was already gone, closing the door behind her.

Heather pirouetted and barked in anticipation, and Lise smiled as she knelt to snap the leash on her collar. "Yes, baby, you get to go out in the most miserable weather you'll ever see, and you think that's fun, don't you?"

Conan asked, "You're not going outside with her, are you?"

"No, she's got twenty feet of rope, and that gives her plenty of leeway. Don't worry, Conan, we've been through this a few times since the storm started. Come on, Heather."

At Lise's nod, Will opened the door, gasped at a blast of arctic air, thick with snow. Against the door, snow had packed solidly into a yard-high barrier. Lise looped the end of the leash to the outside doorknob and shouted, "Go, Heather! Good girl!" And when the sheltie leapt out over the packed snow into the storm, Lise shut the door, leaned against it, whispered, "And don't tarry, for God's sake."

For a while, the three of them waited, no one venturing a word, until Lise looked up at Conan and after a couple of tries said, "I'm sorry I blew up in the kitchen. I know you were trying to get some information, but I—"

"Keep your voice down, Lise." He glanced up the stairwell, then said softly, "I understand your explosion.

By the way, didn't you say Lucas occasionally phoned you while he was in California?"

She nodded. "Not often or regularly, but he kept in touch."

"Did he ever happen to mention Demara Wilder?"

"No, at least not by name. But about a month ago, he said . . ." She flinched, as if some memory had taken her by surprise, but after a moment went on: "He said something about being in love again. Well, that was sort of a running joke. Lucas was always falling in love, but it never lasted. And he said something to the effect that if Dad was shaken when Al brought his Vietnamese war bride home, he'd go ballistic if he found out about *his* new love."

"Did he mean he intended to marry this new love?"

"I didn't think so at the time, but it was hard to tell with Lucas. Sometimes he liked to make a joke of things that were—"

She stopped, suddenly alert, and Conan and Will exchanged glances. They had heard it, too: a faint, thudding pop repeated three times. Identifying the sound against the rush of wind was impossible, and perhaps it was only a branch blowing against the lodge.

Lise opened the door, squinting into the wind and snow, and shouted, "Heather? Where are you?" She waited a few seconds, then pulled at the leash hooked on the doorknob, and obviously there was no resistance. "Heather! Oh, God—*Heather!*" And before Conan could even think about stopping her, she hurdled the barrier of packed snow, stretching the leash taut as she followed it out into the storm.

"Stay here!" Will commanded and plunged after her, leaving Conan to hold the door against the wind to a slit a few inches wide, while he strained to see their shadowy shapes and hear their shouts.

He couldn't have guessed how long he stood shivering, blinded by the gusts of snow and the cold that literally took his breath away, but he had reached a point of desperation where he was ready to plunge into the storm himself, when two blurred forms loomed toward him.

He threw the door open, and Lise, with the sheltie in her arms and Will huddling protectively over her, stumbled into the atrium amid a miniature avalanche of clotted snow knocked from the packed drift. Conan closed the door and turned, aware of the thuds when Kim dropped her load of wood as she came in from the garage; of Mark swinging on his crutches from the living room; of Tiff, Demara, and Loanh hurrying down the stairs, Loanh with her silk-black hair loose, falling below her waist; and above all of Lise, on her knees to lay Heather on the snow-scattered floor, calling her name in a keening wail. Will gazed down at Lise, struck dumb, it seemed, by her pain.

Conan asked sharply, "Will, is she dead?" Then at his blank look, "Heather, for God's sake!"

A tremor shook Will's sturdy body, then he knelt and asked Lise the same question, but more gently.

"No, she—she's still alive," Lise answered. She sat back on her heels, and Conan could see that Heather was panting in terror, the fur on her left haunch soaked with blood. Lise barely touched the area, and Heather loosed a yelp like a small scream.

"Will, you've got to *help* her!" Lise cried. "I can't stand this, I can't stand any more death! Oh, Will . . ."

If she had wept then, perhaps Will might have been able to deal with it more adroitly, but she only stared at him with all her pain trapped in her eyes, and Will mumbled, "But I—I'm not a vet, Lise, I don't know anything about—"

"I'll help you, Will," Conan cut in. "Lise, go up to Will's room and get his medical case."

"No. *I'll* help Will. I won't leave her, I won't!"

Conan pleaded, "Lise, please, you'll only make it harder."

"Come on, Sis." Mark stretched out a hand to her. "Let Will get on with what he has to do."

Her resistance collapsed, and she touched Heather's forehead, then rose and ran for the stairway.

Will swallowed, and once she had gone seemed to recover his confidence. "Kim, you'd better turn the generator back on. I need a good light. And a table. The kitchen table."

Kim objected, "The *kitchen* table?" then shrugged as she headed for the garage.

Will apparently didn't hear her. "Tiff, get some sheets to cover the table. Demara, I better have one of the floor lamps in there." When he lifted Heather, she cried out and struggled, but only briefly.

She seemed small and fragile in Will's arms, and Conan ached for her suffering. And for Lise, who loved her, who had already lost too much.

CHAPTER 14

Within fifteen minutes, the makeshift operating room was in readiness, and the assistants in the preparations ushered out—in Lise's case, reluctantly. The kitchen table, draped in an incongruously flowered bed sheet, had been pulled into the center of the room under the ceiling light, with a brass floor lamp augmenting its light. At one end of the table on a paper that had come out of a plastic envelope marked STERILE DRAPE, an assortment of medical paraphernalia was laid out: gauze pads and rolls, micropore tape; bright steel tools lying atop their crinkled brown sterile wraps; Betadine and antibiotic ointment; suture kit; disposable syringe and needle; a rubber-sealed vial designated XYLOCAINE; and Conan's electric razor. And the surgeon, sleeves rolled up, his scrubbed hands double gloved, stood in a funk of uncertainty, while his patient lay trembling and bleeding on the flowered sheet.

Will was dithering again. "I don't know anything

about dogs. I mean, I grew up on a farm, and we had dogs all over the place, but I don't know anything about them medically. Hell, I could *kill* her if I give her the wrong medication or cut in the wrong place, and Lise . . . well, she'd be all yours then. She'd never forgive me."

Conan stood at the other end of the table at Heather's head, constantly stroking her, acutely aware that if in panic she snapped at his tender fingers the result would be near agony. "Damn it, Will, you're a doctor," he said irritably. "Your patients are mammals. So is Heather. Now, I suggest you start by removing enough fur around the wound so you can see how bad it is. And what *caused* it."

Will repeated, "What caused it?" as if that question hadn't yet occurred to him. Then he took a deep breath and reached for a pair of scissors. "Okay, try to keep her still." He set to work, cutting away the blood-stiff fur and tossing it on the floor.

Heather whined and struggled, and Conan bent over her, elbows on the table, caging both her front and back legs, grateful that it didn't seem to occur to her to use her teeth to escape. When Will had the fur reduced to stubble and began gingerly wiping away the blood with a gauze pad, she yelped and began struggling in earnest. Will desisted, peered at the wound, and Conan leaned closer to see it. It was a furrow perhaps two inches long, angling down from back to front through the muscles padding the femur, and ending in a small, seeping, red circle.

Will said grimly, "This looks like a bullet wound."

Conan only nodded, finding no surprise in that. Questions, yes, but no surprise.

Will, however, was appalled. "Conan, who would— who *could* be out in that blizzard to *shoot* her?"

"I don't know, but I'd appreciate it if you didn't announce it loud enough for everyone in the next room to hear. Is the bullet still there?"

Brows drawn, Will reached for the syringe and the vial of Xylocaine. "Well, I can't probe for it with her flailing around. God knows how she'll react to this, but it's all I've got in the way of an anesthetic." He filled the syringe, then, like a man about to test an electric circuit with his bare finger, began injecting the clear liquid into the skin along the edges of the wound. Heather again struggled, but again Conan managed to restrain her.

Then the three of them waited, Will holding the syringe, Conan holding Heather, the sheltie panting, showing the whites of her eyes, but apparently none the worse for the injection. Calmer, in fact, which meant the anesthetic was working.

Will waited a few minutes more, then released a long sigh, reached for Conan's razor and began shaving off the stubble of fur, absorbing the seeping blood with gauze pads. When he put the razor aside, he swabbed the orange Betadine over Heather's pale, naked skin, then stripped off one pair of surgical gloves and gently palpated the wound with his fingertips. "I can feel the bullet right under the skin. Went in at an angle, so I don't think it did more than tear some muscle."

He took up a scalpel, and with one deft stroke opened the wound an inch further, extracted the bullet with pickups, then placed it on the sheet where it lay dull and gray in the center of a pink chrysanthemum, a blunt-pointed cylinder less than a quarter inch in diameter. As Will pressed another pad to the wound, he asked, "What do you think, Conan? Small caliber. Maybe a twenty-two."

"Where did you acquire your expertise with bullets—on Burnside?"

"I've taken out a few at the storefront."

"Well, you're right about the caliber, and it probably came from a small handgun."

"How can you be sure it's not from a rifle?"

"It couldn't have been fired from any great distance—not in this storm—and if it had been fired from a rifle at short range, it would've gone on through her leg. Besides, a rifle is very difficult to tote around without people noticing."

Will nodded as he took the needle holder out of the suture kit. "Can you get a hand free to mop up the bleeding? Don't touch the wound. You're not sterile."

Heather lay quiet now, with trusting patience, and Conan came around to the side of the table and began soaking pad after pad, while Will, his hands seeming too big for the fine task, wielded the minuscule scimitar of the suture needle and methodically closed the wound with a line of tiny, black knots. Finally he squeezed antibiotic ointment along the line, taped a square of gauze over his handiwork, then wound Heather's leg with strips of gauze to secure the bandage, predicting gloomily, "She'll probably try to chew this off." At length, he removed his gloves and tossed them on the floor with the rest of the bloody detritus of the surgery. "Conan, what are we going to tell those people? That somebody's out in this blizzard shooting dogs?"

Conan stroked Heather's silky head. "No, Will, we're going to tell those people—including Lise for now—that Heather gashed her leg on something unidentified, probably a frozen branch."

"Right. I suppose you want the bullet for evidence?" He didn't wait for an answer, but found a plastic bag in his medical case, dropped the bullet into it, then stowed it away next to the filled specimen bottle.

Conan asked, "When you and Lise found Heather, was her collar off?"

"Yes. Lise followed the leash out to maybe six feet past the steps toward the garage, and the collar was there, but no Heather. I guess she'd slipped out of it. Lise just kept going. Fortunately Heather was lying only a few feet from her collar."

"I doubt very much that she slipped out of her collar without help. If you'd been a second later, you probably wouldn't have found her at all. Will, I can tell you one thing: no outsider just happened through the storm and saw Heather and took a shot at her. Let's clean this place up. I don't want Lise coming in here and seeing bloody gauze all over the floor—nor Kim to be offended by dog hair in the kitchen."

Will looked around and seemed amazed at the mess. While Conan opened drawers until he came up with a paper bag, Will found a broom in the pantry. As they cleaned up the litter, Will asked, "You think somebody here in the lodge shot her? How, Conan? How would they get outside to do it?"

"Mark could've gone out the back door in the kitchen. Demara, Tiff, and Loanh out any of the upstairs windows at the back of the lodge, especially the ones at the east end. Kim could've gone out the outside door of the woodshed. And she already had a parka on."

Conan noticed that Will didn't take exception to the suggestion that Mark might have been agile enough, despite his broken ankle, to make his way around to the front of the house through the storm and back again in a short time.

Will paused to check Heather, who seemed content to lie quietly, then he took his tools to the sink and washed them. "Conan, if anybody'd been outside, we would've seen snow on their shoes."

"Yes, but I was too distracted by Heather's plight to notice anyone's shoes. Did you?"

"No." Will put his equipment in his case, closed it and turned the combination lock, then carefully lifted Heather. "Can you hold her a minute while I clean up this table?" As Conan took her in his arms, Will shook his head. "Poor pup. Why would anybody want to hurt her?"

Conan didn't reply to that obviously rhetorical question, but he was well aware that he had lost his guard dog. He pressed his cheek against her head and whispered, "Sweet lady, you didn't deserve this."

When Will had disposed of the bloody sheet in the trash, wiped the table with bleach, and pushed it back into its nook, Conan said, "You'd better take her in to Lise. I'll take your medical case up to your room." Conan transferred Will's patient into his arms, then picked up the case, careful to keep the weight balanced on the palm of his hand. "Come on, Lise will be waiting."

Will sighed gustily. "Thank God I've got good news for her."

CHAPTER 15

When Conan and Will came out of the kitchen, Lise was sitting on the floor in front of the fireplace, her back against the hearth ledge, a drawing pad on her knees. The paper was covered with an erratic jumble of dark shapes. At her side was a wicker dog bed. She looked up at Will, then tossed the pad aside and came to her feet.

Conan watched the transformation in her face from fear to joy when Will carried Heather to her. "She's going to be fine," Will said softly as he knelt to place the sheltie in the basket.

Lise made a choked sound between a sob and a laugh and knelt with Will, murmuring reassurances to Heather. Then she impetuously flung her arms around him. "Oh, Will, thank you, thank you!"

His face glowed pink, and he seemed incapable of a response. It didn't matter. A moment later Lise was again lavishing her attention on Heather.

Loanh, who had been sitting on the couch reading, rose and leaned down to embrace Lise, her long, silky hair falling forward over her shoulder. "I am so happy for you, Lise."

Lise patted her hand. "Thanks, Loanh."

Tiff didn't move from the armchair at the west end of the couch, and the hectic movements of her crochet needle didn't stop. She observed Lise's joy complacently, opining that at least something had gone right, and perhaps that was a sign that the worst was over. Even the wind seemed to be letting up a little.

Mark sat at the end of the dining table near the kitchen door, fiddling with the portable radio from which snorts of static and garbled music erupted. He glanced at Lise, but made no comment. Nor did Kim. She was sitting in the other armchair, legs drawn up under her, hands pushed into the sleeves of her heavy cardigan. She seemed numbed both physically and mentally by the cold that occupied the room despite the fire crackling in the fireplace.

Conan listened for the wind, and perhaps Tiff was right; perhaps it *was* letting up a little. He wandered casually toward the bar to give the display of guns a visual check, but saw no empty spaces, and the locks on the glass doors were apparently intact. He was wondering where Demara was, when, as if materialized by his thought, she came into the living room from the atrium, carrying a nail file and a bottle of scarlet polish. She was still wearing the black parka and shoulder-strap purse; still apparently ready to depart at any moment. She paused by the couch and asked, "Is the dog okay?"

Loanh rose and nodded. "Yes, she is okay, thank God."

"So, what was wrong with her?"

Will sat down on the hearth ledge, glanced at Conan,

then explained, "She gashed her leg on something. Maybe a frozen branch. It's a deep cut, but I stitched it up, and she'll be okay. Lost a lot of blood. Lise, try to get some water down her. If she was a human patient, I'd have her on a saline IV, but I'm not even sure where to find a vein."

Will's explanation of the cause of the injury was apparently taken at face value. Only Lise, with a lift of her eyebrows, showed any skepticism, but she said nothing. The others seemed indifferent, or simply preoccupied, trapped as they were in the shadow of a tragedy that perhaps only one of them entirely understood. Mark concentrated on the radio, while Tiff's needle looped through the bright strands, and Demara sat down at the other end of the dining table and began filing a long, scarlet fingernail.

Finally Kim rose and said, "I'm going to turn the generator off. Will, would you mind bringing in some wood for the fireplace?" He nodded and followed her toward the atrium, then she paused and asked, "Did any of you leave the lights on in your rooms? They should be turned off when the generator's not running."

Conan shifted the medical case in his aching hand. "I'll check them, Kim. I'm going upstairs anyway."

She nodded as she crossed the atrium to the garage door. "You don't need to check my room. I'm sure I turned everything off."

Will said, "Maybe you should rest a while, Conan."

"Maybe I will."

The thought was appealing as he climbed the steps. He had been too absorbed in the last hour to be conscious of his aching hands and feet, of a pervading weariness. When he reached the second floor, he turned left and opened the first door on the corridor into the room that had been assigned to Will. It was smaller than

Conan's and had a wood stove instead of a fireplace, a single bed instead of a double, but it had its obligatory private bath, and the dormer window on the north would no doubt offer a fine view of Mount Hood, if the curtains weren't drawn against the frigid, white chaos outside.

Conan put Will's case in the closet, checked the light switches, then left the room, closing the door and wishing he could lock it to protect the contents of the case. But this hotel did not furnish locks on the doors.

He crossed to his room and went into the bathroom, where the light went out just as he entered. He frowned at that, not because he was surprised at the sudden quenching of the light—that simply meant Kim had turned the generator off—but because he didn't remember leaving the light on when he left his room this morning. He uncapped the bottle of ibuprofen tablets, swearing at the adult-proof cap that made opening it a painful undertaking, downed four tablets with a glass of water, then looked around the bathroom carefully.

Someone had been here.

At first he couldn't explain that conviction; the evidence was subtle: one drawer was not quite closed; his shaving kit was zipped shut, and he remembered that he hadn't zipped it in deference to his tender fingers; a handkerchief lay on the floor, and it had been in the pocket of his robe, which hung on the hook behind the door.

He went into the bedroom and checked the drawer in the bedside table. His gun was still where he had left it, the magazine still full.

His cigarettes and lighter were also in the drawer, and he shook out a cigarette, accepting the flare of pain in his thumb when he lit it. He eyed the bed longingly, but allowed himself only a few puffs on the cigarette as a respite. Two could play the game of invasion of privacy, and he knew he wouldn't soon have a better opportunity. With any luck, the family would stay near the only heat available—the living room fireplace—for a while. Besides, he had an excuse for being in other people's rooms: he was supposed to be checking light switches.

He stubbed out the cigarette and went into the hall, paused to listen, hearing indistinct voices from below, then padded down the hall in his scuffs to Mark and Tiff's room, next to his on the west.

The door was open, and he left it that way. This room was larger than his, with the fireplace on the left wall, the bed on the right, the bath in the far right corner, but the decor was essentially the same. He dutifully checked the switch by the door, found it in the ON position, and turned it off. For a moment he surveyed the room, knowing he couldn't risk the time for a thorough search, trying to guess where he was most likely to find what he was looking for.

What he was looking for were three small items that could be hidden almost anywhere: a radio detonator, which might be no larger than a remote control for a television; a pill bottle labeled NITROSTAT; and a small-caliber gun. And all three could have been tossed out a window, where they would now be buried under a yard of snow. He had no illusions that he was likely to find them, but he had to try.

He began in the bathroom, noting that Tiff traveled with a small cosmetic boutique as well as a stock of vitamins and herbal medicines and a prescription for Valium, and that Mark took medication for hypertension and ulcers.

Next, he tried the closet. Most of the space was taken up with a colorful array of feminine apparel, with only a small space left for Mark's conservative pants and jackets. Conan knelt to check the shoes, then felt through every pocket in every garment. In the breast pocket of the blazer that Mark had been wearing when he arrived Friday, Conan found a slip of paper from a memo pad. Printed at the top were the words ACE TIM-BER AND WOOD PRODUCTS, INC. A telephone number was scrawled in blue ink below the heading: 503-1212.

Conan memorized the number and returned the memo to the pocket, then took time to go to the door to listen. Hearing nothing to indicate that anyone was approaching, he turned his attention to the chest of drawers by the windows. Mark's billfold lay on top of the chest next to Tiff's patched saddlebag of a purse. Conan went through both, but found nothing more unusual than the antique silver flask in the purse. It was half full of vodka.

The drawers were equally disappointing, as were the drawers in the desk and in the tables on either side of the bed. Four pieces of luggage were stacked near the closet, but they were all empty. Conan got down on the floor to look under every piece of furniture, then turned the pillows down, and finally moved around the bed lifting the mattress enough to feel under it.

Finally, his fingers pulsing with pain, he restored the bed and went to the door. He stood listening, facing the closed door across the hall: the master bedroom; A. C. and Kim's room. He wondered why Kim had been so quick to assure him that she had turned off the lights in that bedroom. *My* room, she had said.

Then he hurriedly stepped back into Tiff and Mark's room. Someone was coming up the steps.

But remembering that he had an excuse, however flimsy, to be in other people's rooms, he emerged into the hall just as Loanh reached the top step. She turned to her left and walked away from him, apparently without seeing him, then made another left turn into the room beyond Will's. He didn't hear the door close. After a moment, he started down the hall, slowing as he passed her door. She was bending over a suitcase open on the window seat, her back to the door.

A pace or so farther down the hall on the right was another closed door: Lucas and Demara's room. Conan went inside. The room was almost a mirror image of his own, but the bed was unmade, every chair and flat surface cluttered with apparel, both masculine and feminine. He checked the light switches, but didn't attempt a search. Not with Loanh so near. He closed the door as he departed.

There were only two more doors, one opening off each side of the hall. These were tiny rooms that had in years past been reserved for children. He opened the door on the north side. Lise's occupation of this room was evident in the drawing pads, the open box of pencils, and the penknife on the desk. Conan checked the switches, then crossed the hall to the other small room, the only unoccupied bedroom.

The air was so cold, his breath came out in clouds. There was one window on the south wall, and the curtain was open. He went to the window, shivering at the cold emanating from the glass—a chill intensified by the realization that the windowsill was damp. And there were damp spots on the floor under the window.

The window was locked, but Conan had no doubt that it had recently been opened. He couldn't be sure when. The moisture would be slow to dry in this unheated room.

There was no ice on the panes. The temperature here was too low to cause condensation on the glass. Conan looked out into the white storm, and he could see shadows of sapling hemlocks only a few feet away. This was the highest point of the hill against which the lodge had been built. Around the corner, along the east side of the building, the ground sloped steeply toward the front of the lodge.

And he realized that the fact that he could see even the shadows of the trees meant the storm was abating. The wind had appreciably lessened. He took a long breath, fogging the glass as he let it out. There was hope, then: hope that they might all escape this white hole.

Hope that an inconvenient witness to murder might live to tell his story.

He left the curtain as he had found it and closed the door when he departed. He walked down the hall, noting as he passed Loanh's room that she was still bending over the suitcase. Again, she didn't seem to hear him.

When he reached the head of the stairs, he checked his watch, surprised to find it was only 11:15. He paused, debating whether to go downstairs or to attempt a search of the master bedroom. He heard no sounds from the living room.

The quiet was abruptly annihilated by a thudding against the front door. In the vault of the atrium the sounds reverberated hollowly.

A muffled voice cried, "Help! Help me!"

CHAPTER 16

"What is happening out there? What is *happening*?"

Conan turned, found Loanh beside him at the top of the stairs, and in her eyes, as dark and unblinking as a startled deer's, he saw the same fear he felt.

It was an irrational thing, this fear, and he knew the last time he had felt anything like it was when he was a child, when he could still believe in phenomena that defied the laws of nature.

Yet that was a human voice he heard pleading for help, and he knew on a rational level that the fists beating at the door were also human, even though he couldn't begin to explain—rationally—how *any* being, human or otherwise, came to be knocking at that door in the midst of a blizzard.

Conan hurried down the stairs, with Loanh behind him, and the atrium was suddenly crowded as the family rushed out of the living room. Then they all stopped, breathlessly silent, facing the door.

The pounding and the cries ceased momentarily, and Will said, "Jesus, who could be out there in that storm?"

The pounding resumed, and Tiff loosed a thin shriek and reached for her husband, nearly knocking him off his crutches.

Conan moved toward the door. "We'd better ask him—or her, as the case may be." Will nodded, stood with his feet planted, ready to do battle with whatever came through the door when Conan opened it.

In a white, frigid blast of wind, a man in camouflage-patterned pants and hooded parka, his beard and eyebrows encrusted with snow, staggered into the atrium. When Conan closed the door, the man sagged against it, gasped through chattering teeth, "Oh, shit, I was afraid nobody was home. . . ."

Confronted with this tangibly human being, Conan's fear gave way to reined exhilaration. He couldn't explain it, but he was convinced that this stranger came bearing answers. Still, he only glanced at the man, then focused on the family.

What he saw were various degrees of shock and fear, which masked any sign of recognition. When the man pushed his hood back, Tiff gasped, but Conan couldn't be sure whether that was anything more than typical theatrics. From the living room came Heather's weak attempt at barking, and Lise hurried away to check on her. The others didn't seem aware of her departure.

Will was first to speak: "What were you doing out in this storm? Where'd you come from? Who the hell *are* you?"

"Name's Jerry Tuttle," the man said in a rasping voice, wiping the snow from his face with a gloved hand. "I'm from Salem. Came up for the weekend to do some hunting. Hey, I'm sorry to scare you folks, but I got caught in the storm. My Bronco's on the highway by the bridge. I saw the sign on your gate, and I figured I could make it half a mile to the house. Damn, I could sure use something warm to drink."

Will seemed to remember himself then. He took Tuttle's arm and aimed him for the stairs. "You need more than that. Come on, let's get you thawed out and let me check you over. I'm a doctor, by the way. Kim, you better turn on the generator again. I'll put him in the little room at the end of the hall, okay?"

Kim's eyes narrowed speculatively as she studied Tuttle, then she turned and headed for the garage door. "You'll need a fire in that bedroom, Will. It'll be freezing."

Lise returned from the living room, offering, "I'll take care of that."

"I'll help you," Loanh put in, and the two of them headed upstairs.

Will and his new patient followed, with Conan a few paces behind. Tiff and Mark, he noted, hadn't moved, Mark frowning in confusion, Tiff's too-green eyes fixed apprehensively on the stranger. Demara had retreated to the arched entryway into the living room from which vantage point she also watched the stranger warily.

Jerry Tuttle, without the snow whitening his facial hair, was younger than he seemed at first. Perhaps in his early thirties. His hair was straight and blond, parted in the middle and hanging to his shoulders. His beard was nearly red. He had the face of a stereotypical Viking: long and narrow, the bones pressing against thin, fair skin darkened by exposure to the sun. His bluish eyes were set deep under prominent brow ridges, eyebrows and lashes thin and so much the color of his skin, they seemed nonexistent. It was obvious that he made his living at some sort of outdoor work; his hands were scarred and callused, embedded dirt dark under the fingernails, and his body was sun-browned from the waist up, pallid from the waist down. A lean and muscular body, with articulated pectorals and deltoids that suggested he spent time lifting weights on a regular basis.

Conan made these observations while ostensibly helping Will warm his patient in the bathroom off the unoccupied bedroom. Conan leaned against the door, savoring the warmth from the wall heater and the steam as hot water poured into the bathtub, while Tuttle lay half submersed, and Will knelt by the tub taking his blood pressure and temperature. Tuttle seemed to be enjoying the attention.

Will removed the cuff with a rip of Velcro, then checked the thermometer. "Normal as apple pie, and you can consider yourself damned lucky."

"Oh, I do," Tuttle responded. The rasp in his voice that Conan had noticed when Tuttle first arrived was apparently a permanent condition. "You'll never *know* how lucky I feel." The askew grin was apparently also a permanent condition.

Conan asked, "How did you get stuck out in this storm?"

"Oh, man, that's a long story. Yesterday afternoon I parked down by the bridge over that little crick—"

"King's Creek?" Will asked as he turned off the water.

Tuttle shrugged, then submerged himself, came up sputtering and rubbing water out of his eyes. "Yeah, I guess so. Anyhow, I headed upstream a ways, and I spotted this buck. Shit, he had the biggest rack of horns I ever saw. I followed him, hoping for a good shot.

Pulled off a couple, but didn't touch him. Well, I lost track of the time, and when I got back to the Bronco, it was dark. I was too damned tired to go look for a place to camp and too damned poor to stay in a motel, so I figured I'd sleep in my truck. Had some food with me, so I just stretched out on the seat and zonked out. You guys got any soap?"

Will was busy putting the sphygmomanometer in his medical case on the counter, so Conan took the small bar of soap by the sink and a washcloth from the towel rack and handed them to Tuttle, who asked idly, "What happened to your hands? You burn 'em or something?"

"No, just a touch of frostbite."

"Oh. You guys part of the King family?"

Will closed the case with a snap, said, "No, we're just friends of the family. I'm Will, and this is Conan."

Tuttle was busy soaping one foot. He gave Will a knowing leer. "Hey, must be nice bein' a friend of *this* family with all those sweet chicks. You guys can sorta take your pick, right?"

Will's big hands curled into fists, but before he could say anything, Conan asked, "Don't you have a radio in your truck?"

"Naw. Well, I had one, but it broke. I guess if I'd had a radio, I'd've known how bad this storm was going to be. Shit, I just figured it'd snow for a while and clear up this morning. Big mistake."

Conan nodded. "I thought Broncos had four-wheel drive. I mean, I'm surprised you couldn't drive out last night before it got really bad."

"Sure, I got four-wheel drive," Tuttle replied as he thrust out a hand to soap his arm pit, "and I probably could've drove out if I hadn't been so zonked. Hell, I didn't wake up till nine-thirty last night. Only reason I woke up then was I had to pee. Hooee, that was a damn cold pee! Must've froze before it hit the ground." He gave that a laugh, then, "When I got back in my rig, I looked at my watch and saw it was nine-thirty. By then, I knew there was no way I could get outta there, four-wheel drive or not, so I sat it out. Ran the heater half an hour on and half an hour off all night."

Will leaned back against the counter, arms folded. "I hope you kept a window rolled down. But you must've, or you wouldn't be here now."

"Shit, I'd still be out there, probably, turning blue."

Conan didn't bother to point out that with carbon monoxide poisoning he was more likely to turn bright pink. "What made you leave the Bronco? Did you run out of gas?"

"Just about. This morning when the gauge hit a quarter, I figured I was either going to freeze to death in the rig or on my way to help, so I waited till the storm let up a little. I remembered the sign on the gate. And the fence. I felt my way along the fence all the way up here. Think somebody'd loan me a blow-dryer?"

With a hint of annoyance, Will replied, "I'll ask around. I suppose some of the ladies—"

He was interrupted by a knock on the door. Conan opened it a few inches and found Lise waiting with a mug of coffee. She beckoned to him, and he came out into the bedroom, closing the door behind him.

"Here's some coffee for Tuttle. We have a fire going in the stove, but it'll take a while to warm this room. Kim found some more of Dad's clothes for him"—Lise nodded toward the bed—"and she looked through his clothes. Conan . . ." She stared at the bathroom door with a piercing gaze that seemed to bore through it. "Who *is* he?"

"A lost hunter—so he says. Were you on hand when

Kim searched his clothing?" Then at her nod, "Did she remove anything?"

"Only a rather efficient-looking jackknife. She said she'd just made a new house rule: guests had to check their weapons at the door."

Conan laughed and took the mug. "Tuttle's in no position to argue that, but I'm sure he'll appreciate the coffee. Oh—and a blow-dryer, if anyone is willing to volunteer one."

"Tiff must have one. I'll ask her."

He returned to the bathroom where Tuttle had emerged from the tub and was toweling himself. He accepted the mug with a grunt that might have indicated thanks, although Conan guessed he'd have preferred something stronger. Conan said, "We're working on the blow-dryer, and there are dry clothes on the bed. Now, if you'll excuse me, three's a crowd in here. I'll put your case away, Will."

Will handed it to him with a quizzical look, and Conan made his exit, but he didn't head for Will's room. Instead, he went to the chair in front of the woodstove where Jerry Tuttle's clothes were hung to dry: a blue plaid shirt, leather hiking boots, fleece-lined leather gloves, and the camouflage-patterned parka and insulated pants.

He didn't expect to find anything unusual since Kim had already been through them. What he found was a set of keys on a ring attached to a plastic disk decorated with a stylized ram in profile. There were two keys with the Ford motif, and three more of various sizes.

And a nearly empty pack of Marlboros and a red Bic lighter.

But of course, Conan reminded himself, Marlboros were a popular brand.

Other than that, Jerry Tuttle had come here without

identification of any sort. Had he left his billfold in his
Bronco when he embarked on the desperate trek to the
lodge? If so, why?

And why were the outer clothes all stiffly new, without a stain or tear, except for a hole in the right pocket
of the parka about two inches long. But that hole was
the result of a badly finished seam. It had no doubt been
there when Tuttle purchased the parka. Even the hiking
boots were new: no wear on the thick soles, not a par-
ticle of mud in the tread. None of the brand names were
unusual, and all these items would be available in any
sporting goods or department store.

Conan turned away and left the bedroom, hearing the
sound of water draining from the tub as he passed the
bathroom. When he reached the hall, he stopped abruptly.

Demara was just crossing the hall to the stairs. She
didn't glance his way before she descended.

Conan left the medical case in Will's room, detoured
into his own room for his cigarettes, then went downstairs to the living room, where Lise was sitting on the
floor in front of the fireplace by Heather's bed. She was
drawing again, her pencil moving incessantly, seemingly of its own volition. She didn't seem to be listening to the conversation going on between Tiff, seated as
usual in the armchair at the west end of the fireplace,
and Loanh, who huddled near her at the end of the
couch. Mark sat at the other end of the couch, the radio
in his lap emitting spurts of static and fragments of music as he turned the dial.

Demara was standing in front of the fire, rubbing her
hands. When Conan entered, she turned, glared at him,
then demanded, "Who *is* that man? Did he have anything to say?"

Conan sat down on the hearth ledge near Lise and lit

a cigarette, then recounted Tuttle's story. Everyone listened attentively, and when Conan finished, Mark shrugged. "Well, I guess it sounds reasonable. It could happen."

Tiff shrilled, "Oh, Mark! I don't believe *any* of it. I mean, you just can't *trust* people these days." She sent Conan an accusing stare. "How *could* you let that man *in* here? You don't know anything *about* him. I mean, for all *you* know, he could be a *serial* killer."

Conan flicked the ashes from his cigarette into the fireplace, thinking that Tuttle might indeed be a killer; he was certainly not what he claimed to be. But he said nothing. Not that Tiff would have heard him if he had.

"You had no *right* to let that man *in*, Conan, I mean, you might've at least *asked* what anybody thought, or if we *wanted* a strange man coming in here, you know, after all that's happened, but you just—"

Lise cut in wearily, "Tiff, shut up. What would *you* have done? Let the man freeze to death on our doorstep?"

"Well, better him than *us*! I mean, you just don't *know* about people any more. It's the good Samaritans that get their *throats* cut, you know, and—oh, I just don't understand. . . . I mean, everything that's happened, I can't *deal* with all this at once, I just *can't*. . . ." She began to make snuffling noises as tears spilled from her tightly closed eyes.

Demara threw up her hands in disgust and strode to the far end of the dining table where she sat down and began noisily shuffling cards, while Mark mumbled, "Tiff, honey, now, don't worry about—" Then he stopped, distracted by the radio.

He hurriedly turned up the volume, making audible a man's voice reciting a list of highway closures. Not surprisingly every pass in the Cascades was closed. The voice added—just before it was drowned in rising static—that the National Weather Service had advised that the snow was likely to continue for another twenty-four hours.

Mark groaned and impatiently switched off the radio. At that, Tiff renewed her weeping, which she had put on hold to listen to the report. Loanh stared at the silent radio apprehensively, and Demara said succinctly, "Oh, shit."

Conan leaned down to stroke Heather's head. She was sleeping, and her eyes fluttered open only briefly. He envied her acceptance of a situation far outside the security of her normal pattern of existence. But then she didn't understand exactly how abnormal the situation was.

"Conan?"

Lise was looking at him, gripping her pencil with white-knuckled tension. He wondered what she was asking of him. The wind in the chimney boomed, and even with the fire at his back, the room seemed suddenly colder. Twenty-four more hours of snow.

"Lise, the weather people have been wrong before." Then he tossed his cigarette into the fire as he rose. "Where's Kim?"

"In the kitchen making lunch. She shooed me out a while ago. We seemed to be getting in each other's way."

He nodded and started for the kitchen as the clock chimed twelve o'clock. Noon. It seemed absurdly implausible in the dusk of this cavernous room.

CHAPTER 17

The door was closed when Conan went into the kitchen, and he pushed it shut behind him. Kim was at the counter on the left wall, taking sandwiches from a formidable stack on a cutting board, bisecting them diagonally with a long, serrated knife, then placing each one on a platter. The stainless steel bowl at the back of the counter was smeared with the remains of tuna salad. She studied Conan with her intense blue eyes, then returned to her work. "Lunch—such as it is—will be ready in a few minutes."

"No hurry, Kim. I just wanted some coffee." He went to the pump thermos, which gurgled as it spewed coffee into a mug, then, holding the mug between his palms, he leaned against the counter near Kim. But not too near. She didn't look up as she asked, "Did you find out anything about our unexpected guest?"

Conan reiterated Tuttle's story, adding, "Strange, though, he didn't have any identification with him."

She shot Conan an oblique glance. "You checked his clothing, too."

"Well, it seemed like a good idea. Kim, when he first came in, did you recognize him? I mean, did he remind you of someone?"

The knife thunked hard against the cutting board, then she shrugged. "No. Why? Did you think I recognized him?"

"I suppose I was just hoping someone had," Conan replied lightly.

She continued efficiently cutting and stacking, while Conan sipped at his coffee. Finally he said, "Lise told me you had made A. C. very happy, Kim, and it was obvious Friday night that she was right."

Kim stopped mid-slice and fixed him with a look that suggested she thought he was mocking her. Then she apparently changed her mind and even smiled. "Lise was the only one of A. C.'s kids who accepted me at all. The rest of them think I married him for his money." She finished the slice and reached for another sandwich. "And I'll admit the money was attractive. I mean, would I have married him if he was a dirt-poor logger? Probably not. But then A. C. wouldn't have been a dirt-poor logger. His money, his power, his ambition—it's all part of what he is. So is his rather old-fashioned gallantry. He always made me think of words like that: gallantry, courtesy, honor."

She turned away abruptly, went to the refrigerator for a carton of milk, took it to the table, and placed it next to a bowl of potato chips. When she returned to her task, she added, "He was also stubborn, narrow-minded, and even ruthless. But he never showed me that side of him. Only the gallantry. I haven't had much luck with men in my life, so I found that irresistible."

"Kim, you're an extraordinarily attractive woman. I should think you'd have had your choice of men."

She laughed, eyeing him curiously. "Oh, my, Mr. Flagg, I do think you have a streak of gallantry in *you*. If you learned that from your father, Pendleton must have produced an amazing generation of men."

"Well, I doubt A. C. and my father were entirely representative."

"No," she said, her smile fading. "They're not representative *anywhere*. Do I sound bitter? Well, I am. I married at eighteen—a football player named McLean Ryder—and my dad disowned me for that. The marriage lasted five years, and the last three were as close to hell as I ever hope to be. Mac acquired about every vice necessary to destroy a marriage, and I was so naive, I nearly died trying to give him a child because I thought that would change everything, that it would change Mac. And one night, while I was in the hospital—*he* put me there—he got drunk and ran his pickup off the I-5 bridge into the Columbia at seventy miles an hour. And that's the best thing he ever did for me. The best thing any man ever did for me. Until I met A. C."

Conan was silenced by that and taken off guard when she gave him an ironic smile and said, "Well, I seem to be spilling my guts for you. I suppose your ability to loosen tongues is useful to a private detective."

What was she telling him? That she knew his questions weren't motivated solely by concern or even curiosity? He asked, "Mac Ryder? Was he related to Jerry Ryder, Al's business partner?"

"Jerry was Mac's uncle." She opened a drawer, took out a stack of paper napkins, and carried them to the table. "Jerry is probably the only true Christian I ever met. He gave Mac a job at his construction company and tried to help him grow up. Then after Mac killed himself, Jerry took me under his wing and not only gave me a job but sent me to night school to study accounting. But four years ago he was diagnosed with ALS. Lou Gehrig's disease. That's when he decided to retire. Now he's in a hospice. Dying." She paused as the kitchen door opened.

It was Lise. She said, "Will just brought Tuttle downstairs."

Kim went to a cupboard for a stack of plates then crossed to the table and put three sandwiches and a pile of potato chips on the top plate. "He can eat at the dining table. I suppose he'll want beer."

Lise nodded. "Probably. There's plenty in the bar fridge."

Kim took the plate and a couple of napkins and went out the kitchen door, propping it open as she passed. Lise glanced questioningly at Conan, but he only shrugged as he followed Kim.

Will stood frowning, his arms folded across his chest, near Tuttle, who was warming his hands in front of the fireplace. A. C.'s cords and sweaters were too long for him, but he filled them out in the shoulders.

Apparently Tiff, Mark, and Loanh hadn't moved since Conan had left the room, and Demara was still at the far end of the dining table with a solitaire game laid out, ignored now while she, like the others, stared warily at Tuttle. Conan studied faces, again seeking a hint of recognition, but all he saw was doubtful suspicion. No one spoke to Tuttle except when Kim indicated that his lunch was served.

"Hey, I really appreciate that, uh, ma'am." There was a querying inflection in that, but Kim didn't offer an alternative to *ma'am*, and Tuttle made a beeline for the table and had begun on one of the sandwiches before

Kim could offer him a beer. This offer he accepted with only a nod, since his mouth was full.

Kim brought a can of beer from the refrigerator behind the bar for Tuttle, then announced to the others: "There are sandwiches in the kitchen. If you want anything else, you'll have to fix it yourself. If it's anything that requires electricity, you're out of luck. I'm going to turn off the generator now."

Will said, "I'll take care of it, Kim," as he started for the garage.

Demara was the first to respond to the invitation to lunch. Mark was next, but it took him awhile to get himself upright and on his crutches. While Tiff was helping him, she asked, "Kim, what kind of sandwiches did you make?"

"Tuna salad," Kim replied curtly.

"Oh. Is it dolphin-free?"

"What?"

"The tuna."

Before Kim could respond, Mark said, "Honey, right now we can't be choosy. Loanh? You know, you've *got* to eat something."

Conan had been moving casually toward the atrium, and by the time the family had filed into the kitchen, leaving Tuttle alone to wolf his sandwiches, Conan had nearly reached the stairs, where he met Will coming out of the garage.

Conan murmured, "Anything new from our house guest?"

"No." Will grimaced irritably. "Just more about how he likes the looks of the *babes* we got here. Aren't you having lunch?"

"Later. Just tell the others I've gone upstairs to rest."

Will studied him a moment, then nodded. "Sure."

But as Will had probably guessed, Conan had no

plans for resting. With the family occupied at lunch, he had to take advantage of this opportunity to continue his invasions of privacy.

He began, for no particular reason, with Loanh's privacy.

Of the three bedrooms over the garage, the center one was the largest, and in fact second in size only to the master bedroom. Lise had always referred to it as Al's room. No doubt he had regarded it as his due as eldest son. Conan surveyed the room, hearing the wind rumbling at the window. He hadn't been listening to the wind for a while, and now it seemed even more vicious, as if it had renewed its energies with the brief lapse he had hoped foretold an end. He shivered, his breath coming out in clouds in the chill air.

Then, consciously releasing the tension tightening his jaw and shoulders, he focused on the task at hand. He began in the bathroom, found nothing unusual, and when he finished there, checked the closet, and by then realized that the closed suitcase on the window seat was Al's and that Loanh had packed everything belonging to him in it. That must have been what she was doing when he passed her room earlier.

The suitcase was unlocked. He opened it and searched its contents carefully. If Loanh looked into the suitcase later, she wouldn't know anything in it had been touched. He found the clothing and shaving kit he expected. And Al's billfold.

It was made of black eelskin with Al's name stamped in gold: ALFRED CHARLES KING, JR. Conan flipped through the plastic envelopes, noting the American Express Gold Card and the Republican Party membership card. No photographs. In the money folder, he found over three hundred dollars, mostly in fifties. He almost missed the receipt mixed with the bills, folded until it was nearly the same size.

It was from the Jacob Palenz Private Investigation Service in Portland for a retainer of one thousand dollars paid by Al King on October 16.

Conan knew Jake Palenz to be reputable and competent, with a staff of ten operatives. He specialized in corporate investigations, but accepted insurance fraud, divorce, and custody cases.

Conan wondered what induced a man who couldn't pay the interest on a loan from his father to give a PI a thousand-dollar retainer.

October 16. That was only ten days ago.

Conan checked for a hidden fold, the kind designed to fool thieves, although any thief—or private investigator—was well aware of them. Apparently this stylish design didn't include anything so prosaic.

He continued his search, his hands aching by the time he turned to Loanh's purse, a practical and tailored design of supple beige leather, which he found on the mantel of the fireplace on the east wall. He found the usual cosmetics, a linen handkerchief, a key ring, a bottle of Excedrin, a rosary with jade beads, and a small, flat purse that served as a billfold. Loanh carried less than fifty dollars in cash with her. The plastic envelopes displayed four credit cards, memberships to the Portland Art Museum and the Oregon Symphony Society, and snapshots of her children and Al, as well as a King family portrait taken at the lodge in happier times when Carla was still alive.

Conan checked for a hidden fold and found one. It didn't contain money, but a color photograph. It was also a family portrait: a woman with graying hair, perhaps in her sixties; two men and two women in their forties or late thirties; five children ranging in age from about ten to twenty. They were all Asian, but the setting was typically American and probably Oregonian. Portland, possibly. They stood in two smiling rows in front of a modest house with a red rhododendron in bloom by the porch, and in the background at the edge of the photograph, Conan saw a white shape that looked suspiciously like Mount Hood.

And he remembered what Loanh had said to Lise: *For me, for my people, family is everything. Without family, one might as well be dead.*

But was this Loanh's family? He understood she had left her family behind in Vietnam when she married Al.

Conan checked his watch. He had been at this search for fifteen minutes, and that was pushing it. He restored the photograph to its hidden fold and the small purse to the larger one, then left the room, walked down the hall to the stairway, and stood listening. He heard the nasal complaints of a country western singer done wrong, interrupted by bursts of static. Perhaps Tuttle was entertaining himself with the radio. Conan heard no other voices, and he could only hope that meant the family was still in the kitchen.

He checked his watch and walked back down the hall to Demara's room. He left the door open.

In its abandoned clutter, the room reminded him of his adolescent second cousin's lair. Some of the clothing strewn about was Lucas's. Apparently Demara wasn't disturbed by such reminders. At least not enough to put them out of sight, as Loanh had.

In the bathroom, the counter was littered with expensive cosmetic products for both women and men. Conan spent little time there, and his examination of the bedroom was equally hurried. And careless. In this clutter, it was unlikely that Demara would notice if anything had been moved, and he couldn't count on much more time.

Besides, he doubted that the three items he was looking for would be here even if they were in her possession. She carried the perfect hiding place in the shoulder-strap purse she had worn throughout the day.

Both Demara's and Lucas's suitcases were open on the floor. Lucas's was empty except for a pair of black silk pajamas. The matching pajamas were in Demara's suitcase, along with various pieces of diminutive lingerie.

And in a side pocket, a blue velvet ring box.

Conan opened the box and smiled. A diamond solitaire, probably a full carat, and a gold wedding band. Inside the band, he found an inscription: LJK & DW FOREVER, followed by a date.

Lucas King and Demara Wilder had been married on September 10. *Forever* had been of short duration for them, or so it seemed.

He replaced the ring box, then straightened, and it was at that moment that he heard a sound.

Behind him. At the door.

CHAPTER 18

Conan's breath came out in a long, shivering sigh. It was Lise standing in the doorway.

"I wondered what you were up to," she said.

"Well, now you know how PIs entertain themselves." He went to the door and took her arm, urging her out into the hall, then closed the door. "Everyone's finished with lunch?"

"Yes, but there are still plenty of sandwiches if you get hungry. Kim, Will, Mark, and Tiff have started a pinochle game, Demara's playing solitaire, Loanh's reading a book—Michener's autobiography—and Tuttle is sitting on the couch with a beer being thoroughly ignored. It doesn't seem to bother him. I get the feeling he thinks it's funny in some perverse way. Is there any firewood left in your room?"

"Thanks for the report. Yes, I think there's still a little wood."

"Come on. I'll get a fire going. You're going to re-freeze yourself."

Conan followed her into his room without asking why he should warm himself there rather than down-stairs by the living-room fire. He wasn't surprised that she closed the door. He went to the armchair by the fireplace and waited while she laid a small fire.

When it was burning well, she sat down in the straight chair and asked coolly, "Was it Tuttle who shot Heather?"

Conan almost laughed. Obviously Lise hadn't been convinced by Will's story that Heather had cut her leg on some unknown sharp object.

"No, Lise, Tuttle didn't shoot her. But you're right, she *was* shot. Will extracted a bullet. Small caliber. Tuttle didn't have a gun of any caliber when he arrived. Of course, he could have disposed of one by simply throwing it into the snow, but there was a lapse of about an hour between the time she was shot and the time Tuttle appeared at the door. I doubt he was wandering around in the storm all that time."

"Then who *did* shoot her? And *why*?"

"I don't know, but it had to be someone here in the lodge."

"Oh, God. The nightmare just gets worse, doesn't it?" For a moment, something fragile, ready to shatter, re-vealed itself in her gray eyes, then they turned opaque with the sheen of steel.

Conan asked, "What about the guns in the display case downstairs? Who has a key to the case?"

"Dad always keeps . . . kept that key on his key ring. But none of those guns can be fired. No firing pins. They're just for display."

"Do you know if he kept any working guns here?"

"The only working gun around is the .38 revolver

Dad gave me two years ago. He was worried about my being here alone so much."

"Where is it?"

"In the studio."

The studio. Conan felt a sharp adrenaline surge. He hadn't included the studio in the scenarios of murder he had constructed last night. Yet if either Al or Lucas had left camp just before the explosion, the blizzard might have intensified enough so that he couldn't reach the highway and his getaway vehicle, and in that case, he might have sought shelter in the studio. There he would have food, a woodstove, and running water. All the comforts of home. And a gun.

It wasn't the .22 with which Heather had been shot, but under the circumstances, any unaccounted-for weapon as potentially lethal as a .38 made Conan distinctly nervous.

"Lise, did you go up to the studio Saturday night?"

She was watching him intently. "Yes. After we got the generator started and realized this might be a serious storm, Will went to the studio with me to get some of my things."

"What time was that?"

"Oh . . . right before eight-thirty. We didn't stay long. I just had to pick up some clothes and drawing pads and a few things for Heather. I doubt we were in the studio more than ten minutes. Why, Conan? What are you thinking?"

He was thinking that Al or Lucas might at this moment be hiding in the studio waiting for the storm to abate, but that possibility Conan wouldn't discuss with Lise until he was sure. She'd be chagrined enough if Al was the mastermind behind the murders, but she'd be devastated if it was Lucas, the twin she loved so unequivocally.

"Lise, I'm thinking so many things, nothing makes much sense. I wonder if you could do something for me. A portrait."

She looked at him quizzically. "A portrait? Of whom?"

"Jerry Tuttle. But *sans* beard and mustache."

"All right. I assume you don't want him to know about it?"

"Nor anyone else."

"Why, Conan? I mean, why do you want his portrait?"

"Possibly to jog someone's memory or simply for shock value. I don't think Tuttle is a perfect stranger to everyone here. One thing I'm sure of, he's not a hunter. He said he'd been tracking a buck yesterday. But deer season is over. It's elk season now, and any hunter would know that and would certainly know that male elk are called bulls. He also described this apocryphal buck as having the biggest rack of horns he'd ever seen."

"Horns?" Lise gave that a curt laugh.

"And there's more. Remember, he said he saw the sign on the gate and figured he could make it half a mile to the lodge. All the sign says is 'King.' To a stranger, that might suggest a house up the road, but it doesn't say how far away the house might be, and *this* house is not visible from the highway even on a clear day because of the curve in the road. So how did he know he only had half a mile to go?"

She asked in a husky whisper, "You think *he's* the killer?"

"He might be an accomplice. The other accomplice—or perhaps the mastermind, for all I know—is the person who tried to kill me last night, and that certainly wasn't Tuttle. It was someone who was here in the lodge last night, someone who was on hand to filch the Nitrostat from Will's case in the confusion while he was thawing me out."

She pushed shaking hands through her hair. "But, Conan, you can't be sure about the Nitrostat. I mean, that it *was* in the toddy."

"No, but I *can* be sure that someone came to my door at two in the morning. If that had been an innocent visit, why didn't this shadow person stay when Heather started barking?"

Now Lise's whole body was shaking, and in her eyes the steel sheen dissolved. "I can't—I can't handle this, not with Dad and Al and . . . oh, *Lucas*—"

"Yes, you *can* handle it." Conan leaned forward and took her hands. "Lise, where's your rage? Hold on to it, for God's sake!"

She held on to his hands for now, and he tolerated the pain she didn't know she was inflicting. Finally the shaking stopped, and she said in a voice so coldly harsh he hardly recognized it, "I guess rage is all I've got, and if I find out who murdered my father and my brothers, maybe your problem then will be to stop me from killing the killer."

"I'll stop you, Lise, if it comes to that."

She took two deep breaths, let each out slowly, and he could feel her hands go still as her eyes again reflected the steel sheen. Then she looked down and pulled her hands away. "Oh, Conan, I'm sorry. Your fingers must be sore enough without my crushing them."

"Are you all right now?"

"Yes. It's just . . . once in a while I lose my grip. Maybe it's a good thing you have Will if I fall apart." She mustered a smile as she added, "You know, he's an uncommon man. A man of courage. He spends half his working life in that storefront clinic, and a lot of his patients there are crazy and quite capable of killing him, yet he calls them his friends—and means it. And today when I begged him to save Heather, I didn't think what a terrible burden I was putting on him if he *couldn't* save her. But he accepted that burden without a second thought."

Conan, who had witnessed Will's many second thoughts on that burden, only smiled and said, "He loves you, Lise."

"What?" Then she shook her head. "Oh, Conan, what Will needs is a woman who'll be a proper wife and a mother for his children. I couldn't be that kind of woman, even if I wanted to."

"I doubt Will would be a good husband for that kind of woman. He's too absorbed in his work. That will always come first for him."

She seemed to need to think about that, and Conan rose, putting his back to the fire. "Meanwhile, I have a problem other than trying to figure out who masterminded these murders. If Tuttle *is* involved, I have to worry now about *two* people trying to dispose of me."

Lise winced. "And I can't offer Heather as a guard dog now. Maybe . . . maybe that's why she was shot."

"That occurred to me," Conan said grimly. "At any rate, I don't think I can continue teasing information out of the family without revealing why I want it. I don't have time for that. I'm going to have to tell them the truth."

"Well, that should throw everyone into a state— especially Tiff."

"Probably. Come on, we'd better go downstairs." He started for the door, then stopped. "I almost forgot. I found a telephone number this morning, and I was wondering if you recognized it: 503-1212."

"That's Al and Loanh's home phone. Where did you find it?"

When he told her, she didn't comment, but she was frowning as they left his room and crossed the hall to the stairway. They paused there. Jerry Tuttle was coming up the stairs, booted feet thumping on the treads. He stopped when he saw Conan and Lise.

"Just headin' up to my room," he said, his voice raspier than usual as he inspected Lise, head to toe, with a slow, challenging grin. "Thought I'd sack out for a while. Didn't get much sleep last night."

Conan said, "You'll probably have to stoke up the fire."

"Yeah, I know." His grin stretched into a complacent smirk. "Seein' as how I don't have nobody to warm up the bed for me." With that, he thumped on up the stairs and down the hall.

Lise said irritably, "Typical case of testosterone glut. Someday medical science will come up with a cure for that." Then she added with an oblique smile, "When there are more female medical scientists."

Conan only laughed as they descended the stairs. He was wondering if sleepiness was the real reason for Tuttle's retreat to his bedroom. But then perhaps he might find it less chilling than the atmosphere in the living room.

And with Tuttle absent, Conan knew he must take advantage of this opportunity for a family conference.

He wasn't looking forward to it.

CHAPTER 19

Conan stopped under the arched entry into the living room. As Lise had reported, Kim, Will, Mark, and Tiff were engaged in a pinochle game at the card table set up between the bar and the fireplace. Tiff, he noted, had a rocks glass, half full of Scotch, at her side. Loanh was curled up at the east end of the couch with an afghan and a book, and Demara was at the dining table dealing out a game of solitaire. Mark, frowning at the fan of his cards, offered a starting bid of two-fifty.

While Lise went on into the living room, Conan caught Will's eye and signaled for him to come out into the atrium. Will made a show of studying his cards, then put them down and said, "I'll pass. It's up to you, Kim." The players watched him as he departed.

Conan retreated to the foot of the stairs to wait for him and kept his voice low when he spoke. "Will, I'm going to have to tell the family what really happened at the camp, and I'd better do it now while Tuttle's up-

stairs. I just want to be sure he doesn't decide to eavesdrop. Would you mind standing watch at the top of the
stairs?"

"Sure." Will glanced into the living room. "Is Lise
okay?"

"As far as I know, yes."

Will hesitated a moment, then nodded and started up
the stairs.

Conan went into the living room and crossed to the
fireplace, where Lise was sitting on the hearth ledge by
Heather's basket. The sheltie was asleep, and she didn't
wake. He found everyone in the room staring at him,
the card game suspended. Finally he said, "I have
something to tell you, if you'll gather around."

They gathered, silently. Tiff carried her glass to her
usual chair, pulled her crocheted creation out of the
sewing bag beside the chair, and began knotting a
strand of purple yarn with fidgety flourishes of her needle. Kim took the other armchair, and Mark swung over
to the couch and sat down near his wife, while Demara
stood behind the couch, arms folded, hooded eyes flash-
ing with impatience. Loanh slipped a place marker into
her book and put it aside. Her silky black hair hung
about her shoulders like a mourning veil.

Conan began, "For what seemed compelling reasons
at the time, I've been less than honest with you. I didn't
tell you the whole truth about what happened last night
at Loblolly Creek."

Kim raised an eyebrow. "You mean about the rock
slide?"

"I mean about what *caused* the rock slide. It was *not*
a natural phenomenon. It was preceded by an explosion.
In other words, it was triggered by dynamite or some
other explosive."

Predictably that pronouncement was followed by a

long silence, and in every face the doubt and shock seemed genuine. Then everyone began talking at once, except for Tiff, whose commentary took the shape of incoherent wails. Only Loanh had nothing to say.

Mark's voice carried over the others' with what seemed to be the consensus: "That's crazy! You're talking about *murder*!"

"Yes, I am," Conan said quietly.

"Why would anyone want to murder Dad and Al and Lucas, for God's sake? And you? But of course *you* got away without a scratch, didn't you? And we've only got *your* word for what really happened."

"Mark, don't be silly," Lise said. "Why would he lie about it?"

Demara said bitterly, "God, we should never have come here!"

"Oh, I *knew* it," Tiff wailed. "I *knew* somethin' *awful* would happen. I mean, when *Lucas* showed up, and Al was such a bastard—"

Loanh cut in, "Tiff, you must not say such things!"

Before Tiff could reply, Conan said, "There's one obvious reason why someone might want to kill A. C.: a forty-million-dollar reason."

That elicited more noise, mostly in the form of denials, and Conan cut through it with, "But A. C. wasn't the only victim, and I don't even know if he was the *intended* victim. One thing I'm sure of: The person who masterminded these deaths knew your family traditions and knew A. C. and his sons would be camping at Loblolly Creek last night."

The clamor ceased while they looked at each other with sudden suspicion. It was Kim who asked, "What about Tuttle? Maybe he wasn't out hunting. Maybe he was parked by the bridge because *he* set the explosives."

Tiff shrilled, "Didn't I *tell* you? That man has an

aura, an aura of *evil*, and now we're *trapped* here with him, and who *knows* how long this storm'll last. Oh, we're *all* gonna *die!*"

While Mark patted his wife's hand, Conan managed to make himself heard over her sobs. "Kim, you could be right about Tuttle, but what motive would a stranger have to kill A. C. or Al or Lucas? Does anyone know Tuttle? Did any of you recognize him?"

Tiff's hiccuping sobs stopped, and there was another exchange of wary glances. Conan asked, "What about you, Tiff? For a second when Tuttle first arrived, I got the feeling you'd seen him before."

"Me?" She sprang out of her chair, the crocheting dropping in a heap of spectrum colors at her feet. "I never saw him before in my *life*, and why're you asking *me*? Oh, this is just too *much!*" She began stuffing the yarn into the sewing bag. "I'm gonna go up to our room. It may be cold, but at least I *won't* have to listen to this—this *crap!*"

Conan sighed. "You needn't bother, Tiff. I'm going to the kitchen for some lunch." He leaned down and said into Lise's ear, "You can tell Will he's off duty."

She nodded, and Conan headed for the kitchen. Silence followed him all the way, but as he closed the door, he heard an erupting babble of voices. At least he'd given them something to think about.

With any luck, something to talk to him about privately.

He went to the table and filled a glass with milk, then put a sandwich on a plate and sat down at the end of the banquette. He was a little surprised that he was so hungry, but then it was after two o'clock. And Kim made an excellent tuna salad sandwich, with thick brown bread, plenty of mayonnaise, and a subtle mix of spices. He had started on a second sandwich when the door opened. It was Mark. He pushed the door shut behind him and limped to the table.

Mark limped simply because the cast and walking shoe put him off balance. He was not using his crutches.

He slumped into one of the straight chairs, his tight mouth giving him an expression verging on a pout. Conan waited, chewing at his sandwich. At length Mark announced, "I've got something to tell you."

"No doubt something about your miraculous recovery? It must've been amazing. Did you throw your crutches aside and shout, 'Praise the Lord, I can walk!' "

"Will said you'd figure it out." Mark sighed and added, "There's a perfectly good reason for it, but I realize . . . well, it looks bad."

"In view of what happened on the hike you missed because of that supposedly broken ankle—yes, it looks bad, Mark."

"I know, I know. But I just didn't want to go on that hike. I didn't want to spend a whole day and night playing buddies with Dad!"

"Why not?"

Mark averted his eyes, fixed them on the plate of sandwiches, and after a moment reached for a half. "That's private."

"Nothing is private in a murder investigation."

"Investigation? You're not a policeman, Conan. You have no right to invade anyone's privacy, murder or not."

That silenced Conan, especially the part about invading privacy. He watched Mark bite into the sandwich, jaws churning in quick, nervous motions as he chewed. Finally Mark said, "Hell, you'll probably find out anyway from Lise. The truth is, I didn't want to spend all that time with the man who tried to *rape* my daughter."

Perhaps Mark expected Conan to be shocked, but he didn't pretend to be unaware of Karen's accusation against her grandfather. He asked, "Mark, do you really believe A. C. tried to rape Karen?"

"Yes!" Color flooded unevenly into his face. "I know Karen's had a lot of problems, but it hasn't all been her fault. When a kid has to be raised by a nanny—well, what can you expect? I'm not blaming Tiff. She . . . she just couldn't cope with the girls. She tried. She really did. And Diana and Nancy have never given us a bit of trouble, but Karen always was high spirited." He put his sandwich down, fixed Conan with a look in which there was no prospect of concession or doubt. "But I *know* my little girl wouldn't *lie* to me! Not to *me*!"

Conan didn't venture a comment on that. Instead he asked, "When did you decide on the subterfuge with the broken ankle?"

Mark picked up the sandwich and took another bite. "It was in September. September thirteenth, actually. I remember because it was my birthday, and Lucas phoned to wish me a happy birthday. Not that he'd ever noticed my birthday before unless somebody reminded him. Just a whim. Poor Lucas. He was full of whims, always running off half-cocked. Hell, it was *his* idea, the broken ankle. That's the sort of outrageous thing he was always thinking up. Normally, I wouldn't have considered it, but I was dreading this reunion and the hike so much . . . well, it sounded like a good idea at the time."

"Why didn't you just stay home?"

Mark munched at his sandwich then shrugged. "No guts, I guess. Look, I have to work with Dad every day. As far as he was concerned, that business with Karen was finished and forgotten. It was just easier to go along with him and keep up the sacred family traditions. But I couldn't face that stupid hike. My God, we're none of us kids anymore. His boys. He still calls us his *boys*." Mark hesitated, and for a moment he looked very much like a frightened boy. "You know, I still can't really believe it. I mean, that Dad and Al and Lucas are . . ."

Conan cautiously wiped his tender hands with a napkin, then rose to get a mug of coffee, and when he returned to the table lit a cigarette and took a long drag. "It was Will who applied the cast?"

"Yes. I had a hell of a time talking to him into it, but we've been friends a long time. Since our football days at OSU. He finally said he couldn't see any harm in it, so he fixed me up with this thing. What he didn't tell me was it takes special tools to remove a Fiberglas cast, and naturally he doesn't have the tools with him, so I'm stuck with the damn thing till we get back to Portland."

Obviously Mark saw no humor in that, and Conan managed to keep a straight face as he took a puff on his cigarette and said noncommittally, "I hope it isn't too uncomfortable."

"It's *damn* uncomfortable. Itches like hell. Anyway, I just wanted you to know why I did it. I mean, I can see how it might look like I was giving myself an excuse not to go on the hike because I knew . . . well, like I knew what was going to happen."

A convincing excuse, and one that Conan had no doubt Mark would not have revealed had his accomplice in the subterfuge been less honest. Perhaps sensing Conan's doubt, Mark leaned closer. "You've *got* to believe me. Jesus, why would I do something like that?"

Conan could think of a few reasons, but he didn't voice them. Instead he tapped the ash off his cigarette and asked, "What's going on between you and Loanh? Why did you take her aside for that secretive little conference Friday afternoon?"

Mark drew back, his face turning waxy. "I can't talk about that."

"Why not?"

"Lawyer-client confidentiality. I'm acting as Loanh's counsel in a private matter."

"A divorce?"

"I *said* I can't talk about it."

Whether Conan might have been able to break down the stone wall Mark had erected became abruptly moot as the door swung back and closed again behind Tiff, who stormed into the kitchen looking like a well-insulated Fury. She fixed Conan with a baleful look the effect of which was diminished by the difficulty she seemed to be having in focusing.

"Okay, Mr. Private Detective, you *rilly* wanna know who mighta killed ol' A. C. and Al, maybe you oughta take a good close cook—look at *Ms.* Kimberly Kaiser. Right! *Cute* little Kim!"

Mark rose, put his arm around his wife. "Sweetheart, don't say anything you might regret."

"Regret?" She pushed him away. "Why should I *regret* tellin' the *truth*?"

"Honey, you've had a little too much to drink. Let's go—"

Conan put in, "Mark, I want to hear what she has to say."

Tiff smirked triumphantly, then leaned on the table, brought her face close to Conan's. "Did you *know*, Mr. Detective, that Kim and Al were *lovers*? Yes, they were. Went on for *years*. That was when Kim was workin' for *Al*, you know, back when it was still King 'n' Ryder Construshion Company, but when Jerry Ryder retired, well, *that* was when Kim cut out. Took a job at Ace Timber and dug her fingernails into *poor* ol' A. C., and all she was after was his *money*, you know, and poor Carla hardly in her *grave*—"

"Tiff, please!" Mark pulled her away from the table. "That's just gossip. Now, come on."

She jerked out of his grasp and flounced to the door. "I *said* all I had to *say*!"

The door swished shut behind her, and Mark sent Conan a pallid smile, muttered, "Don't pay any attention to her. She's just ... on edge," and hurriedly followed his wife.

Conan remained at the table, finishing his coffee and cigarette and contemplating Tiff's information—or gossip. Obviously Kim had not made a friend of Tiff, and perhaps that was understandable. Tiff didn't appreciate having to share A. C.'s estate with a Janie-come-lately.

An uncharitable thought, no doubt, and he wondered, with equal lack of charity, how drunk she actually was. Something about her display hadn't rung true. Did she think she'd be held harmless for a vicious bit of gossip if it could be blamed on drunkenness? Or was she simply reinforcing her role as an airheaded, middle-aged lush, certainly not the kind of person to be taken seriously as a suspect in a murderous scheme that required careful planning and singleminded ruthlessness.

The problem now was to find out if there was any fire behind the smoke of gossip, if Kim *had* been Al King's lover.

It would probably be fruitless to ask Kim, but Conan had found that in such matters the betrayed spouse was usually very much aware of the betrayal, even if he or she remained silent about it.

He put out his cigarette and went into the living room, where the pinochle game had been abandoned. Will was gathering the cards and returning them to their box. Tiff had also abandoned her crocheting, and it still lay in a rainbow heap on the floor by the armchair where she sat peering into her glass, as if seeking an answer in the amber liquid. Mark sat on the arm of her chair, absently patting her shoulder. Kim occupied the other armchair, a lighted cigarette in one hand, the ash long and on the verge of falling, as she stared at the ceiling. Demara had returned to the far end of the dining table, where a solitaire game was laid out, but she slumped with her elbows on the table, hands supporting her head, the cards forgotten. Loanh was absent.

Conan knew he was the object of covert glances, but no one spoke to him or otherwise recognized his presence. Lise was again on the floor by Heather's bed, knees raised to support her drawing pad.

He sat down near her on the hearth, while the thick, black-leaded pencil moved across the paper as if she had set her hand in motion and was simply watching what it did. Her subject was Tiff. The drawing would not have pleased its subject, who probably wouldn't have recognized herself in it, yet it captured in strong, questing lines the erratic, brittle essence of Tiff's face.

On the floor beside Lise lay several sheets from the pad, and on the topmost sheet was a study of Will Stewart. It was a far gentler drawing, hinting at laughter and naiveté, venturing close but not crossing the line into caricature.

The pencil stopped, and Lise looked up at Conan, said softly, "Just practicing."

"And making perfect. Where's Loanh?"

"I guess she went up to her room."

Conan rose. "If anyone asks, I'm going upstairs for some medicine."

She nodded, and the pencil was set in motion again. Conan watched it for a few seconds, consumed with inconsolable envy, then headed for the stairs.

No one spoke as he departed.

CHAPTER 20

The upstairs hall had the chill, dark feel of a mine tunnel, as if untold tons of impenetrable substance pressed upon its ceiling. A dim light was cast into it from the open door of Loanh's room. Every other door—including Tuttle's—was closed.

Conan stopped at Loanh's door. She had built a small fire and sat hunched in a multicolored afghan in one of the two armchairs facing the fireplace on the right-hand wall. He tapped on the door, but it was still a moment before she looked around at him. She said nothing.

He asked, "May I join you?"

She gestured toward the chair beside her. "If you wish, Conan." She watched him as he sat down, then turned to the fire, and she seemed to be talking more to herself than him when she said, "A person's life is changed past knowing in a matter of hours sometimes. I had forgotten that feeling. It happened to me many times when I was growing up. In my country lives were changed, even destroyed, every day, every hour. Then I could adjust to such changes, but now I have had too many years of peace and safety. I am not sure I can still adjust."

She seemed so fragile, so vulnerable, that Conan was inclined to leave her without asking the questions that had brought him to her. But he had long ago learned to doubt appearances and learned that he had no right *not* to ask the questions that might uncover the truth.

"Loanh, did you know Al had a reputation as a womanizer?"

Her gaze remained fixed on the fire. "Al treated me like a princess. When we first met, that's what he called me, his princess. He was a good husband and father, and I knew always that he loved me, even if he needed other women sometimes."

Conan wondered if she considered the belligerent attitude Al had displayed toward her Friday the kind of treatment due a princess.

"You knew about the other women?"

"Yes."

"Is Kim one of them?"

"She was. For four years. But that ended when she quit the company. I was relieved at that, because I believe Kim was the only other woman Al truly loved. He was . . . obsessed with her. I think that was because he knew she didn't love *him*. Al needed very much to *be* loved. When he was angry at her, he called her the Black Widow."

"Did Al discuss his feelings for Kim with you?"

Loanh gave that a bitter laugh. "Of course not. I never worried about his women, but still, I needed to know about them. So I listened to his phone calls. He often made such calls from the phone in his den, and I sometimes listened on an extension. I don't think he knew I listened, and I never talked to him about what I learned. Why should I?"

Conan didn't try to answer that. He waited, hoping she would go on, and at length she did, fine lines like the veining in a ginkgo leaf showing around her eyes. "I wish I *could* have talked to him about Kim. I mean, I wish he could have talked to *someone* who might have helped him."

"Helped him how?"

"To free himself. When she ended it with him, Al could not accept that. It has been another four years since, and he still phones her, still begs her to come back to him."

"Even after she married A. C.?"

"Especially then." Loanh took a deep breath and let her head rest against the back of the chair. "So much went wrong for him since Jerry retired. That year Al got the contract to build the Greenwood Mall in Portland, but when it was nearly finished, there was an explosion at the site. Al thought it was sabotage, although the police found no evidence of that. His insurance didn't cover all the damage, and he lost a lot of money. After that, there were fewer contracts. He said it was the recession. The last two years were so bad, sometimes I was afraid . . ."

When she couldn't seem to finish that, Conan asked gently, "Afraid of what, Loanh?"

"Perhaps . . . afraid that he might break under so much pressure."

"Al owed A. C. money, didn't he?"

"Yes." She sent Conan a look in which animosity lurked. "How did you find out about that?"

"I inadvertently overheard a conversation between Al and A. C. Friday night."

"Oh. Yes, Al owed A. C. money. When Jerry retired,

Al had to buy his half of the partnership. A. C. should have known Al would repay the loan if he only had more time. He had borrowed money before and always repaid it. Al said Kim turned A. C. against him."

"Do you think that's true?"

Loanh shrugged. "I don't even know if Al believed it. He still wanted her. Only a week ago, he still wanted her. He called her, and I heard him say that if she didn't come back to him, he would tell A. C. they had been lovers, even tell him they *still* were lovers."

Conan felt a shiver at the back of his neck. "What did Kim say?"

"She said she didn't care what he told A. C., then she hung up."

"What would A. C. have done if Al *had* told him that?"

"I think he would have been very angry. He might have divorced her. Perhaps that was what Al hoped for."

Conan considered the tangle of motives for murder Loanh was revealing so carelessly—or perhaps so artfully?—and wondered if Al had thought Kim *would* come back to him if A. C. divorced her, and if so, would Al then divorce Loanh to marry the Black Widow, his obsession?

And could anyone be as tolerant of betrayal as Loanh seemed to be?

"Loanh, did you ever consider divorcing Al? You certainly had grounds."

"Never," she replied flatly. "What does it matter if a husband has other women? What matters is that he provides for his wife and children and treats them well. Al always did. Besides, there is another reason: I am Catholic. I grew up in that faith, and it is very important to me. No, Conan, I have never even thought about divorce."

"Had Al ever thought about it?"

That seemed to shock her, and she didn't reply immediately. At length she said, "I doubt it, because a divorce would mean admitting to his father that he had made a mistake to marry me—a foreigner and a Catholic. That was the only time in his life that Al stood against A. C. In every other way he tried to please him, to be *like* him."

"It must've been hard for you, coming into this family as a bride."

"Yes, it was hard," she admitted. "A. C. did not make me feel welcome—not until Charles was born—but Carla accepted me from the beginning. She was a second mother to me. I miss her. I *still* miss her."

Conan waited a respectful moment before he asked, "Do you know why Al hired a private investigator on October sixteenth?"

Her composure vanished. She stared at him, her voice little more than a smothered whisper: "Are you sure? How do you know that?"

Since Conan had no intention of answering that question, he remained silent, waiting. Her delicate hands curled into fists, yet she wasn't looking at him but at some point in memory and at something that frightened her. "When did you say? October sixteenth?"

"Yes."

The sound of his voice seemed to rouse her, and she made an effort at composing herself, casually pushing her hair back from her face.

"I cannot guess why he did such a thing." Then she added firmly, "And I do not wish to answer more questions. I came here to be alone."

Conan accepted that less than subtle hint. "Loanh, I'm sorry to have to burden you with my questions, but

I have no choice." She didn't respond as he rose and left her to her solitude.

October 16. What had happened on that date? Why did it alarm her so much?

Whatever happened, he knew he wouldn't find out from Loanh.

He glanced down the hall at Tuttle's room, saw that the door was still closed, and went to his own room. Perhaps another dose of ibuprofen was a good idea. He had used his hands badly today, feeling under mattresses and into the recesses of private lives.

He found the pill bottle and glass almost by feel in the near darkness of the bathroom. Even in the bedroom, the light had the quality of late dusk. As he crossed to the window and opened the curtains, he checked his watch: 3:20. The ice on the panes had melted. Snow still rushed past the window, but the wind had again diminished. These signals wakened no hope in him. The storm had slackened this morning before Tuttle arrived, only to revive again.

At the sound of the bedroom door opening, he turned, his pulse hammering, betraying an underlying state of apprehension he didn't like to admit.

His unannounced visitor was Kim.

Without preamble, she demanded, "Conan, are you sure about that rock slide? If you're not, this farce about murder is unforgivable, considering the state of everyone's nerves."

He replied curtly, "For God's sake, Kim, do you think I'd *invent* something like that?"

For a moment she was silent, eyes narrowed, then she frowned and strode to the fireplace, where a few embers still glowed. "What are you trying to do, get another case of hypothermia?" She began building up the fire with the few scraps of kindling and wood left in the wood box.

Conan went to the armchair, turning it so that he could see the open door, waited until she finished her task, then while she stood watching the burgeoning fire, waited to see if she had more to say.

She didn't, apparently, but on the other hand she made no move to leave. Finally he said, "Al King wasn't a graceful loser, was he?"

"No, I don't suppose he was." She turned to face Conan. "What are you talking about?"

"Your affair with Al. His reluctance to admit it was ended—if it was. His threat to tell A. C. about it."

She laughed and sat down in the straight chair. "Well, you've been busy. Or probably Tiff has. Yes, I had an affair, as you put it, with Al, but as far as I was concerned, it was finished four years ago. I don't know why Al couldn't seem to let go. I never really loved him, and I didn't pretend to. He was just . . . an indulgence, I suppose. He could be charming, you know. He liked to think he knew what women want, and to some degree he did. He just didn't understand what human beings want. Al was a user, but I didn't choose to be used. In fact, I probably used *him*, and he didn't know how to deal with that."

"It must have been a new experience for him," Conan commented, wondering at that passionless assessment of the situation.

Kim studied him, a faint smile curving her lips. Her blonde hair seemed frosted, a phenomenon of the cold. "Yes, it was a new experience. It made him possessive. When Jerry retired, I decided to make a clean break from Al, so I told him I didn't want to see him again and quit King and Ryder. Well, it was just King Construction by then."

"And went to work at Ace Timber."

"There was a vacancy in the accounting department, and I applied for it. I didn't know A. C., and I certainly didn't foresee marrying him. It was just a good job, and good jobs are hard to come by these days."

"But Al was singularly persistent. Only a week ago he threatened to tell A. C. about your affair and even to tell him it had never ended."

Her fair skin reddened, and she started to speak, then thought better of it and instead crossed to the window and pushed the curtain aside to look out. Conan rose, watching her and again waiting.

At length she turned and said, "That had to come from Loanh. I always wondered if she didn't eavesdrop on Al's phone calls. He was so arrogant, he didn't think she'd dare. Yes, he tried to blackmail me. I don't know what kind of relationship he thought we'd have if I *had* been coerced into going back to him, but he wasn't thinking straight. He hadn't been thinking straight for a year or so. He was a man on a collision course with . . . with something. Maybe himself."

"You weren't concerned that he might carry out his threat? I can't imagine that A. C. would've been pleased with the news. He might even have divorced you."

Kim eyed Conan coolly. "And you think that gives me a motive to kill him? That any divorce settlement wouldn't begin to equal the inheritance I'd get as his wife if he died?"

Conan didn't reply, and she nodded. "You didn't know A. C. that well. Nor do you know me. When Al threatened me, I realized the only way to pull his teeth was to tell A. C. myself."

"What was his reaction?"

She returned to her chair, smiling pensively. "He was

hurt at first, but I think he was more hurt to find out a
son of his could be such a fool. He said who I
loved—or made love to—before we married was none
of his business. No, I have no proof of that. It was a private conversation. Just A. C. and me. And he's . . . beyond verifying it."

Conan sat down, resting his aching hands on the arms
of the chair. She was convincing, he had to admit, and
strangely it was that contained lack of passion that
made her so convincing. He changed the subject, asked,
"Didn't Al owe A. C. a lot of money?"

"Yes. He borrowed nearly a million dollars when he
bought out Jerry's half of the partnership four years
ago. He kept up the interest payments for a couple of
years, but since then he hasn't paid a cent. A. C. didn't
believe his sons should expect special treatment when it
came to business dealings. He said they had to make
their own way."

"But Al was having a hard time of it?"

"So he said. All A. C. was asking was for Al to bring
the interest payments up to date. He wasn't asking for
anything on the principle."

"What collateral did Al put up?"

"The only thing he *had* to put up: King Construction
Company, lock, stock, and contracts."

"Would A. C. have foreclosed on his son?"

Kim brushed bark fragments off the sleeve of her cardigan. "Probably. But he wouldn't have let Al and
Loanh and their kids starve."

"How would he rationalize that sort of charity?"

"Oh, I'm sure it wouldn't have taken the form of
charity. A. C. probably would've offered Al a job at
Ace Timber."

Conan tried to imagine how Al would have reacted to
such an offer. He reached into the pocket of the

Pendleton shirt that was the top layer of his Charlie Brown winter ensemble—the shirt off A. C.'s back, in fact—for his cigarettes. He offered one to Kim, but she said, "Thanks, I have my own," and pulled a pack of Marlboros out of the cardigan pocket. He lit her cigarette, then his own.

"Kim, have Mark or Lucas ever borrowed money from A. C.?"

"If so, the loans were made and paid off before I married A. C. I doubt it, really. I don't think Mark ever made the kind of investments that required a lot of capital, and if Prince Charming borrowed any money, it was probably from Carla. And it was probably never repaid."

Conan noted the bitterness in her tone. "Lucas was always a con man at heart, wasn't he?"

"Of course, but no one in this family ever saw that. Not even A. C., although he didn't really trust Lucas, even before he made such an ass of himself at the wedding reception. Did Lise tell you about that?"

"Yes, and she said you dissuaded A. C. from disinheriting Lucas."

"Well, that was for A. C., not Lucas. Family came first with A. C., and I knew he'd eventually regret it if he cut Lucas off entirely." Her blue eyes turned glacial as she added, "I said A. C. hadn't loaned Lucas any money, but I didn't say Lucas hadn't asked. Damn him, he didn't even speak to his father for two years, and when he did finally break the silence, it was to ask for money."

Conan took a slow drag on his cigarette. "When was that?"

"Only a couple of months ago. Late August. It seems the fair-haired boy got himself in deep doo-doo with the

IRS. In fact, two hundred and fifty thousand dollars deep."

"Was that the 'little problem' he talked about Friday afternoon? The one he said he'd taken care of?"

"Yes. A. C. told me about it Friday night. He wanted so much to believe Lucas, to believe he really meant that apology."

"I think A. C. *did* believe it before he died."

"Thank God for that." Her eyes were downcast as she drew on her cigarette.

"How did A. C. feel about Mark? I know about Karen's accusation."

Kim's lips curled toward a sneer. "That little bitch. And Mark's such a fool. But A. C. understood. He told me Mark *had* to side with his own daughter. A man had to be loyal to his own flesh and blood. What's wrong?"

She had no doubt caught the shift of Conan's attention to the open door. Jerry Tuttle was slouched against the jamb, mouth slack, pale eyes slyly intent.

Tuttle said, "I was just wondering if you folks've got any more wood. The wood box in my room is empty."

"Yes, we have more wood," Kim said as she rose and tossed her cigarette into the fire. "And all the boxes need filling. You can help with that."

"Be glad to . . . ma'am." Kim marched out of the room, and Tuttle stepped aside to let her pass, then sent Conan a wily grin. "Shit, Conan, that is one sweet-assed little fox."

Conan made no reply, although several came to mind, none of them friendly. Tuttle stood a moment longer, and the grin turned chillingly sardonic as he raised his right hand, index finger pointed at Conan, thumb cocked. He squinted one eye as if he were looking down the sights of a gun and made a hissing, "Pow!" The hand that had become a gun recoiled realistically, and Tuttle turned with a rasping snigger and followed Kim, his boots thudding on the stairs.

There, Conan thought, was a man destined for an early demise, a typical victim of what had been termed *righteous slaughter.* He would swagger through life, goading the people around him into states ranging from annoyance to anger, until eventually someone would cross the fine line into uncontrollable rage.

Conan hadn't been goaded beyond disgust, but there were elements of fear and, perversely, satisfaction in it. Fear because that contemptuous, self-indulgent gesture had been nothing less than a threat. Satisfaction because with that threat, Tuttle had revealed himself. He might as well have put it into words: *I'm going to kill you.*

And he might as well have admitted that he was involved in the murders Conan had witnessed and admitted that he recognized Conan as a liability that must be disposed of.

So. Conan inhaled on his cigarette and watched the curls of smoke. What was Tuttle's role in the murders? Rather, his job. He was undoubtedly simply a hired hand in this conspiracy. Wheelman, almost certainly. The headlights Conan had seen from the clear-cut before the explosion probably belonged to Tuttle's Bronco. He said he had parked at the King's Creek bridge. He obviously wasn't there for the hunting, and Conan assumed he was there because he was waiting for something or, more likely, someone.

Why else would he stay at the bridge so long that he got trapped by the storm? Not because he had slept until nine-thirty, unaware that the storm had turned into a full-fledged blizzard. The pounding wind would have kept anyone enduring it in a flat-flanked vehicle awake.

Nine-thirty. Conan's eyes went to black slits as he made an absent attempt at a smoke ring. That time meant something to Tuttle. He had mentioned it twice. Was that the time agreed on for the rendezvous at the bridge?

Who had Tuttle been waiting for?

Al or Lucas. Tuttle wouldn't have been waiting for anyone who was at the lodge Saturday night. Only Al or Lucas needed a means to escape the scene of the crime.

But neither had reached Tuttle's Bronco. If either had, Tuttle wouldn't have come to the lodge this morning. Al and Lucas knew about the studio, and if one of them had reached the Bronco and been trapped there, he and Tuttle would have gone to the studio this morning. It wasn't that much farther than the lodge. But Tuttle obviously didn't know about the studio, and in his desperation, he had come to the lodge, and he had come alone. If his employer had reached the Bronco, he definitely wouldn't have stayed there to freeze to death when Tuttle departed.

Was Tuttle more than a driver? Was he also the explosives expert that any of the suspects would need? Conan could at least be sure that Tuttle made his living working outdoors. Possibly in construction.

He took a last puff on his cigarette and flipped it into the fire. He still didn't know who the lodge accomplice was. Nothing he had learned today eliminated anyone. Either Al or Lucas might have conspired with any of them. Al wasn't likely to have conspired with Demara, since he apparently hadn't met her before this weekend, but he might have conspired with Loanh, with Mark and/or Tiff, or even with Kim, his obsession, his Black Widow. Perhaps she wasn't as indifferent to his appeals as she claimed.

Lucas might conspire with Demara, his secret wife and heir; or with Loanh—and for her, Al might be the intended victim—or, again, Mark and/or Tiff might be the lodge conspirators. Mark had admitted it was Lucas who suggested the subterfuge of the false cast.

Conan rose and went to the window. The wind *had* slackened. Snow still fell, but not in the blinding surges of only a few hours ago.

So much for National Weather Service predictions. Maybe.

But if he was right about Al or Lucas being forced to take refuge in the studio last night, and if this was more than a temporary lull, a window of opportunity was approaching. As soon as the lull became a definite trend, the highway department would send out snowplows, and when that happened, the person in the studio would have a chance to reach the highway and escape in Tuttle's Bronco. Tuttle had said there was still a quarter of a tank of gas left when he departed for the lodge. That was more than enough to reach a filling station.

Let it be Al, Conan thought. For Lise's sake, let it be Al who conceived this vicious, bloody-minded scheme.

CHAPTER 21

As Conan neared the foot of the stairs, the door into the garage opened, and Kim emerged with an armful of wood, followed by Demara, Will, and Tuttle with similar loads. Kim directed Tuttle to accompany her, while Demara and Will headed upstairs. Conan followed Kim and Tuttle into the living room, where they deposited their loads with rumbling thuds in the wood box by the fireplace, then started back to the woodshed for more.

Lise sat at the card table with her drawing pad and a kerosene lamp. She had moved Heather's bed next to the table. Loanh sat on the couch, concentrating on Michener, or at least staring at the open pages, while Tiff worked at her multicolored creation with an intentness that suggested she was finding concentration difficult. The glass beside her was still, or again, half full. Mark had also begun the happy hour early; he sat at the end of the dining table, one hand curled around a glass, staring morosely at the silent radio before him.

Conan knelt to greet Heather, who responded to his petting with a feeble thrashing of her tail. "Well, pretty lady, you're looking better."

Lise looked down fondly at the sheltie. "She *is* better. Will said if a cold nose really is any indication, then she's recovering beautifully."

There was a hint of fondness in that, too—for Will— and Conan smiled as he rose and glanced at the drawings torn off the pad. "May I?"

"Sure." She pushed the stack toward him, her voice low as she added, "Whatever else these are or will be, they're at least therapeutic. You can't think about anything else when you're drawing."

Conan looked up as Kim and Tuttle made another trip to the wood box. He waited until they had dropped their loads and again set out for the woodshed before he began leafing through the drawings.

The entire cast was represented, executed in a brooding, agitated style. The last drawing was only a beginning, a few lines and shadows, but already there was no doubt who its subject was: Jerry Tuttle.

Conan slipped Tuttle's likeness under the pile. The drawing on the pad was also in the early stages. Demara Wilder. Along the margins of the sheet were studies of Demara's long, strong hands.

"These are beautiful, Lise." But she didn't seem to hear him. Her pencil was again in motion.

He crossed to the French windows and pushed the drape aside, looked past a fringe of icicles into a world steeped in dusk and leached of color except for the scarlet of a vine maple on the far edge of the lawn, and he knew the fact that he could see that color at all was a miracle. In the short time since he had looked out his bedroom window, the snow had lessened, and the flakes were big and slow.

He turned, saw Kim, Will, and Demara going upstairs with more wood, while Tuttle brought another load to the living room. Conan went over to Mark. "Have you tried for a weather report lately?"

Mark shrugged. "What's the use?"

"Try it," Conan said irritably. "The snow has almost stopped. I'd like to know if this is just another lull or the beginning of the end."

Mark looked at him, his soft features doughy in the wan light. Then he blinked, surged to his feet. "It's stopped *snowing*?"

"It's *almost* stopped—Mark!"

But Mark was already limping to the window. He nearly tore the drape as he flung it back, then he shouted, "Tiff! Hey, everybody, it's stopped snowing! I mean, it's *almost* stopped! It's almost *stopped*!"

His shouts attracted everyone, even the wood detail from upstairs. He opened the drapes as far as they would go, and the family gazed hungrily, hopefully, into the white dusk. But the cries and laughter of relief died quickly, and something like dread seemed to overcome them. Perhaps it was the realization that escape from this white hole was possible, even imminent, but then they would have to deal with real-world problems, such as grief. And murder.

Conan switched on the radio, rotating the dial through spurts of static and snatches of music. He could find nothing resembling a weather forecast. Finally he left the tuner set on the strongest station and lowered the volume. When he looked up, he found that the radio was now the focus of everyone's attention.

Kim checked her watch. "It's only four-fifteen. We should get a weather report at five. Come on, let's finish filling the wood boxes."

The wood detail joined her as she again headed for

the woodshed. Mark sighed and went to the fireplace to build up the fire, while Tiff returned to her crocheting, muttering a running commentary that no one seemed to hear. Lise returned to her drawing, Loanh to her book. Each of them seemed suddenly more isolated, more withdrawn.

No doubt they were all thinking about tomorrow and the possible end of the siege by storm. Conan was thinking about tonight, about the person who might be hidden in the studio waiting to make his escape.

And he was thinking that if the siege was in fact ending, tonight would be the last chance for the lodge accomplice and/or Tuttle to silence the sole witness to the murders of A. C. King and his sons.

Conan returned to the French doors. The light had dimmed to a muted gray, and the color in the vine maple faded. The air next to the glass was frigid, but he didn't have the heart to close the drapes and shut out the light, however dim. Instead, he went to the fireplace to escape the chill, stood staring at the whispering flames until the wood detail returned. Demara sank down on the couch, rubbing her chilled hands, while Kim checked the wood box and announced, "We've used over half our wood supply, and there's only about fifteen gallons of gas left for the generator. I hope to God the storm *is* letting up."

Will sat down on the hearth ledge near Conan. "Well, I guess we could siphon some gas out of the cars, Kim."

"Sure we could—if we had any siphoning equipment. We don't even have any garden hoses. The landscaping here is limited to what Art can do with a lawn mower."

"What happened to the dog?" Tuttle asked as he slouched over to the card table. When he extended a hand to Heather, she responded with a growling display of teeth. He quickly withdrew his hand.

Offering no apology for Heather's unfriendly attitude, Lise replied, "She cut herself on something outside."

"Yeah? Well, ain't it nice having a vet in the house— even if he *is* a doctor." Tuttle seemed to find that irresistibly amusing. He was still laughing when he leaned over Lise's shoulder, oblivious to her annoyed glare. "Hey, that's good. That's real good. Ms. Black Beauty, herself."

Demara turned, her glare echoing Lise's. Then she came over to the table and studied the drawing. "That *is* good. Would you sell it to me when you're done?"

Lise didn't get a chance to respond to that. Tuttle was eyeing Demara with a grin that hovered near a leer as he said, "Maybe she oughta do a *real* art picture—Ms. Black Beauty in the buff."

Demara drew a hissing breath and snapped, "Just shut up."

"Hey, it was just a *joke*. What's wrong with you people, anyhow? You all act like you're at a funeral."

This he also found amusing, even when it brought every eye into burning focus on him. Tiff sprang to her feet, her birdlike features strained with outrage. "A *funeral*!" she spat out. "Yes, that's *exactly* right! Three people we all loved *died* yesterday—as if you didn't *know*!"

"Now, just a goddamned minute!" Tuttle retorted. "Hell, Tiff, how was *I* supposed to know? I'm just a guy come in out of the storm."

Demara took a step toward him, her open hand connecting with his face with a cracking slap that rocked him. She shouted, "I wish you'd *stayed* out in the storm! You owe everybody here an apology, *Mr. Tuttle*!"

Heather barked frantically despite Lise's attempts to restrain her, and Tuttle scowled at Demara, his hands in potent fists, his gaunt face chalky except for the red mark left by her palm. Conan, like Will, rose, ready to intercede in the explosion that seemed inevitable.

But it didn't come. Tuttle's scowl slackened, then he said in a conciliatory tone, "You're right, I was outta line, and I apologize." He turned to Tiff, added, "I just didn't know what I was saying. Sorry."

This met with silence, but it seemed a silence of surprise more than anything else. Then Demara nodded regally and stalked over to the fireplace, while Tiff slumped into her chair and reached for her glass. The apparently chastened Tuttle went to the bar, hitched himself up on the stool nearest the wall, and busied himself lighting a Marlboro. He took a long drag and turned his attention to the gun collection.

Given time, Conan thought, Tuttle's arrogance would unmask him. He couldn't seem to resist a bit of sly goading. Was it typical that he backed down so easily?

Kim was the first to speak. "I think we should have an early supper and a proper one. Doris left a couple of fryers in the fridge. I can microwave them. Will, would you mind turning on the generator?"

Will nodded, casting a hard look at Tuttle as he passed on his way to the garage. Loanh and Demara volunteered for kitchen duty, and for the next half hour the crackling of the fire and muted scraps of music, voices, and static from the radio were the loudest sounds in the room. Lise returned to her drawing, Tiff to her crocheting, while Mark closed the drapes against the chill, then joined Will by the radio for a game of gin. Tuttle remained at the bar, smoking one cigarette after the other, moving only to help himself to a beer.

Conan had unfinished business upstairs—he hadn't yet searched the master bedroom—but he wanted to be here if the radio coughed up a weather report, so he preempted Demara's solitaire deck, losing every game he dealt out.

At five o'clock, Mark's announcement that he was getting a weather report on the radio ended the unnatural quiet. Within seconds, everyone in the living room— even Tuttle—had gathered around the radio, while a shout from Will brought the cooks out of the kitchen.

The announcer detailed rising temperatures in northwestern Oregon and southwestern Washington. The freezing rains that had plagued the coast and the Willamette Valley had stopped, and high-wind warnings were canceled. The report ended with, "An Oregon Department of Transportation spokesperson announced that snowplows have already been dispatched into the Cascade Mountain passes, and all of them should be open by early tomorrow morning."

Amid the expressions of hope and relief, Tiff emitted a shriek of joy. "Oh, thank *God*, oh, I thought we were gonna be *trapped* here *forever* and nobody'd *ever* know what happened. I mean, I thought we were gonna be *buried* here like—like . . . oh, it's been so *awful.* . . ."

Mark took her in his arms, offering a reassuring, "We're going to be okay, sweetheart, we're going to be okay."

The cooks rose to the occasion for dinner, despite electrical limitations, but it was largely a silent meal, with Jerry Tuttle as the ghost at the banquet, polite and generally quiet. Again the relief engendered by renewed hope had dissipated to be replaced by an equivocal tension.

Afterward Kim and the other women—with the exception of Tiff, who slumped in her chosen chair with yet another Scotch—accepted help from Will and

Conan in clearing the table, then sent them away, declaring them an unnecessary crowd in the kitchen.

Since the dishes had to be done by hand—the dishwasher put too much demand on the hot-water heater and the generator—and Conan could be sure Kim would be occupied for some time, he slipped upstairs to take care of his unfinished business in the master bedroom. He had no illusions that he'd find anything there, but it satisfied him to try.

He stopped first in his room for a flashlight, switched on the ceiling light so it would show under the door, then went on to the master bedroom. He closed the door, but didn't turn on any lights, depending on the flashlight.

He set about his task methodically, noting in passing the bright blue, yellow, and white Wedding Ring quilt decorating the bed on the west wall; the old, two-man saw, at least six feet long, hanging on the east wall; the small bronze sculpture of a mounted cowboy on the chest of drawers, an excellent copy of a Remington, if it wasn't an original. The mantel provided a showcase for photographs of friends and family. In one, Carla posed formally with the four children when Al was perhaps fifteen, Mark about ten, Lucas and Lise no more than five.

Conan studied that portrait with an aching regret that approached grief: regret for promises unfulfilled, hopes extinguished.

But he was roused from his reverie by the sound of footsteps in the hall. He went to the door and listened, feeling his quickened pulse in his throat. He would not relish trying to explain his presence here to Kim.

But it wasn't Kim. Tiff and Mark. Tiff was rambling through one of her chaotic monologues, while Mark worked in a reassuring comment now and then. With the sound of a closing door, their voices ceased.

Conan let his breath out and continued his search, extending it to the bathroom, which had been modernized with an ostentatious spa as its centerpiece. When he had done as thorough a search as he felt he had time for and had found nothing—no gun, no detonator, no Nitrostat bottle, and nothing to link Kim with the murders—he went to one of the windows flanking the bed and looked out. The snow had stopped altogether, and no wind moved the trees. The moon hid behind a thin layer of clouds as it had last night before the blizzard swept down, and the diffuse light glowed softly on the clean expanse of snow that blanketed the lawn. Not a track on it.

Last night. Only last night. It seemed something remembered from a long time past. *A life is changed past knowing. . . .*

Conan vacated the bedroom, went to his room, where he left the flashlight and turned off the ceiling light, then hurried downstairs. In the living room, the fire burned hectically, and every light was on as if someone were preparing for a party, giving the room a forced cheeriness that failed to dissipate its claustrophobic atmosphere. Lise and Will were kneeling on opposite sides of Heather's bed, which had been returned to its place in front of the fire, Will frowning intently as he checked Heather's bandage, while Lise offered her a bowl of water and regarded Will with a hint of speculative surprise, as if she were studying a familiar object that had occupied the house of her life for years, but one she had never examined closely.

Conan sat down on the hearth ledge, savoring the heat at his back, noting that Tuttle had taken Mark's place at the radio from whence a reedy female voice bewailed the vicissitudes of love. Tuttle slumped, a beer can in one hand, watching Will and Lise with a gaze that was both cold and curious, yet underlying both, monumentally indifferent.

When the grandfather clock sounded seven-thirty, Kim, Loanh, and Demara emerged from the kitchen. Kim frowned at Tiff's empty chair as she crossed to the armchair at the other end of the couch. "Have Tiff and Mark gone upstairs already?"

"Yes," Lise replied. "Tiff . . . well, she was getting a bit wobbly."

Loanh murmured, "She is under a great strain. She has never had to learn how to deal with . . . with trag-edy."

"I know, Loanh," Kim said, almost gently. "None of us are very good at that. Except you, perhaps." Then as if she felt she was slipping out of character, she added briskly, "If that weather report was right, I guess we can afford to leave the generator on a little longer tonight."

"I hope to hell it *was* right." Demara sighed as she sank into Tiff's vacant chair. "God, I don't think I'll ever be warm again."

Will said lightly, "Heck, Demara, we figured you'd be buying a cabin up on Mount Hood so you could spend the winters here. Damn good skiing."

"I don't think I'll ever ski again, either," she said with a brief laugh. "I've had enough snow this weekend to last a lifetime."

"This weekend has been a lifetime," Loanh said softly, as she picked up her book from the couch, then crossed to the bar. "I think I will need something to help me sleep tonight." She poured a gin and tonic with little tonic and no ice, and headed for the stairs.

With her departure, an uneasy silence set in. Finally Kim looked across the room at Tuttle, who still sat with his beer, watching. Her nostrils flared, as if she were trying to identify a strange scent, then she rose. "I'm going upstairs. Lise, are you staying down here with Heather tonight?"

Lise looked vaguely startled, perhaps because Kim had called the sheltie by her name instead of *the dog*. "Yes. I don't want to have to move her upstairs. I'll just bed down on the couch."

"Well, you can turn the generator off when everyone settles down." Kim too made a stop at the bar, fortifying herself for the night with a brandy. She departed without another word.

Within a few minutes Demara made her exit, but without a stop at the bar. Will, Conan, and Lise sat in silence in front of the fire, and finally Tuttle turned off the radio, sauntered to the bar for another beer, and drawled acidly, "Well, good night, folks. It's been a blast."

Conan waited a few seconds, then went to the atrium to be sure Tuttle had gone upstairs. Satisfied, he returned to the fireplace and said quietly, "I'm going to the studio tonight. Just to check it out."

Will asked, "Check *what* out?"

Lise answered for Conan, her voice flat, wrung dry: "To see if Al or Lucas is hiding in the studio."

"Yes, Lise," Conan said, a little surprised. "It's a possibility I have to eliminate."

"Well, if you find anyone there, it'll be Al. Lucas didn't have it in him to kill anyone. For God's sake, I grew up with him. He was . . . he was my dearest friend."

Conan didn't attempt to reply to that, and after a while Will said, "I'll go with you, Conan."

"Thanks. Lise, do you have a key to the studio with you?"

"I didn't lock it."

"But someone else might have."

She seemed to need a moment to digest that, then she nodded as she came to her feet. "My keys are upstairs. I'll go get them."

"By the way, that gun A. C. gave you—where do you keep it?"

"In the drawer in the bedside table." She turned to leave, then stopped and about-faced. "Conan, you *won't* find Lucas there."

Conan nodded, wondering if she had thought past that defensive assertion, if she understood that if Lucas wasn't in the studio, he was buried under tons of rock at Loblolly Creek.

Perhaps of the two options, she preferred the latter.

CHAPTER 22

At the moment, Conan could think of nothing that would instill in him more dread than what he was doing: stepping through the back door into the frigid world outside the lodge.

He stood shivering on the deck in snow up to his knees, gasping out steaming puffs of breath, hands deep in the pockets of his parka, left hand curled around a flashlight, right hand grasping the Ruger P-85. The snow had stopped, the wind had died, yet the cold was still stunning, and in spite of his boots and borrowed mittens, it struck immediately at his vulnerable hands and feet and set them aching miserably. The memories revived by that pain, by the sensation of freezing air in his lungs, awakened in him, briefly, a black panic.

Will Stewart, similarly bundled up and steaming, closed the back door, muttering, "Damn, Conan, nobody in their right mind would be outside in this. Must be twenty below."

Conan looked across the field of snow that had so recently been a lawn where people could toss Frisbees, now bordered by trees transformed into bizarre snowmen, and he found himself thinking of Robert Service and particularly of Sam McGee. The sky was still overcast, the glow of the moon providing a pale light that stripped everything of dimension and substance.

"Come on, Will. Let's get this over with."

Conan pushed through the snow to the steps at the end of the deck, nearly fell when he miscalculated the loca tion of the first one, then set off along the south perimeter of the lawn. The only sound in this silence, so profound that it made his ears ring, was the crunching shuffle of their footsteps.

They had traversed perhaps fifty yards through knee-deep snow, which left both of them panting and a plowed trail behind them, when Conan stopped and looked back at the lodge, a gray monolith against a slope brocaded with snow-burdened trees. There was a light behind the curtained windows of the master bedroom. On the back wall, he could see the dark windows of Tiff and Mark's room, then his own. A clutter of branches hid Demara and Tuttle's windows.

Will said, "Looks like Kim's still awake."

Conan nodded as he turned and slogged on to the opening in the trees that marked the beginning of the path to the studio. The snow under the alders was still up to his knees, but when he reached the conifers beyond, it was only half as deep. It was pristine, devoid of tracks. The light in the shadow of the firs and hemlocks was only a few degrees short of darkness, but Conan glanced back at Will, said, "Don't use your flashlight. If anyone's in the studio, we don't want to give him fair warning."

Will grunted as he stumbled over a snow-hidden root.

"Okay, but if you get us lost, I'm not treating you for hypothermia again."

Conan laughed and tramped on. The snow at least made following the path easier. It seemed to have a crepuscular light of its own. For a long time the silence, punctuated by their squeaking footfalls, held. Finally Conan realized that the shadow shape above and to their left was not indigenous to the wintry landscape.

The studio. He stopped, heart pounding with an equivocal mix of dread and doubt. No trace of light shone behind the windows.

"Will, when you and Lise came up here Saturday night, did you close the curtains?"

"Yes, and we left water running in the kitchen and bathroom to keep the pipes from freezing." He gave that a caustic laugh. "Probably froze anyway."

Conan squinted at the roof, trying to separate the chimney from the tree trunks beyond the building, but he couldn't tell which shadow was the chimney, much less whether any smoke was coming from it.

The lack of light from the studio was not conclusive. Even if the curtains were thin enough for light to show through, there might be no candles or kerosene lamps available or in use right now, and the wood stove was enclosed and would emit no light even if it were burning at full capacity. A lack of smoke *would* be conclusive, but the darkness precluded that test. He asked, "You have the key handy?"

"Right here in my pocket."

With Will only a pace behind, Conan made his way around to the south side of the studio and moved cautiously across the porch. At the door, he pushed his hood back and leaned against the screen to listen.

Silence. But even that meant nothing.

He removed his right-hand mitten and took the gun

out of his pocket, gasping at the electric pain as his bare hand closed on the cold metal. He pushed off the safety and whispered, "Will, get ready with your flashlight." He heard the rustle of Will's parka, then eased the screen door open, forcing it back against a bow wave of snow. Will slipped the key into the lock, turned it, and whispered, "It's not locked."

"All right. Get ready to open it." Conan took a deep, chill breath then shouted, "Now!"

Will shoved the door open, his flashlight coming on as they rushed into the studio, the light moving in quick arcs around the room, while Conan followed the light with his eyes, the gun raised and ready.

Nothing.

The only movement was a rattle of brushes scattering on the floor when Will accidentally knocked them off the palette table.

Conan's racing pulse slowed, dread and doubt giving way to chagrin and—what? Anger? Whom could he rationally be angry at? Himself for being so obviously wrong? Al or Lucas for not being here?

The icy scent of the air in this room was evidence enough that there had been no fire in the stove since the blizzard began. The water in the jar where Lise had cleaned her brushes was frozen, and in the sink in the kitchen area, a thick icicle hung from the faucet.

Conan returned the gun to his pocket. "I was wrong, Will. No one took refuge here. And that means both Al and Lucas are dead."

Our center is gone. . . .

So Lise had said of Carla King's death, and now she had lost almost all of the rest of her family—her father and two brothers, including the twin she loved so intensely and forgivingly.

Conan turned his flashlight on the unfinished painting

on the drafting table with its bold washes of sienna, raw umber, and cerulean. Then, the muscles in his jaw rigid, he crossed to the bedside table, and opened the drawer, found the .38 revolver. It, too, was painfully icy in his hand, but he opened it, saw that all the chambers were loaded, then snapped it closed and handed it to Will. "You'd better keep this."

Will took it with only a momentary pause and put it in his pocket. "So what do we do now?"

"Go back to square one." Conan gingerly pulled his mitten on. "And for now, go back to the lodge."

"What do we do about Tuttle and his friend at the lodge—whoever that might be?"

"Wait for them to make the next move."

Will headed for the door. "Maybe we should just wait till the snowplows come through, and we can get out and talk to the police."

"And tell them what?" Conan asked bitterly. "That's the irony of this thing. I really don't have a shred of solid evidence. I'm not even sure I can prove that the murders occurred."

They stepped out onto the porch, where the cold waited in ambush, going for the jugular. Rather, for Conan's hands and feet. Will led the way down the path, his flashlight guiding him. He asked, "What about the missing Nitrostat? And the bullet from Heather's leg?"

"If an analysis shows Nitrostat in the toddy, it proves that someone was trying to poison me, but there's no way of knowing who, since I didn't find an empty bottle of Nitrostat anywhere. Nor did I find the gun that fired the bullet you extracted from Heather's leg."

Will tramped on for a while then turned, inadvertently shining his flashlight in Conan's eyes before pointing it downward. "Sorry. Damn it, Conan, you heard an explosion. You know that rock slide wasn't an accident. If the police start looking around the slide, they'll find the proof—wire or pieces of wrapping from the dynamite or whatever."

"Not necessarily. The technology of explosives is rather sophisticated these days. On the other hand, someone is obviously worried about the fact that I witnessed something at Loblolly Creek. Maybe because a police investigation will tie up the probation of A.C.'s will indefinitely, or maybe because the killer thinks I know more than I do, but for whatever reason, that person is worried enough to try to kill me. And that is, perversely, my only hope."

"You mean all you can do is wait for Tuttle and the killer to tip their hand? By trying to kill you again?" Will sounded annoyed, as if Conan were being unreasonably recalcitrant.

"If we can catch Tuttle tipping his hand in an incontrovertibly criminal manner, then maybe he'll be willing to plea bargain with the identity of his accomplice. He doesn't strike me as a man capable of great loyalty."

Will sighed and turned away, continuing down the path. Conan didn't try to renew the conversation, but followed in silence as they moved into the alders and finally to the edge of the open plain of the lawn. There Conan stopped, a groan escaping him.

"My God, Will, it's snowing again."

The air was full of fine, pale flakes, whirling in a reviving wind. Already the plowed furrows of the tracks that Conan and Will had made no less than half an hour ago were filling, blurring.

Will swore in a furious monotone, employing a vocabulary undoubtedly learned in the seamy shadows of Burnside, while Conan looked at the back of the lodge and saw a glow of light in one of the windows.

His window.

CHAPTER 23

When Conan and Will reached the lodge, they found Lise wrapped in a satin comforter on the couch, facing the fireplace. All the lights were off, and she looked up at Conan with firelight reflected in her pale, questioning eyes.

But he made his excuses and left it to Will to tell her what they had found—or not found—at the studio. He went upstairs, treading as quietly as possible on the stairway.

There were no lights in the hall or under the closed doors. He paused outside his door, listening, but heard nothing except the creak of timbers in the wind and the distant hum of the generator. Finally he took his gun out of his pocket and opened the door onto darkness. He flipped the ceiling light switch. The room was empty. He checked the bath and closet, went to the window and turned on his flashlight to check the lock. It was closed, the bright circles of screw heads glinting.

Frowning, he looked around the room. There was no evidence that anyone had been in here, yet he had seen a light in this window, and it seemed he could all but smell an unknown presence.

His breath shivered out in a sigh as he returned the gun to his pocket and sat down in the armchair by the fireplace, where ashes swirled in the wind moaning in the chimney. He considered removing his boots to rid his toes of their painful constriction, but refrained finally. Tonight he wanted the assurance of solid footing.

He rose and crossed to the bathroom for a dose of ibuprofen before he turned out the lights and left the room. On his way downstairs, he detoured into Will's room. The medical case was still in the closet, the combination lock intact.

When he reached the living room, he found Lise and Will sitting close together on the couch. Will was holding her hand, and she had been crying, but she had herself under control now, her steel-hued eyes dry and fevered, as if she were in thrall of a pernicious illness.

She said, "I finished the portrait, Conan. It's over on the card table at the bottom of the pile."

Conan went to the table, found the drawing of Tuttle, and took it to the hearth to examine it in the light of the fire, wondering how she had captured, in nothing more than lines and shadows, the arrogance and the underlying indifference in Jerry Tuttle's face. The chin and jaw were educated guesses, since she had, as requested, deleted the beard and mustache. The chin was slightly receding, emphasizing the tendency to an overbite that Conan hadn't consciously noticed before.

"This is perfect, Lise." She only nodded, and he returned the drawing to the bottom of the stack on the card table, then sat down on the hearth ledge by Heather's bed, leaning forward to run his hand along her head. He asked, "Lise, did Will tell you it's snowing again?"

"Yes. God, I hope it doesn't mean another blizzard coming in."

Will said, "We should try the radio for a weather report at nine."

Conan checked his watch. It was only 8:45, but it felt like midnight. "I'd be grateful if you'd leave the generator on tonight, Lise. If Kim objects, I'll take the blame."

Lise managed a smile. "Good. I don't want to get into an argument with her. Just remind me, I'll have to fill the tank again." Then her tenuous smile faded. "Conan, what are you going to do?"

He glanced toward the atrium, and even though he had kept his voice down to this point, he lowered it further to reply, "I'm going to bed. But not to sleep. And Will is going to wait behind his door, keeping it open a crack so he can see my door."

Will nodded. "Right. That way I'll be at the killer's back—with Lise's trusty thirty-eight."

Lise winced at that, then said soberly, "By the way, I have something to report. About twenty minutes ago, I went up to my room to get some fixative for the drawings, and just before I reached my door, I heard voices from Tuttle's room."

Conan's mouth felt dry as he asked, "Did you recognize them?"

"No. Well, I'm sure one was Tuttle, but maybe that's just because I expected it to be him. The other—I couldn't guess. All I could hear was a sort of muttering."

"Could you guess whether the second voice was male or female?"

She shook her head. "It was low-pitched, but not so

much that I could be sure either way. Besides, the voices stopped after a few seconds. I went into my room and took my time finding the fixative. I even waited at the door a while. Nothing. But I know what I heard wasn't just the wind, Conan. I *did* hear someone talking."

"I believe you." And he believed beyond a doubt that Tuttle had at that time been speaking to the lodge accomplice, the person who had tried last night to dispose of that inconvenient witness, Conan Flagg.

And at the time of this perhaps fateful meeting, that witness had been absent from the lodge in pursuit of a chimera. Even now, that witness was absent from the room that had been the scene of one attempted murder and tonight might be the scene of a second attempt.

Conan came to his feet, trying to maintain a casual attitude. "Will, why don't you stay here till nine and see if you can get a weather report? I'm going up to my room. Don't worry, I won't be asleep."

"No, I don't figure you will." His red thatch of eyebrows lowered in a frown. "I'll let you know what we hear on the radio."

Conan nodded. "Good night, Lise."

"Be careful, Conan."

As he made his way to his room, he wondered how he could be more careful than he was being now.

He turned on the lamp by the bed, crossed to the fireplace, and after donning his mittens to protect his fingers, built as big a blaze as the small hearth would safely accommodate. Then he sat down in the armchair and watched the flames while he contemplated the error of his ways.

Rather, the error of his assumption that Al or Lucas would be in the studio. Was it possible that both were simply victims, intended or incidental, that neither of them had been the mastermind?

No. Jerry Tuttle made that premise untenable. He had been waiting at the King's Creek bridge for someone. But whoever he was waiting for hadn't even reached the studio, much less the Bronco.

Conan took off his mittens and lit a cigarette, blew out a web of smoke, bitter frustration coiling within him. He didn't even know who Tuttle was or what his relationship with any of the victims—or with any of the beneficiaries of the murders—might be, and he had no way of finding out.

Not in this white hole.

He looked around the room, intensely aware of the walls, the low, sloping ceiling. He had always suffered a tendency to claustrophobia, yet at the same time always felt a need for privacy that induced him to close curtains and doors. He generally balanced the warring inclinations by responding to them alternately. When he had a choice.

He had no choice now. And the wind was still rising. The lodge, this frail fortress, might again be under siege by a storm beast.

And the beast within?

It wasn't Jerry Tuttle. Conan closed his eyes, savoring a long pull on his cigarette. Tuttle was only a tool. Dangerous, yes, but only a tool. The beast within this besieged keep was capable of subtle deceit and ruthlessness entirely beyond Tuttle's scope.

Still, for the moment, Tuttle was the key.

A light knock at the door, and Conan surged to his feet, muscles knotting. Then he sank back into his chair as Will Stewart came in, closing the door behind him.

"Will. Any luck with the radio?"

With a sigh, Will sat down in the straight chair. "I got

a short weather report. There's a new cold front coming in, but the weather people aren't committing themselves yet about how bad it'll be. And it's still snowing. I looked out the front door before I came up. Not as bad as Saturday night. Not yet, anyway."

"Any reports on the highways?"

"Hell, it's a Portland station. They figure one minute every hour for the weather is plenty. They've got their thermostats set at seventy, so it's on to Billy Ray Cyrus." He slumped in his chair, frowning. "I've got some friends out on the streets in Portland, guys who can't go into the shelters. They've been locked up one place or another too long, and they can't stand walls."

Conan could sympathize with an antipathy for walls, but he made no comment. He asked, "How's Lise?"

"Okay, I guess. Damn, I just want to—I don't know. Make it all go away, all the pain. But it won't go away for a long time. All I can do is be handy." Then he added, with a trace of bitterness, "Like a big brother. Somebody to make up for the brothers she's lost." He cast an almost accusing glance at Conan.

Conan took a puff on his cigarette, turning to face the fire. "You're lucky, Will, to have Lise as a surrogate sister. I consider myself lucky just to have her as a friend, to be an awestruck fan."

Will squinted at him suspiciously, then his eyebrows went up, and he started to respond, but apparently changed his mind, instead pushing his sleeve back to check the time before he rose and crossed to the door. "I guess the vigil starts now. I'll be at my post, ready and waiting."

"Thanks, Will."

"We're going to finish this thing tonight—one way or another."

Conan nodded, hoping there was more prophecy than bravado in that.

After Will's departure, Conan finished his cigarette, then removed the gun from his pocket, took off his parka, and prepared for his own vigil. He propped pillows against the headboard and lay down, pulled a comforter over himself, turned off the light, and cradled the bitingly cold metal of the gun in his right hand. The fire cast its amber light on the ceiling and walls, yet they still seemed too close, compressing the air. He looked at the window then at the door with an irrational sense that both were as solid as the walls and would never again open.

He closed his eyes and composed his thoughts for patience. He had kept long vigils before. They required a particular mind-set and a high degree of confidence. Patience would not survive a failure of hope.

Yet as he counted his slowing heartbeats, he realized that the worst problem he faced now was something as simple—and as potentially dangerous—as sleepiness. After the exhausting trek down from the camp and the resultant hypothermia and frostbite, after a night of alarms and anxiety and little rest, after a day of more alarms and anxiety and constant chill, his body claimed the right, even at the risk of his life, to the recuperative hiatus of sleep.

He fought that claim with mental exercises, silently reciting poems and limericks; calling up historical dates; adding, subtracting, multiplying, and dividing numbers—many derived from the sum of minutes and seconds revealed by the glowing numbers on his watch—and again and again reviewing the murders and everything he knew about them, everything he didn't know.

Still he found himself repeatedly sinking into sleep.

Never a deep sleep. The smallest sound jarred him awake, adrenaline sending his pulse rate soaring. The room grew constantly colder and darker as the fire burned down. The seconds ticked tediously into minutes, the minutes into hours, and he was surprised at how much light filtered through the curtains. Moonlight, snowlight . . . first light I see. . . .

Again. He had slipped over the edge into sleep.

He wasn't sure what wakened him this time. He heard nothing. The fire had burned out, and the only light was the diffuse glimmer from the window. From his watch glowed the numbers 11:42.

There. A soft scraping. He held his breath, mouth open to keep his teeth apart so they wouldn't chatter with the chill. The steel of the gun burned cold as he flipped off the safety and slowly moved his hand out from under the comforter. Otherwise he didn't move a muscle, but lay waiting, half turned toward the door.

The scraping sound again, louder; a small metallic rattling, and his eyes registered a subtle brightening of the light that struck the door. Yet it hadn't opened.

The window.

Conan threw the comforter aside as he twisted around to face the window.

Open. The window was open, the curtain pushed back, and against the fey snowlight, a black shape moved toward him in a silence crystalized out of the icy wind, a shadow shape fixed in the crystalized moment, so close it blocked out the strange light. Conan felt himself engulfed, frozen in the black shadow.

The icy silence exploded.

Two shots, and a bullet thudded into the headboard. Too low, the flashes were too low, but he didn't have time to make sense of that, not before reflex closed his finger on the trigger. The silence again exploded, and he felt the surging recoil of three shots, flinched at the glare of the flashes, kneeling upright on the bed, and he had no memory of even moving, no memory of gripping the weapon in both hands, arms straight before him.

A single hoarse shout, and the shadow vanished, the snowlight poured in. The thud sounded like a falling boulder.

No, something still—again—blocked the snowlight. Two more flashes that seemed strangely separate from the crashing detonations. Conan reeled backward, staggered by the hammer blow that tumbled him off the bed, dragging the comforter with him. He crashed to the floor in a tangle of soft, swishing material, tried to crawl to the foot of the bed so he could see around it to the window.

Too late. A pounding crash, a blinding burst of light, a shout of chagrin.

"What the hell's going on?"

CHAPTER 24

On his knees, crouched against the bed, Conan began shaking, overwhelmed with relief, and at the same time—and only now that he recognized the voice, understood that the crash was the door flying back against the wall under the impetus of Will Stewart's dramatic entrance, that the blinding light came from the ceiling fixture—now he was overwhelmed with pain that clamped his left shoulder in an invisible and unforgiving vise.

"Conan! You okay?"

Overwhelmed, too, with frustration as he focused on the window. Empty, the snowlight lost in blackness, errant flakes whirling in on the frigid wind.

He got to his feet, right hand still clenched on the gun, and swayed toward the window, passed the sprawled shape on the floor. He leaned out into the wind and snow. In the light fanning from the window he saw indentations of tracks striking east along the wall, but the falling snow obliterated them as he watched, and there was nothing, no one moving against the pale drifts. He winced at the burning ache in his fingers as he relaxed his hold on the gun and thrust it into his belt, then he pushed the sash down, cutting off the icy wind.

"Conan?" Will hovered near him, frowning at the dark, sodden circle to the left of the collar of Conan's red plaid Pendleton jacket "You were hit. Figures. Sounded like a damn shooting gallery in here."

Will's anxious solicitude roused in Conan only annoyance. He stared at Jerry Tuttle, face down on the floor, right hand loose on the grip of a small semiautomatic that seemed a plaything in his big, callused hand. Near his right foot lay a knife, its long blade reflecting the ceiling light. It looked like a carving knife. It looked like it belonged to the knife set in the kitchen. And it probably did.

Conan was distracted by shouts and footsteps in the hall. He folded his left arm against his body to immobilize the shoulder as he strode to the door, reached it in time to see Mark thumping down the dark hall with Tiff clinging to his arm, Kim hurrying from the master bedroom, while Loanh approached from the other direction, ghostly in a white robe, black hair veiled around her shoulders. Next came Demara, tying the sash of a floor-length, black satin robe, then Lise, racing up the stairs. Mark reached the door first, and when it became obvious that Conan didn't intend to step aside, Mark stopped abruptly, mouth open in an incongruous O as he peered past him.

"Christ, what *happened*? Is that Tuttle? Is he *dead*?"

At that, Tiff threw her arms around Mark's neck, emitting panting shrieks. Lise demanded, "Conan, are you all right? Where's Will?"

Will moved up behind Conan, but any reassurance he had to offer was drowned in the cacophony of questions punctuated by Tiff's continuing shrieks. Conan held up his right hand. "Be quiet! Everyone, just be *quiet!*"

The cacophony stopped as if he'd turned a spigot, but he knew it wouldn't last. He said quickly, "I'll explain what happened later. Right now, I want all of you to go downstairs and wait until—"

"Wait?" Mark objected. "I'm *damned* if I'm going to wait—"

Will cut in, "Mark, just give me a little time to take care of the casualties. Please."

That elicited some grumbling, but Mark was apparently ready to accept the request coming from his friend, and he gathered Tiff under his arm and headed for the stairs. "Come on, everybody. Kim, any coffee left?"

Kim regarded Conan coolly, then shook her head. "No, Mark, but I'll make some." She started downstairs, and after a moment, Loanh and Demara joined her.

Lise made no move to follow them, and Conan said firmly, "Lise, go downstairs with the others. I want to know if any of them leave the room at any time for any reason."

She looked past Conan at Will, then nodded and set off down the stairs. Conan closed the door, leaning against it as he looked across the room. Will had turned Tuttle onto his back and was bending over him, seeking a pulse or breath.

Finally Will said, "He's gone."

Conan found a cold irony in that euphemism. *Gone.* Why did doctors, who so often witnessed death, find the word so hard to speak?

"He came in the window?" Will asked. "Didn't you lock it?"

"Of course I did." Conan crossed again to the window. "I checked the lock when we got back from the studio."

But now the entire lock was missing, leaving a pale imprint in the wood and two empty screw holes. He searched the floor and found the lock near the baseboard and a bright, silvery screw a few feet away. He leaned down to pick them up, teeth clenched at the motion that tightened the vice locked on his shoulder. When he straightened, he had to wait for a transient dizziness to pass before he examined his find.

The screw was new, as was its mate, which was still caught in one of the holes in the dark brass of the lock. He took the screw to the window, dropped it into one of the screw holes.

Simple. The original screws had been replaced with these, which were too small for the holes. Raising the sash had dislodged them, sent the lock flying. That's why there had been a light in this window when he and Will returned from the studio. Someone had been exchanging the original screws for these. And where would that person find these screws and a screwdriver?

In the garage, neatly arranged in the cabinet above the worktable next to the tools. Art Rasmussen was an orderly man.

Conan put the screw and lock on the windowsill. "The lock was sabotaged, Will."

"Damn, I should've stood guard in here." He blew his cheeks out with an audible sigh and began unzipping Tuttle's parka.

Conan's dizziness returned with a wave of shivering as he made his way to the bed and sat down just before his knees gave way. He was wondering if he could keep his supper down. That physical reaction was, he knew, only in part a response to the gunshot wound. He could deal with that, with the pain, the chill lightheadedness.

What he found difficult to deal with was the flaccid corpse of Jerry Tuttle in his camouflage-patterned clothing, eyes half closed, mouth sagging. Conan denied himself the urge to turn away while Will unbuttoned Tuttle's shirt and revealed three small, red craters, perhaps six inches apart, forming a nearly equilateral triangle in the center of his sunburned, well-muscled chest.

Will sighed again and closed the shirt. "Good shooting."

Conan's eyes squeezed shut. Good shooting? It had been nearly point-blank range. How could he have missed?

"Hey, Conan . . ." The bed shifted as Will sat down beside him. "Damn it, you had no choice. He was shooting at you."

Conan opened his eyes to stare down at the gun still lying on the floor near Tuttle's body. "No, Will, he *wasn't* shooting at me."

"What do you mean?" Will demanded. He leaned down and picked up the gun, sniffed at the barrel. "This *has* been fired."

Conan winced at Will's cavalier handling of evidence, but he didn't comment on it. This crime scene had already been hopelessly contaminated, and at the moment proper crime scene procedure, and even the concept of the Law itself, belonged to a remembered world somewhere beyond this white hole and were quite meaningless here.

"Yes, Will," Conan said wearily, "I know it was fired. One of the bullets is embedded in the headboard and another in my shoulder. There are two more somewhere in the walls, probably."

"I'm going to have a look at the one in your shoulder as soon as I get some heat in here. Hell, you might as well be sitting in a refrigerator." He went to the fireplace and began building a fire on the remaining coals. "What do you mean, Tuttle wasn't shooting at you?"

"I mean Tuttle came in here with that knife. It's probably from the kitchen. He didn't have it with him when he first arrived, nor did he have the gun. Will, I want the bullet out of the headboard for comparison with the one you took out of Heather's leg."

"I'll take care of that later." He stared into the flames licking at the wood. "You figure that gun belongs to whoever shot Heather?"

"Yes."

"Maybe they gave it to Tuttle."

"Then why did he come in here armed with a carving knife?"

"Beats me. Come on over by the fire." Will watched Conan closely as he walked to the armchair. "Okay, just settle till I scrub up and get my case." He turned on his heel and hurried out of the room.

Conan settled, taking a moment to remove his gun from his belt and put it on the mantel before he eased himself into the chair. He looked at his watch. 12:10. Monday. A new day.

When Will returned with his medical case, he said briskly, "Before I can look at your shoulder, I've got to get rid of a few layers of clothes."

He put the case on the straight chair and took out a pair of scissors, but Conan objected, "I'm not having you cut up someone else's clothing. Help me get the right sleeves off, and the rest will be easy."

That was perhaps optimistic, but together they managed the disrobing—the Pendleton shirt and two wool sweaters—but when Conan was down to a red-stained

T-shirt, shivering in spite of the fire, Will resorted to the scissors. He slit the cloth, pulled the shirt out from under Conan's belt and tossed it into the fire, then leaned close to study the wound. Conan craned his neck to peer at it. The bullet had found the hollow below the clavicle perhaps an inch from the attachment of the deltoid.

Will said, "Lean forward a little." Conan complied, and Will noted, "No exit wound. The bullet got stopped by your scapula."

"I know."

"Right. Just sitting there rubbing against the bone every time you move."

"Something like that."

Will reached into his case. "You're depleting my Demerol supply."

"No!" Conan met Will's annoyed stare with a faint smile. "The pain is bearable, and tonight comfort isn't as important as alertness."

Will considered that, then nodded. "Well, all I can offer you is more ibuprofen. Might as well start now." He went into the bathroom and returned with the pill bottle and a glass of water. As Conan downed the four tablets he handed him, Will asked, "You say Tuttle *didn't* shoot at you? You want to explain that?"

Conan nodded, trying not to flinch while Will cleaned the wound with gauze pads soaked in Betadine that was cold against his bare skin.

"The flashes were too low, Will. And I know someone else was in this room. The shot that hit me came *after* I . . . after I shot Tuttle. Someone slipped in through the window behind him. With the gun."

"Someone? Like who?"

"The person I've been calling the lodge accomplice. But now that person can be called a killer."

"Then it was this accomplice/killer who fired first?"

"Yes. The trouble is, I didn't register the fact that the flashes were too low and probably came from *behind* Tuttle before I fired at him."

"Well, it wasn't the sort of situation where you ask questions first." Will sighed disconsolately. "Conan, I'm not equipped to take this bullet out. Hell, you're just lucky it didn't hit an inch lower and go into your lung. Or three or four inches south, and it might've hit your heart."

Three strikes, Conan thought, but the killer wasn't out. In this game, the killer was still at bat.

"At least there's not much bleeding," Will said. "But all I can do is clean it up and bandage it. I just hope to hell we can get out of here tomorrow. Today. Whatever. Okay, what I want to know is why that gun was in Tuttle's hand if he didn't fire it?"

"Probably the person who *did* fire it put it there before making a fast exit out the window. I was supposed to be dead, and when you and the others came in, you'd assume Tuttle and I shot each other—*and* that Tuttle was responsible for the murders at Loblolly Creek."

Will applied antibiotic ointment, stacked three gauze pads to make a bandage, and centered it over the wound. "Hold this a second." Then while Conan held the pads in place with his right hand, Will ripped a strip of tape off a roll and began securing the bandage.

Conan stared at Tuttle's body. "We were set up, Will. Both Tuttle and I. Two birds with one stone: an inconvenient witness and a potentially dangerous accomplice and perfect scapegoat."

"Yeah. Okay, that's all I can do for you except a heavy dose of penicillin." He reached into his case for a bottle of tablets.

Conan swallowed two of them, thinking about how

Tuttle and his partner had managed to communicate with each other. They'd had a conference in Tuttle's room tonight when it seemed everyone else had gone to sleep—the conversation Lise had overheard—but it had been the middle of the afternoon when Tuttle, with gratuitous arrogance, had pointed that imaginary gun at Conan, in effect announcing his intent to kill him. Was it significant that he used the image of a gun? Possibly not. What that gesture told Conan now was that Tuttle had at that time already communicated with the lodge accomplice, and he had been told that Conan was a liability and must be killed.

"Okay, Conan, better get you dressed again, unless you prefer to go around half-naked in this refrigerator."

"Well, I prefer not to add pneumonia to what ails me."

The process of getting dressed proved more painful than the dressing of the wound. Will loaned him a clean sweater to go over Conan's clean T-shirt, but he had no choice but to don a blood-spotted sweater and the Pendleton shirt for the outer layers. Finally, Will removed the case from one of the pillows on the bed, casually slit it all the way down one side and halfway down the other to make a sling.

"How does that feel?" he asked as he tied the loose ends around Conan's neck. "Too tight?"

"It's fine, Will." Conan sank back into the chair again, surprised to find his cigarettes still in the shirt pocket. He lit one, closing his eyes as he inhaled, feeling the edge of tension slacken. "You'd better put the gun and knife in there."

Will was busy straightening the contents of his medical case. "I don't have any more bags. I'm not set up for forensics, you know."

Conan laughed. "Forget the bags. You've already

handled the gun. If a real forensics technician by an incredible chance ever examines them, he can sort your fingerprints from any others."

Will stepped around Tuttle to get the gun and knife, brought them back to his case, then closed it with a decisive snap. "So what do we do about him?"

Conan turned to regard the body. Finally he took another drag on his cigarette and said, "Tuttle is the key, Will."

"He's also . . . dead."

"But none of the people waiting downstairs—no doubt impatiently—know that."

"Jesus, Conan, what are you up to now?"

"A trap. The only way we'll ever learn the identity of the lodge accomplice—the killer—is to set a trap."

"With Tuttle as the bait?"

"Exactly. The killer wanted to silence Tuttle as well as me with that choreographed shoot-out. Tuttle was more of a liability than I am because he knew a great deal more than I do. And if he *had* survived the shootout, he'd be a bit piqued to realize he'd been set up and probably quite willing to spill his guts. And the killer has to be aware that if we ever get out of this white hole, Tuttle might do his gut-spilling to the nearest officer of the law."

Will put his medical case on the floor and slumped wearily into the straight chair. "You want me to tell everybody he's still alive?"

"But seriously injured. And it has to be convincing. When they come upstairs, they must be able to look into this room and see Tuttle in that bed tucked in like a proper patient."

"Then what?"

"Then once everyone settles down to sleep, you and

I will lie in ambush here until the killer comes to deliver the *coup de grâce*."

"Oh, boy." Will glared at Tuttle's body balefully, then he nodded. "Well, I can't come up with a better plan."

"We need to make the trap as attractive as possible. You'll have to establish that Tuttle is in critical condition, and you won't be surprised if he doesn't live through the night. That way the killer will think that insuring his demise won't arouse anyone's suspicion."

"Look, I'm not sure I can . . ." Will's mouth compressed into a tight line, then he came to his feet. "Okay. I guess the first thing to do is get my patient into bed."

Will set about his grim task, even agreeing to removing Tuttle's boots and outer clothing so that they could be hung on the straight chair in clear sight. While Will pulled the bedclothes back, then heaved the body onto the bed, Conan took Tuttle's clothing to the chair. It was only habit that made him check the pockets of the parka, or perhaps it was some subtle sound, an anomalous shifting.

He reached into the left-hand pocket and found the key ring with the plastic ram medallion. But one of the keys was missing: one of the car keys. He put the key ring in his pants pocket, then checked the right-hand pocket of the parka.

And his hand slipped through into the lining. Frowning, he turned the pocket inside out and saw that the small hole in the badly finished seam had been enlarged forcibly. Zigzags of thread trailed around an opening big enough for a large hand.

He restored the pocket, pushed his own hand through the hole, all the way to the elbow, and finally his fingers closed on a smooth surface and a square corner.

He pulled the object out, sagging into the armchair as

he studied it. A manila envelope, about six by nine, its contents giving it a pillow shape, perhaps an inch thick. It was addressed and stamped for mailing. The address was typed on a blank, paste-on label: SAM CLEMENS, GENERAL DELIVERY, PORTLAND, OREGON 97367. There was no return address.

"Will, does the name Sam Clemens mean anything to you?"

Will smoothed the comforter over Tuttle's chest and folded the sheet down neatly before he went to Conan's chair to look over his shoulder at the envelope. "The only Sam Clemens I know of was a writer. Used the pen name Mark Twain. Where'd you find that?"

"It was in the lining of Tuttle's parka. Stamped but never mailed. There's no post mark." He turned it over and felt a satisfying acceleration of his pulse.

A message had been written on the back of the envelope in black ink. Block letters spelled out: HE'S DEAD. FLAGG KNOWS WHAT HAPPENED & WHO YOU ARE. DOESN'T HAVE A GUN. GET RID OF HIM. BURN THIS!

This, then, was Tuttle's first communication with the killer. Probably it was left in his room while he was downstairs. Certainly it was left at a time when he and the killer had no opportunity to talk to each other, otherwise it wouldn't have been necessary. It also explained why Tuttle came through Conan's window tonight with nothing but a carving knife. He thought his intended victim was unarmed. But the killer knew Conan had a gun. Someone had been in this room this morning and carelessly left the light on in the bathroom.

Will commented, "Tuttle didn't follow orders very well. He didn't burn the thing. Conan, damn it, what's inside?"

The flap had been torn open. Conan opened it, whistling under his breath. There were two rubber-banded stacks of one-hundred dollar bills. He counted them. There were two hundred, with Ben Franklin smiling enigmatically from each of them.

"I'll be damned," Will whispered reverently when Conan announced the total. "I've never even *seen* twenty-thousand in cash. Makes a neat little bundle, doesn't it?"

"I know Tuttle didn't have this neat little bundle when he arrived. I suppose this is the final installment on his fee. For services rendered."

"Why would anybody plan on sending twenty-thousand dollars—in cash—through the mail? Sounds a little risky to me."

"Not necessarily. Actually, for all the horror stories you hear, the USPS loses very few pieces of mail. The odds are high that any particular piece will get through, and the mail has one advantage: It doesn't leave a paper trail like the private delivery services do. But why wasn't this envelope mailed? It was probably supposed to be waiting for Tuttle in Portland when he finished his job here."

"Sounds like somebody meant to double-cross him."

"Yes, it does." Conan slipped the bills into his pillow-case sling between his arm and the cloth and handed the envelope to Will. "You'd better put this in your case along with—"

But before Will could take the envelope, Conan's fingers tightened on it, and he stared at the block-lettered message with a tingling sensation at the back of his neck.

"Conan? What's wrong?"

"Nothing. Only that a lightbulb just went on."

"What kind of lightbulb?"

"He's dead."

"Tuttle? Yes, I know, Conan, but—"

"Not Tuttle. The message, Will."

"Oh. Maybe it was to tell him his mission was accomplished."

Conan read the message again, eyes down to obsidian slits, and shook his head. "Why would the lodge accomplice have to tell Tuttle he had accomplished his mission? The money itself would tell him that."

"Right. Besides, Tiff blabbed it when she told him why everybody was acting like they were at a funeral. So what about this lightbulb?"

"Tuttle didn't need to be told that his intended target was dead, but he *did* need to be told that the mastermind was dead, so he'd know he had to deal in future with the lodge accomplice."

"The mastermind?" Will leaned back, folding his arms. "You mean Al or Lucas. You still think—"

"I know Tuttle was waiting for someone at the bridge—someone who never arrived—and it couldn't be anyone here in the lodge."

"Okay, but that doesn't shed any light on your lightbulb."

"How did the accomplice *know* the mastermind was dead?" When Will only shrugged at that rhetorical question, Conan added, "Because the accomplice killed the mastermind."

"What?"

Conan turned to the fire, watching the flowing patterns of flames. "Neither Al nor Lucas would risk taking the detonator on a camping trip. It could be too easily discovered in such intimate surroundings. So he had to trust someone else to trigger the explosion. Tuttle? I doubt it. He wasn't a man to inspire trust, and probably the only reason he waited at the bridge so patiently was that he wouldn't get his final installment until he drove his employer to safety. Only then would the mastermind tell him where to pick up his money in Portland."

"But that envelope never reached Portland."

"No, and I doubt it was the mastermind who planned to bilk Tuttle out of his final installment. Tuttle wouldn't let him live to start a new life in that case. But the question that has haunted me since Tuttle's arrival is why he waited so long at the bridge that he got trapped by the blizzard. The explosion occurred at eight o'clock. Lucas or Al could've left the camp at, say, seven-thirty. We'd all retired to our tents by seven, and I know at least two of us were asleep at seven-thirty. If he could average twelve minutes per mile—and that isn't asking too much of a man in good physical condition, which both Al and Lucas were—he could've reached the bridge by eight-thirty. It didn't start snowing until eight, and even if the blizzard was well under way by eight-thirty, he and Tuttle could've driven out then with four-wheel drive. Why did Tuttle wait at least an hour longer?"

Will stared at Conan. "You think . . . what? That Tuttle wasn't expecting Al or Lucas to show up till an hour later?"

"I have no way of knowing what the original schedule was—and obviously it didn't include the blizzard—but I think whoever was entrusted with the detonator changed that schedule."

"And set off the explosion early."

"Yes."

"Damn."

Conan nodded. "Dishonor among thieves—an extraordinarily ruthless and coldblooded dishonor."

Will looked intently at Conan. "Do you know who it is—this accomplice?"

"No. All I've seen is the tracks of the beast, and

they're deep and bloody." He heard the distant tolling of the grandfather clock and looked at his watch. One o'clock. "We've kept those people waiting downstairs long enough." He rose, finding it necessary to pause a few seconds until the dizziness passed, then crossed to the door, looking back at Tuttle. "Will, maybe we need a little less light on the subject."

Will nodded and went to the bedside table to turn on the small lamp there, then on his way out into the hall flipped off the ceiling light.

"You want the door left open?"

"Yes, Will. I want everyone who comes up the stairs to have a clear view of your patient."

CHAPTER 25

Heather watched Conan and Will approach with the same intent gaze as did the human occupants of the room, a combination of fear and doubt and profound bafflement. Lise was again sitting on the floor by Heather's bed, and Will took a stand on her right with his back to the fire, hands in his pockets, while Conan sat down on the hearth ledge on her left. He looked around at the rapt faces, and he didn't doubt that when these people first gathered here, there had been a great deal of speculation and argument, but now a silence had fallen, webbed in the white noise of the generator's hum.

Even Tiff was silent, sitting in her usual chair, her shaking hands engaged with her crochet needle, but Conan doubted that the last rows of this creation would hold together. Her staring eyes seemed blanched. She wasn't wearing her bright green contact lenses. A glass of Scotch stood ready on the end table. Mark slumped on the right arm of her chair, clutching a glass whose contents were no doubt similar, although there was so little left, Conan couldn't be sure.

Kim occupied the other armchair, wearing a wool plaid robe that had probably been A. C.'s. She sat with her legs crossed, apparently at ease, but she was smoking with quick, impatient puffs that betrayed her anxiety. Near her, Demara lounged with one arm along the back of the couch, her long legs stretched out before her, ankles crossed. Her maroon suede boots made an incongruous combination with the black satin robe, yet she made it seem oddly glamorous. Her hooded eyes moved languidly from Conan to Will.

At the other end of the couch, Loanh huddled in a nearly fetal position, wrapped in the bright afghan, her dark hair shadowing her face. She regarded Conan with spent resignation, as if she had remembered, finally, how to deal with daily terror.

It was Lise who asked, "Conan, what happened to your arm?"

"I was hit by one of the bullets flying around my room when Tuttle came in via the window. Apparently he didn't know I had a gun. He was hit, too."

Like a bottle uncorked, Tiff came to frothing life. "I was *right*! Oh, I knew it, I *knew* we should *never* have let that man into this house. I knew what he was. I mean, you could *see* it in his eyes, a drug-crazed *mad*man come to kill us all, one by one, but thank God, he started with the *one* person here who just happened to have a *gun*! And I'm *glad* you killed him, Conan. I'm *glad*!"

Mark put his arm around her shoulders. "Oh, Tiff, you don't really mean that."

"Yes, I *do* mean it! I'm glad because he *deserved* to die!"

"I'm sorry to disappoint you," Conan said, "but I didn't kill him."

Kim demanded, "Then he's still *alive*?" Her cigarette was trembling between her fingers, and as Conan replied she hurriedly stubbed it out in the ashtray on the table beside her.

"Yes, he's still alive," Conan said. "Barely. Will can tell you more about that."

Will sat down on the hearth ledge, running a hand through his hair, and Conan held his breath, wondering if this honest physician could carry off his role.

"Like Conan said, he's just barely alive," Will began, then went on with more confidence, "He took a bullet in the lung. What he needs is a fully-equipped ICU. There's not much I can do for him."

Conan allowed himself a sigh of relief before Demara leaned forward to ask, "Did he say anything?"

And Mark added, "He must've had *some* reason to want to kill Conan."

"He's *crazy*!" Tiff insisted. "That's his only *reason*."

Will shook his head. "No, he didn't say anything. He never regained consciousness."

Loanh asked in little more than a whisper, "Will he live?"

"Like I said, he should be in an ICU." Will glanced fleetingly at Conan, then added, "He's young, of course, and in good physical condition, but unless we can get him to a hospital soon . . . well, I just don't know. I really don't expect him to last the night."

Tiff reached for her glass and muttered, "I *still* say he was trying to kill *all* of us, and I always had, you know, a sort of *sixth sense*. I mean, a way of seeing *into* people."

"Yes, you did seem to see something in him," Conan said casually, then changed tack. "There's certainly an aura of mystery about Tuttle. He came here without a shred of identification, and we have nothing but his word for it that his name really is Jerry Tuttle."

Tiff thrust her empty glass at Mark. "Sweetie, I need a refresher." He took her glass and limped over to the bar with his own glass, while she went on, "What *difference* does it make what his name is, I mean, a *name* doesn't mean anything, you know, and *I* saw through him—"

"It's not his name per se that concerns me," Conan cut in. "I think he knew at least one of you, and you knew him."

The sound of Scotch gurgling into glasses was audible in the ensuing silence, and Mark asked, "Anybody else want something?"

Demara turned her eyes upward and muttered, "*Jee-sus!*" but no one else responded to Mark's question. Conan waited until Mark made his way back to his perch on the arm of his wife's chair, then he said, "Lise, may I have that drawing?"

Lise crossed to the card table, took a sheet from the bottom of the pile, and when she returned handed it to Conan. He studied it, feeling a chill dizziness when he realized that since he had last seen this portrait, he had killed its subject. Then he rose and offered it to Tiff.

Her breath came out in a grunt of shock. "Oh, this is *awful*, I mean, it's like . . . like, you know, a *death* mask!"

"Where's his beard?" Mark asked, leaning over her shoulder.

Conan ignored that. "Do either of you recognize him?"

Tiff denied it vehemently and verbosely, and Conan took the drawing, passed it to Loanh, who at first seemed loathe to touch it. Finally she took it by one corner and examined it perfunctorily. "No, I do not know who he is—with or without a beard."

Next Conan offered the drawing to Demara, who barely glanced at it before waving him away. "How the hell should *I* know who he is?"

Kim irritably took the drawing and seemed ready to dismiss it, then she rested it on her knee and picked up her pack of Marlboros, shook one out and lit it, all the while studying the drawing. Conan waited, watching her perplexed frown give way to surprise.

She said, "Sam Clemens."

Will made an odd coughing sound, and Conan was hard put to keep a straight face. Apparently the name on the manila envelope hadn't been an alias and certainly had no literary overtones.

Mark surged to his feet and stood with his soft hands in fists, but Conan was too focused on Kim to more than glance at him.

"Kim, you knew Tuttle as Sam Clemens?"

"I didn't exactly know him. Not well enough to recognize him with all the fuzz on his face. And he didn't have long hair back then."

"Back when?"

"Back when I was working for King and Ryder. So was Clemens. He was another one of Jerry Ryder's orphans. A high-school dropout, a foul-mouthed, tough kid off the streets who thought he wanted to be a boxer, but found out he didn't have what it takes. Jerry was such a sucker for a hard-luck story. I don't know what Clemens's story was, but Jerry took him under his wing, just like he did . . ." She concentrated on her cigarette, leaving the sentence unfinished.

"Ryder hired him for construction work?" Conan asked.

"Of course."

"In what capacity?"

Kim's mouth twitched into an ironic smile, and she looked directly at Conan as she replied, "He blew things up."

Tiff loosed a squeal, but Mark said flatly, "Just shut up, Tiff." She seemed so shocked at that peremptory order coming from him, that she did. He turned away from her, leaning against the mantel, and said huskily, "For God's sake, Tiff, *you* should've recognized him."

Uncharacteristically, she had no reply, only sinking deeper into her chair, eyes closed as if she were trying to make herself invisible, while the others looked on with the uncomfortable shock of people witnessing a private disagreement made embarrassingly public.

It was Will who asked, "Mark, what do you mean? Why should Tiff recognize him?"

"Never mind, Will. It doesn't matter."

Conan said irritably, "Like hell it doesn't!"

"Well, I mean . . ." He looked at his wife, who still seemed to be hoping for invisibility. "Tiff, Chuck Hughes at the club told me about it. Only the name, of course. He thought I should know. I didn't care, really, because I understood, and . . . well, I knew it wouldn't last."

Lise came to her feet, staring at her brother. "Mark, what are you talking about?"

"Oh, Lise, I know I'm no Robert Redford. I never expected to be able to keep a woman like Tiff tied to me. I was just happy she wanted to be my wife and the mother of my children. If she needed, well, a little fling now and then, I could live with that." Tiff buried her face in her crocheting with muffled cries that sounded like a kitten mewing.

"You people need a *reality* check here!" Demara snapped as she rose and stalked to the bar to pour a snifter of brandy. She remained there, watching contemptuously, while Mark leaned over Tiff, gently patting her shoulder, and Tiff's mewing hit a high note. Will shook his head, and Lise, apparently torn between laughter and tears, sat down again.

Conan sank down on the hearth. His knees had an inconvenient tendency to turn to jelly when he remained standing too long. He asked, "Mark, when did this . . . little fling take place?"

Mark glared at him. "About four years ago."

Tiff straightened, putting on an air of beset dignity. "It was after Al *fired* Sam, and he got a job in the fitness program at our club. I mean, he was really just, well, a *maintenance* man, you know, for the exercise equipment, oh, Mark, I didn't want you *ever* to have to *know*."

"Or anyone else, obviously," Conan said acerbically. "Kim, can you tell me more about Clemens's proclivity for blowing things up?"

She gave that a curt laugh as she laid the drawing on the end table. "A lot of building sites required some use of explosives, and Jerry Ryder was an expert. He took Clemens on as a sort of apprentice and taught him everything he knew. He told me he thought it was a safe outlet for Clemens's violent tendencies."

Conan nodded, thinking that at least one of his theories had been verified: Sam Clemens *was* the expert accomplice who designed the explosion that triggered the rock slide. The idealistic Jerry Ryder had been in error. He had simply given Sam Clemens a more deadly means to express his violent tendencies. Jerry. Had Clemens chosen the first name of his alias as a backward homage to his mentor?

"Kim, how long did Clemens work for King and Ryder?"

"I don't really remember. Two or three years, probably. He was still working there when Jerry had to retire and Al took over the partnership. That's when I left K and R. I heard it wasn't long afterward that Al fired Clemens."

"Did you hear anything to explain why Al fired him?"

"No, but I can guess. Al never liked Clemens, and he had no sympathy for Jerry's orphans."

"You were head of the accounting department at King and Ryder?"

"Yes."

"Did you handle the payrolls?"

"Of course I did."

"Then you had access to addresses and Social Security numbers for all employees."

"So what?" she demanded sharply as she crushed out her half-smoked cigarette.

Conan ignored that and turned to Loanh, who seemed to curl tighter into her fetal position. "Loanh, what did Al say about Clemens? The name *is* familiar to you, isn't it?"

"The name, yes, but I never met him. Al talked about him. He called him a troublemaker."

When she didn't seem inclined to volunteer more, Conan prompted her with: "Was there any connection between Clemens's firing and the explosion at the Greenwood Mall?"

"Al always said so. It happened only a week or so after he fired Clemens, and Al was sure Clemens did it in revenge for the firing."

"But the police didn't agree?"

"They said they found no evidence of sabotage."

Kim put in with studied indifference, "Greenwood Mall. Wasn't Lucas the architect on that project?"

"Yes," Loanh replied. "That was LJK Design's first big project."

Conan waited to see if Kim had more to say on that subject, but she didn't. He asked Loanh, "Are you sure you never met Clemens? Maybe when you were visiting Al at the office or at a construction site?"

"No!" She sat up on the edge of the couch, the fear in her dark eyes overlain with the bravado of the survivor. "If I did, I cannot remember. And what difference is it whether I knew him or not, whether *any* of us knew him? You said the rock slide at the camping place was caused by an explosion, so there is your answer. Clemens came here to kill *Al*. He hated Al enough to destroy all his work at the Greenwood Mall with an explosion, so is it not reasonable that he hated him enough to want to . . . kill him?" With the last words she seemed to lose her emotional charge, and she curled against the back of the couch again, pulling the afghan around her.

Demara left the bar and returned to the couch, warming her snifter in the cup of her hand. "It sounds damned reasonable to me."

"Well, at least it explains what that lunatic was after," Mark said with a gusty sigh. "He was after Al the whole time. Who knows how long he's been waiting for his chance."

Conan listened to these reassuring arguments, saw the nods and signals of relief. Sam Clemens did indeed make a perfect scapegoat.

"I agree," Conan said, "that Clemens engineered the explosion. But if he was waiting all these years for a chance to kill Al, he was very casual about it. It's possible he wasn't even living in Portland recently." Conan reached into his pants pocket for Clemens's key ring and handed it to Will. "What does the design on this medallion mean?"

Will squinted at it. "That's the logo for the L.A. Rams." Then with a wry smile, he added, "The football team, Conan."

"Yes, I've heard of them. This key ring belongs to Sam Clemens, and the interesting connection is Los Angeles."

Demara dismissed that with an annoyed, "Oh, hell, anybody anywhere can get Rams souvenirs."

"True. But I have other evidence that Clemens wasn't driven by a compulsion to kill Al in retribution for a job lost four years ago, evidence that he was only a hired hand employed by someone who knew about his expertise in explosives." Conan reached into the sling and pulled out the bundle of bills, fanned them out for everyone to see. "These are hundred-dollar bills, and I found them in the lining of Clemens's parka only a short while ago. They were acquired since he came here. I'm sure of that because I searched his clothing carefully within minutes of his arrival. That means one of you gave him this money, probably as the final installment of his fee for a job well done."

A pocket of pitch crackled and hissed in the fireplace, and Tiff loosed a startled "Oh!" but nothing distracted anyone's attention from the bills in Conan's hand. He closed the fan and returned the bills to his sling, while Mark, Tiff, Loanh, Demara, and Kim all erupted at once with questions and offended disclaimers.

Conan held up his hand for silence, waited patiently until he got it, then: "Sam Clemens wasn't the only one who had motive to kill Al—or A. C. Kim, Al was blackmailing you, in a sense, with the threat of telling A. C. about your supposedly defunct affair with him, and A. C.'s response to that knowledge might conceivably have been divorce." Kim shot forward in her chair, ready with an angry denial, but before she could speak, Conan turned to Loanh. "And Al's affair with Kim—his obsession with her—provided you the classic motive. Not to mention what his death—*and* A. C.'s—would do for your financial profile."

Unlike Kim, Loanh didn't attempt a denial. She only stared at him, unblinking. He didn't relish asking his next question. "Loanh, what about your other motive? The one that drove you to tears Friday night and to the assertion that without family, one might as well be dead."

Her gaze flickered, flashed to Lise, then fixed again on Conan's face, her lips parted for quick, shallow breaths. Still, she didn't speak.

Conan asked, "What family did you mean? Not the Kings. They aren't blood relations. Not your children. They're both of age and can't be taken away from you in the usual sense. Loanh, who are the people in that photograph hidden in your purse? It was dated only two years ago and probably taken in Portland. Certainly not in Vietnam. Aren't they your true family?"

She began shaking visibly, then with no warning unleashed herself like a coiled spring, a cry of despair trapped behind her clenched teeth as she flung herself at Conan, hands knotted in flailing fists.

It was Will Stewart who stopped her. Conan was for milliseconds too long mesmerized by her terrible, sudden rage. She struggled in Will's confining embrace, while Lise leapt to her side, calling her name, softly, pleadingly, and Heather barked in confused panic.

Conan reached down to restrain Heather, and as abruptly as it began, it was over. Loanh yielded to Lise, sobbing against her shoulder as Lise guided her to the couch and held her like a hurt child.

Will slumped down beside Conan, and for a span of seconds a shocked silence held. Finally Mark broke it. He had come to his feet, and now he pulled his shoulders back and regarded Conan with a calculating frown. All he needed was a three-piece suit to complete the image of the attorney-at-law considering a hostile witness.

He asked, "Can you explain how you knew about a photograph that was, by your own admission, *hidden* in Loanh's purse?"

"I searched her room," Conan replied flatly. "For God's sake, what did you expect, Mark? Not only did one of you conspire to murder A. C. and two of his sons, but you almost succeeded in killing me in the process, and there have been two more attempts on my life since. Did you expect me *not* to do everything I could to find out which one of you is a murderer? Yes, I searched Loanh's room. I searched all your rooms— without benefit of a search warrant—and if I survive to get out of this white hole, you can sue me for invasion of privacy, but right now I have more serious problems to deal with."

That served to erode Mark's persona as attorney-at-law, and no one else ventured a comment. Demara even had a crooked smile for Conan as she raised her snifter to take a sip of brandy.

He turned to Loanh, and her face seemed carved of white jade, cool, perfect, except for the fine lines etched around her mouth and eyes. He asked, "Loanh, why did Al hire a private investigator on October sixteenth? I can't believe he thought he might catch you in a tryst with a lover. It wouldn't have occurred to him that you might be capable of anything as outrageously independent as taking a lover. It had something to do with your family, didn't it?"

She shook her head. "No. I do not *know* why Al hired a private investigator."

"Loanh . . ." Lise took Loanh's hand in hers, said softly, "You don't have to keep the secret any more."

As if Lise had delivered a stunning blow rather than a gentle reassurance, Loanh pulled her hand away, and her searching gaze went to Conan's face. It rested there only a split second before she averted her eyes, but Lise caught it, and perhaps she came to the same conclusion Conan did: Loanh was particularly worried about keeping her secret from Conan.

He watched Lise's eyes narrow. Her tone was still gentle, yet there was an unmistakable resoluteness in it now. "This is not the time to hold on to old secrets, Loanh."

Mark again took his lawyerly stance. "Loanh, you don't have to say a word." And obviously he hoped she wouldn't.

But Loanh ignored him, her gaze focused on Lise, and Conan wondered if it weren't Lise's resoluteness that induced Loanh to let go of this particular secret. She said, "Once every week I visited them, and Al never knew. But he followed me that day. October sixteenth. He saw me with them, and he knew who they were. He told me he would see that they were deported."

"Deported?" Conan asked. "How could they be deported unless there was something illegal about their immigration?"

She answered obliquely, "They have lived here for nearly twenty years, my mother, my brother and sister, her husband, their daughter. They have become American citizens. Married and had children. Worked hard and bought a home. Voted and paid taxes. But there is no statute of limitation for immigration fraud."

"Then that's why Al hired the private investigator—to find out if they had entered this country illegally?"

"I can think of no other reason."

"And you knew there was fraud for an investigator to discover?"

"Loanh, don't answer that," Mark counseled firmly.

"For God's sake, Mark," Lise cut in, "it doesn't *matter* anymore."

"What do you know about this?"

"Everything." She looked at Loanh, added, "Mom told me about it before she died."

Mark sagged down on the arm of the chair. "Oh, no . . ."

"The only people who might've called in the INS are *dead*, Mark. Al and Dad. They're . . . dead."

"Lise, there are legal ramifications in this matter that you're not aware of, and I strongly advise you—"

"Not here, Mark!" she cut in, her face nearly as pale as Loanh's. "In this place, there are no legal ramifications." Then she turned to Conan. "No one did anything *wrong*—even if it was illegal."

Conan waited, while Lise looked at Loanh, who didn't seem to respond in any way, yet Lise apparently found a signal of acquiescence in her silence. Lise began, "Al once told me he fell in love with Loanh the moment he saw her. Like a ton of bricks, he said. I don't think he ever really understood that. But he didn't want any part of the Nguyens, her family, and he refused to do anything to help them immigrate. He said he didn't want any more *gooks* in this country. Yet her father was a general in the Vietnamese army and died fighting for the same things—whatever they were—that Al was there to fight for. Of course, Al came by his bigotry naturally enough from Dad. Not from Mom. She loved Loanh dearly, and when she found out about the Nguyens—that was right after Charles was born—Mom made up her mind to reunite Loanh with her family."

Loanh said, "Your mother was a wonderful woman, Lise."

"Yes, she was. Anyway, she went to Mark. He'd just passed the Oregon bar and gone to work for Dad in the legal department."

Mark groaned. "Lise, I'm warning you."

Again, the warning was ignored. "Mark found out that the only way to get Loanh's family into the United States was for an employer to file a form with the INS saying he wanted to hire her brother and brother-in-law for specific jobs."

"That was only the first of the forms," Loanh said. "Form I-129. I remember that number because it was so full of hope for us. And we were lucky. My brother and brother-in-law had gone to university in California. Thien had a degree in chemical engineering, and Tuong studied computers. He didn't finish his degree before my father was killed, and they came home. Then they could not leave Vietnam again. But Tuong's training was enough. Computers were at their beginning then. He says he is now one of the grandfathers of the field, and he is barely forty." She managed a fleeting smile with that.

Lise took up the story: "Dad had talked about trying computers at the research center in Sublimity, and since they were experimenting with laminates there, they could always use a chemical engineer. But of course Mom knew Dad wouldn't approve of bringing in specialists and their dependents from Vietnam. He'd consider that un-American. So she made some sort of pact with the director of the Sublimity center—she didn't give me any details on that—and she had Mark draw up the INS forms, listing Dad as the employer requesting the services of these foreign aliens. Oh, she hated that term. As if they came from Mars. Anyway, *she* signed the forms. She forged his name."

Mark loosed another despairing groan, but Lise went on: "Mom signed Dad's name all the time on household checks when he was too busy to do it, so I guess she was pretty good at it. Eventually, the Nguyens all became citizens, and the men found jobs with other companies. Mom said she never regretted what she'd done, because Dad should have been willing to sign those forms himself."

Conan leaned back with his right arm as a prop, feeling something between disbelief and admiration for Carla King, a woman who thought in straight, clear lines. But she was dead now, and the lines she had drawn had wavered and blurred.

He said, "A delicate situation. If Al *had* discovered the fraud, he might've succeeded in getting the Nguyens deported, obviously something you feared, Loanh. And beyond that, in secretly abetting your family's immigration, you defied him flagrantly, and I doubt Al King would accept that. He'd have the option of divorcing you, and I wonder where that would leave you financially."

Loanh didn't respond to that, but there was in the lift of her chin a hint of cold resentment. Conan turned his attention to Mark, who slumped bonelessly on the arm of the chair, looking like a man who has just been informed that he faces an IRS audit.

"A delicate situation for you, too, Mark," Conan observed. "Carla isn't alive to take the blame for the forgery, if it were exposed. No, Lise, what she told you doesn't constitute proof, and I'm afraid you were in error to dismiss the legal ramifications in this matter so lightly. One is that if the fraud is uncovered, the lawyer who expedited it would be in a very precarious position. Isn't that right, Mark?"

Mark said wistfully, "Damn it, she was my mother. I never could say no to her, and she kept insisting it was all for a good cause."

"No doubt, but the ramifications for you might include disbarment or even prison. And I can't help but wonder what Al's reaction would have been when he learned his brother had abetted his wife's defiance. Or what A. C.'s reaction would have been when he learned that a son of his had perpetrated a fraud against the United States government."

Tiff had remained rarely silent for some time, but now she couldn't seem to contain herself. "Oh, that's *ridiculous*. I mean, to think that Al would, you know, even *care* that Mark had anything to do with . . . well, whatever happened. And why would he betray his own *brother*? Family was very important to Al. And A. C.—well, he'd *never* turn against his own son. I mean, he wouldn't blame him for something *Carla* did, and he'd believe Mark if . . . well, I mean, he *wouldn't* cut—"

"Tiff, please," Mark said. "You're only making things worse."

Conan nodded and leaned forward, trying, with little success, to find a more comfortable position for his shoulder. Mark had stopped Tiff almost in time, before she finished a phrase that in all likelihood ended with *cut Mark out of his will*. But Conan didn't have an opportunity to pursue that line of thought with Mark or Tiff.

Demara abruptly came to her feet, looking down imperiously at each of them in turn. "Jesus, you're all over the edge—*all* of you! And you, Conan—why in hell do you have to rake over all these stupid, *dead* secrets, things that happened years ago and don't matter a damn? Why are you trying to make everything so complicated? Maybe a streak of sadism, for God's sake?"

Conan didn't reply, but he was aware that the others seemed to find merit in her questions. He was the object of speculative looks while she went on, the satin in her voice gone hard. "What happened here and at that camp is simple. The answer is upstairs, and I'm with Tiff—I wish to hell you *had* killed him! The only so-called evidence you've shown us is that twenty thousand dollars, and we've only got *your* word for it that Tuttle—or Clemens, or whatever he calls himself—did *not* have it with him when he first came here. I know this is none of my business. I'm not family. But, damn it, I think we've all been through enough shit in the last couple of days without you adding to it!"

There were mutterings of agreement, and Tiff launched into another convoluted monologue, but Conan focused intently on Demara and said, "But you *are* family, Demara. You're Lucas's wife."

Mark blew out a spray of Scotch when that revelation caught him with his mouth full, and Tiff was obviously at a loss for words. Like Loanh and Lise, she turned to stare at Demara, while Kim paused as she lit another cigarette and said, "I'll be damned."

"And as his wife," Conan added, "you're also his heir."

Where Loanh's face had seemed carved in white jade, Demara's was planed in polished bronze, patinated to rich translucence. Here was a face, Conan thought, to trip a thousand shutters, to beguile a thousand lenses with its absolute perfection. The hooded, onyx eyes glinted with anger, and she hissed, "You *bastard*!"

Yet a moment later, the anger collapsed, and her eyes

slowly closed. She whispered, "Lucas didn't want to tell any of you yet. He thought it would be better . . . easier . . . to wait and see if . . ."

Tiff said, "Oh, my dear, oh, if only we'd *known*—"

"I'm not your *dear*!" Demara countered, turning on Tiff, anger surfacing again. "What would you have done if you'd known? You lily-white bitch, you'd have been the first to look down your cute little nose and toady up to old A. C. about how *awful* it was, Lucas bringing home a nigger woman, and oh, how *embarrassing*, and *really*, you know, just *unforgivable*!"

Tiff answered that acid imitation of herself with a self-righteous, "I would *not* have said anything of the sort, because I've *always* done everything I *could* to open doors for people of color wherever they—"

"And some of your best friends are *niggers*?"

"Oh, that's the *trouble* with you people. I mean, *I* can't help it what A. C. thought *or* what he *said*, you know, but *I* never did *any*thing, not one *thing*, to deserve to be treated like *this*!"

Mark was gripping Tiff's shoulder hard, but to no effect, and it wasn't she who ended the brief argument. It was Demara.

Her rage drained away suddenly, and she sank down onto the couch and said in a voice raw with pain, "God, we never should've come here. It was my idea. Lucas didn't want to come. No, I think he *did* want to come, but he was afraid, because he didn't think any of you, especially A. C., would welcome him. But I told him . . . I told him he had to make peace with his dad. He couldn't go on living with . . ."

She didn't try to finish that, nor did she weep, but her bronze face might have been a sculpted icon of grief. No one spoke or even moved, except finally Loanh, who reached out and placed her small, pale hand on Demara's long, dark, red-nailed hand.

Kim stubbed out another half-smoked cigarette and rose. "This is going nowhere," she said irritably, then stopped while the grandfather clock tolled the hour. Two o'clock.

Conan asked, "Where's the radio? Maybe we can get a weather report."

"It's over here," Mark said as he limped to the dining table to turn the radio on.

At the burst of static and garbled music and voices, Conan leaned close to Will and whispered, "Make sure you're in my room with your patient before anyone else gets upstairs."

Will nodded, but didn't reply. Mark had found a clear station.

". . . second front should reach the Blue and Wallowa Mountains in Eastern Oregon by midmorning. An additional twelve inches of snow has been reported in the Cascades at Timberline and fourteen inches at Sisters and Mount Bachelor, and all Cascade passes have been closed again. But according to an Oregon Department of Transportation spokesperson, snowplows will be dispatched again this morning, and the passes should be open by ten o'clock. In sports news, Portland Trail Blazers' coach P. J. Carlesimo said in an interview yesterday that there is no truth to the rumor that the Blazers plan to trade Clyde Drexler—"

Mark turned off the radio with a short laugh. "Trade Clyde the Glide? That's nuts." Then he looked around, apparently realizing that his levity was inappropriate, and said soberly, "Well, it sounds like maybe tomorrow there's a chance we'll get out of here."

No one seemed to have the energy to show any enthusiasm at that prospect. With resigned sighs, they began moving toward the atrium. Will hurried for the stairs, saying, perhaps too loudly, "I'd better check on my patient."

Kim said, "And I'd better check the generator."

Lise volunteered to take care of that, and Kim turned to Conan. "I guess you'll have to sleep in Tuttle— Clemens's room tonight. I'll change the bed. Loanh? Do you mind helping me?"

While the living room emptied, Conan remained on the hearth ledge, with Heather at his feet nervously watching the exodus. In the silence of the cavelike room, he lit a cigarette, closing his eyes as he inhaled, and considered the tangled webs woven in this family. He wondered if it would endure as a family now, with the heart of it destroyed. Perhaps the survivors would drift apart slowly like the remnants of a stellar explosion.

A few minutes later, he looked up as Lise returned and sat down beside him. "We'll probably lose our lights in about half an hour," she said. "I didn't add any more gas to the generator. The tank is nearly empty, but there's only a gallon or so left in the last jerrican. If we don't get rescued tomorrow, the gas might last a couple of hours."

Conan frowned. He had hoped the generator would be on-line to provide immediate and ample light when he and Will sprang their trap—if they did. But under the circumstances, they would have to make do with flashlights. He asked, "How's the wood supply?"

"Well, we may have to start burning the furniture." She mustered a smile, but it faded quickly as she asked, "How are you feeling?"

"I was lucky, Lise. Nothing vital was hit." And he didn't want to focus on the constant ache occupying his shoulder, nor on the vaguer discomfort in his feet and hands.

"Conan, you're probably wondering why I didn't tell you about Loanh's family before."

"No. It was something your mother told you in confidence, and you had no reason to think it was connected with the murders." Then lowering his voice, he added, "I stayed to tell you that Clemens is dead. Will and I are keeping him 'alive' in the hope that the killer will try to make sure he's dead. If so, we'll be waiting."

She sighed wearily. "For God's sake, be careful, both of you."

He rose, took a last puff on his cigarette before he threw it into the dying fire. "A few more hours, Lise. One way or another, it will be over in a few hours."

CHAPTER 26

The generator ran out of gas, and its constant thrum died at two-thirty A.M., leaving a silence in which the dirgelike chimes of the clock downstairs were audible in Conan's bedroom despite the closed door. He heard each quarter hour marked, culminating in the tolling of the hours. Three o'clock. Four. And now, five o'clock.

He sat in the straight chair—Will had invoked his physicianly prerogative to insist that Conan use the chair—which had been placed just outside the bathroom door, facing the bedroom. The bedside table was only a few feet to his left, the interior wall close enough on his right for him to touch it with his elbow. If he stretched his legs, his feet would touch Will, who, armed with a flashlight and Lise's .38, sat against the wall, where he would be behind the door when it opened, out of sight of whoever entered.

If the door ever opened.

And if the killer didn't opt again for the window.

Conan sat numbed with cold and immobility in his
parka, right sleeve on, left draped over his aching, stiff-
ening shoulder, his right hand in his pocket clasping the
bitterly cold grip of the Ruger, his feet turning to painful, icy lumps in his boots. And the conviction had
taken firm root in his mind that this ambush was not
working.

Of course, he expected the killer to wait until everyone in the lodge was well asleep. But not this long. It
would be dawn soon. He wasn't sure exactly how soon,
and when he thought about it, he realized that at this
latitude and this season, dawn wouldn't come earlier
than six-thirty.

Still, this ambush had been carelessly designed. There
hadn't been time enough to work out the details. Or perhaps he simply hadn't been thinking clearly.

When Conan had come upstairs a few minutes after
two, Tiff, Mark, Demara, and Loanh had been standing
in the doorway of his bedroom like strangers at a car
wreck. As Conan approached, Loanh told him the bed
in Clemens's room was made, then hurried to her room
and closed the door. Conan went into his room, noting
that Will was taking his patient's blood pressure. A nice
touch, Conan thought, that rather surprised him. He
went into the bathroom for his shaving kit and another
dose of ibuprofen, and when he emerged, Demara had
departed, but Mark and Tiff were still watching. Will
put the blood-pressure cuff in his medical case and
tucked Clemens's arm under the covers, then frowned
toward the door. "What is it, Mark?"

Mark shrugged uneasily, like a voyeur caught in the
act, and Tiff chirped, "Oh, we just *wondered*, you know,
if there was anything we could *do*, I mean, I thought
maybe—"

"There's nothing you can do for him," Will said

grimly, glancing at his patient. "Just go to bed, Tiff, and try to get some rest. Mark, you can make sure there's a fire in Clemens's room for Conan."

"Oh. Well, sure, I can take care of that." Mark glanced at Tiff, then the two of them disappeared from the doorway in opposite directions.

Will blew out a sigh and muttered, "I never thought I'd be taking a corpse's blood pressure."

"You were very convincing about it," Conan said, moving close to him, keeping his voice down to a murmur. "Will, we can't leave our bait unguarded for a moment. As soon as I get to Clemens's room, I'll go through the motions of settling down, then I'll wait half an hour. If the coast is clear, I'll come back here. Then you can go to your room—making sure anyone who's listening hears your door close. No," he added, "before you go to your room, make a trip down the hall ostensibly to check on me. Talk to yourself a little."

Will nodded. "Then I go back to my room and act like I'm going to bed, then after a while sneak in here, right? How's the shoulder?"

Conan gave that a brief laugh. "Never better."

"Sure. Damn it, *you're* the one who should be in this bed."

"Not considering what's occupying it now." Conan looked down at Clemens's face in the oblique light of the table lamp. From a distance, he might seem unconscious, but from here, a yard away, there was no mistaking the terrible repose on those slack features.

Conan reached into his sling and removed the stack of bills. "Here's something to add to the collection in your case, Will."

Will took the money with a sigh, and Conan left him. In the hall he noted that the master bedroom door was closed, as was the door into Tiff and Mark's room.

Lines of light glinted under both of them. Loanh's door was also closed, and as he approached, the light under it went out. Demara's door was open, casting a wedge of light into the hall, but when he glanced into the room as he passed, he didn't see her.

In the small room at the end of the hall that Sam Clemens had so recently occupied, Mark was leaning over the wood stove. He clanked the stove door shut and straightened, brushing his hands together. "That should last a while, Conan."

"Thanks, Mark. The heat feels good."

"Yeah. A few days like this makes a person think about moving to Phoenix. You, uh, need any help?"

"Will said he'd come check on me later. He can get me tucked in."

"Right." Mark seemed relieved that nothing more was expected of him and hurried to the door. But there he paused. "You figure Clemens will live long enough to tell anybody what really happened?"

Conan said wearily, "I don't know."

Mark nodded, and when he departed, Conan moved around in the bedroom and bath, making the expected sounds, then switched off the ceiling light and crossed to the window. His breath came out in a sigh of relief. Perhaps the National Weather Service had it right this time, and the second front had passed. Clouded moonlight lay soft on the flawless snow, and no fresh snow was falling.

Finally he went to the bed, turned back the covers, and stretched out to wait, tracking the time by the glowing numbers on his watch. The drone of the generator ceased only minutes after he lay down, and the grandfather clock chimed the half hour.

He forced himself to wait a full thirty minutes, even though he heard no sounds in the lodge. Then he rose, found the flashlight in the bedside table and left it in the bathroom, switched on so that its beam showed under the closed door. Anyone looking into this room would see the rumpled, empty bed and might assume Conan was in the bathroom.

Then he felt his way down the dark hall to his bedroom, where Will had the kerosene lamp lit. They communicated sparingly in whispers until Will blew out the light and departed. When he returned, after making his pretenses at checking Conan in Clemens's room and retiring to his own room, there had been no communication at all. They had maintained perfect silence for over two hours.

The lodge had been perfectly silent during that frigid span of time, except for the periodic striking of the grandfather clock.

Conan methodically flexed and relaxed his muscles, from head to toe, even the muscles in his left shoulder, finding a perverse comfort in the brief intensification of the pain that throbbed against his shoulder blade. It meant he was still capable of sensation, and he was beginning to wonder if when the time came to move he would be able to do so.

On the other hand, he had great faith in adrenaline.

The fire had burned out, but there was still some light perceptible to his dark-accustomed eyes: snowlight, sifting through the curtains, falling on the lifeless face of the man in the bed.

The involuntary flexing of his muscles came with a disturbance of the silence. Muffled creakings that might be footfalls on a cold, oak floor; water running. From Demara's bathroom. He checked his watch: 5:10. The sounds faded and weren't repeated. He heard a rustling and a sigh near him: Will Stewart, his doughty Watson for this adventure, willing and brave. And patient.

At 5:21 Conan heard movements and running water again, and, briefly, a murmur of voices, but this time from Tiff and Mark's room.

Again, silence closed in. Conan let his thoughts wander, not surprised that they turned so often to home. Beyond this white hole, far to the west on the edge of the sea, stood a house he called his castle, and the venerable and cranky Holliday Beach Book Shop, which he called his albatross and/or *raison d'être*. He imagined going to the shop in the morning, finding the steadfast Beatrice Dobie at her post behind the cash register. He would say, "Good morning, Miss Dobie." And she would reply, "Good morning, Mr. Flagg," then, noting his pillowcase sling, she would ask, "Did you have a nice weekend?"

Conan shook his head, closing his eyes tightly and opening them wide. Sleepiness was threatening this second vigil as it had the first.

5:32. He heard a sound he couldn't identify. A metallic clang. Distant. He couldn't guess how distant, but he was sure it wasn't in the lodge. Some phenomenon of thawing ice perhaps? It wasn't repeated.

He couldn't rid himself of the conviction that this cold, wretched vigil was in vain. But then, he reminded himself, clenching his teeth against a wave of shivering, doubt was almost inevitable in a vigil so long and conducted under such miserable circumstances.

When the clock chimed its twelve-note, three-quarter-hour reminder, Conan leaned forward slightly, his right hand tightening on the gun in his pocket. Under the sonorous ringing, he had heard something in the hall. Footsteps, perhaps. Will heard it, too, although he didn't move. Conan could feel his tension as if it were an electric aura emanating from him.

A faint click. The doorknob turning, the latch bolt disengaging.

Conan pulled the gun soundlessly from his pocket, holding his breath to listen. The door opened by inches to let in a flashlight beam. A shadowy figure followed the flashlight.

But it was all wrong. Not tall enough, the hair too long.

Lise.

She whispered, "Will? Conan?"

Will was on his feet in one quick movement, pulling her inside the room and closing the door carefully. He murmured urgently, "Douse the light, Lise."

She did, and the three of them felt their way into a close huddle. Conan whispered. "Lise, what is it?"

"Heather woke me up a few minutes ago, growling, and I thought I heard something in the garage. I took her into the kitchen to keep her quiet, then I went to the garage door and listened. Someone's *in* there."

"Damn it!" Conan didn't bother to whisper, and the words were startlingly loud and sharp. He thrust the gun into his belt, shrugged off the parka and the sling, and grabbed his flashlight from the bedside table. When he turned it on, the beam caught Lise and Will staring at him in astonishment, but he was already reaching for the doorknob.

Lise asked, "For God's sake, what's wrong?"

"She outflanked me *again*. Come on."

Will reached out with one big hand and held the door closed. "Wait a minute! *She*? She *who*?"

"Demara," Conan replied bitterly. "Who else?"

Lise reacted with a strangled, wordless cry, and Will muttered, "Sure. Who else?" as he flung open the door.

CHAPTER 27

Lise took the lead down the stairs, impatience making her descent recklessly noisy. She was oblivious to Conan's sotto voce warnings, and he remembered something she had said—when? Yesterday? Time was so distorted in this white hole, he wasn't sure.

If you ever find out who murdered my father and brothers, maybe your problem then will be to stop me from killing the killer.

"Lise!" he whispered. "Wait!"

But she didn't seem to hear him. At the foot of the stairs, she reached for the knob of the door into the garage, and Conan caught her arm, jerked her around to face him and the glare of his flashlight, and whispered urgently, "Damn it, Lise, just slow down!"

Nor did she seem to see him, her pale eyes too occupied with rage and grief. Will said softly, "Lise, take it easy, or you'll get us all killed."

That got through to her. At least she nodded, and

Conan felt the muscles in her arm relax. But they tensed again at a sound from inside the garage: a metallic clatter.

Conan pulled the Ruger out of his belt, thumbed off the safety, then glanced at Will, who stood ready with the .38 in one hand, flashlight in the other. Conan murmured to Lise, "Stay behind us."

He opened the door.

A light vanished at that moment: a flashlight switched off. He was assailed by the reek of gasoline fumes as the beams of his flashlight and Will's sliced into the cavernous dark, glinting on the rank of cars, on the generator centered on the right-hand wall. The shine on its metallic surfaces was too bright. It had been doused with liquid, and the wall behind it was soaked with wet splashes. On the concrete floor, a spattered trail stopped a few feet short of the woodshed door on the far wall. There an olive-drab jerrican lay on its side, apparently empty.

The woodshed door was open, and their flashlights almost in unison fixed on that rectangular space, on Demara Wilder, who stood framed within it, wearing her parka, ski pants, suede boots, and a red knit cap, with a bulky duffel bag slung over one shoulder.

She had an unlit cigarette in one hand, a lighter in the other.

Will lowered his gun, recognizing, no doubt, as Conan did, that although either of them might disable or even kill her with a shot at this distance—no more than twenty-five yards—the shot would ignite the spilled gasoline and the fumes that filled the garage.

Yet clearly ignition was her intention, and Conan knew there was no way to stop her. Her means of escape was the outside door at the north end of the woodshed.

Demara stood squinting into their lights and shouted, "Back off, Conan! You're too late!"

At the sound of Demara's voice, Lise lunged between Conan and Will with an anguished cry: "*Why?* Damn you, *why!*"

Will caught Lise, dropping his flashlight in the process, before she could rush into the garage. He locked her in a bear hug, containing her furious struggles stoically. Demara shouted, "Why *what?*"

Lise's struggles ceased abruptly. Her voice breaking with rancor, she yelled, "You bitch, you *murdered* them, all of them! You murdered Lucas, and he *loved* you!"

Demara casually shifted the duffel bag on her shoulder. "The murders were *his* idea, Lise. Well—except for one. His."

And with that, she turned and vanished into the woodshed.

Conan shouted a warning. Will lurched backward with Lise still enfolded in his arms, and Conan slammed the door. Within seconds—as long, he knew, as it took for Demara to open the outside door of the woodshed, light a cigarette, then toss it into the garage—he felt a thudding explosion, and the floor shook, panes crackled in the windows flanking the front door.

For a moment, he couldn't breathe against a paralyzing terror. Yet at the same time, he was surprised that the explosion was so brief, even surprised that the house hadn't come down around them. But then Lise had said there was only a gallon or so of gasoline left.

And it might be enough.

Enough to start a fire that couldn't be stopped. Enough to make bombs of the four cars in the garage. He flung open the door, only to be enveloped in a cloud of reeking smoke. Within the smoke, flames raged.

The gasoline had been consumed in the explosion, but the wall behind the generator seethed with flame. The generator was a wreck, its fuel tank burst open, shrapnel fragments littering the floor, the windshield of Al's convertible webbed with cracks. Will was already bounding up the stairs, bellowing the alarm, and Lise pushed past Conan, making an abortive reach toward the shelves by the door. "The fire extinguisher's gone!"

"Where's the nearest hose—hell!" He remembered then that Kim had said there were no hoses at the lodge.

"Conan, the *cars*! We've got to move them, or the gas tanks will blow!" Lise slapped the switch just inside the door, and with a rattling rumble, the two garage doors rose, drawing the bitter brown smoke that spilled from the flames, and Lise cried, "We *can't* get them out!"

Conan heard voices, footsteps thudding on the stairs, as he stared at the rampart of snow, four feet high, that had drifted and packed against the garage doors. None of these cars could plow through that.

But a moment later, he shouted, "Lise, there's our *water*!" and raced between the wall and A. C.'s black Cadillac toward the garage doors, then behind the cars to the east wall, where Art Rasmussen had so neatly hung his tools. He snatched the snow shovel from its outlined position, plunged it into the drifted barrier, carried the load of snow between the XK-E and Lucas's Mercedes, and flung it into the conflagration around the generator. A sizzle of steam in the choking smoke was his only reward, and he sprinted back to the white rampart, nearly collided with Lise who was running toward the fire with a snow-filled bucket. Shouts heralded the arrival of Will and the rest of the family. Conan dumped another load, returned to the snow barricade, filled the shovel, and sprinted again toward the fire, glimpsing

Lise on the other side of the Mercedes, heading back for another bucketful.

Will was shouting instructions, and within seconds, everyone had found a shovel or container, and like bizarre wraiths in layered sweaters and fluttering robes, they ran back and forth from the snow drift to the fire, flinging their loads to steam away in the smoke, going back for more, settling after a few awkward encounters into a frenzied rhythm, harried faces unrecognizable in the flickering glare.

There was no counting the number of trips made, nor how much snow was instantly volatilized into steam. At some point, Conan saw that the portion of drift from which he was loading his shovel was shrinking, almost down to the concrete in one place, yet it seemed to make no difference. The flames were spreading both laterally and vertically along the wall, but it was impossible to see how far they extended with the shimmering smoke boiling around them.

Back and forth, snow to fire, fire to snow, the frantic wraiths plied. The heat made its own wind, or so it seemed, until finally Conan realized that the open door into the woodshed was creating a draft that spurred the fire.

He flung yet another load of snow against the blazing wall where bones of studs showed through blackened plywood and browned, bubbled whitewash, then he struck out through the stygian swelter toward the woodshed door, holding his breath, eyes stinging as if he had dropped acid into them. He hit the fender of the XK-E, shifted course a few degrees, right hand outstretched, left hand clenched on the handle of the shovel. Choking and retching when he could no longer hold his breath, he reached the east wall, found the door, and plunged through it, slammed it shut behind him.

His eyes registered nothing but the flaring afterimages of flames. Even here, smoke saturated the air, and he felt his way toward the outside door, nearly falling over the gas cans scattered on the floor, clanking hollowly as they crashed against each other. He reached the door, staggered out into a thigh-deep drift, and leaned on the shovel, gasping for the clean, icy air.

It was perhaps a minute before he could stop coughing, before his inflamed eyes functioned well enough for him to see that the sky was beginning to pale. Stars glinted against a deep, sweet blue.

He could hear shouts and desperate cries of encouragement as he pushed through the snow to the corner of the garage, following a track already plowed by other feet. When he reached the front of the garage, the glare of fire garishly illuminated the pouring smoke and the plain of white covering the parking area. Snowy lumps hid Lise and Will's vans and Mark's Lincoln. A furrow of tracks vanished into the darkness. He saw a distant light playing on the snow. A flashlight. Demara Wilder.

Demara Wilder King.

"Conan! Where are you?"

He slogged through the drifts into the garage. "Here, Will!"

"You okay?" Will materialized out of the smoke near Conan.

"I just made a detour to close the woodshed door."

Will nodded, then scooped up a pailful of snow and strode back into the inferno. Conan dug his shovel into the drift and followed suit.

Rage drove him, overcame the hopelessness.

What kind of human being would make a funeral pyre of this building, a pyre for six people? And why?

Lise's question. *Why?* Why had Demara murdered a

father and two of his sons, one of whom she had taken as her husband?

Why had she choreographed Sam Clemens's death? For a share of A. C. King's estate? For money?

What could that money conceivably buy that would justify its cost?

Panting and coughing, muscles quivering with fatigue, he drove his shovel yet again into the snow, raced toward the fire yet again.

CHAPTER 28

Only half a mile, Sam had said. Quarter of a mile to the gate, another quarter to the Bronco. *Only* half a mile. Stupid bastard.

Stupid and dangerous. She'd *had* to give him the money. No choice there, knowing Sam. He'd cut her throat as soon as look at her. Now Flagg had the money. Not that it'd give him any joy, and she had enough cash to get to L.A., but she still felt cheated.

Demara Wilder plodded through snow up to her knees. Damn snow had gotten inside her boots. It was like walking barefoot through ice cubes. Her panting breaths came out in clouds as she paused, moving her flashlight back and forth to catch the two lines of fenceposts thrusting out of the snow on either side of her, dwindling toward a vanishing point in the darkness. They were her only guide. The road was buried under the snow.

She looked behind her. She couldn't see the lodge;

too many trees in the way. But she could see the glow of firelit smoke.

And she laughed. No way could they stop that fire.

Of course, that son of a bitch Flagg had almost screwed up everything. If it weren't for him, nobody in that pile of a house would've known what hit them till the gas tanks in the cars exploded.

But Flagg was only delaying the inevitable, wasn't he? He couldn't stop the fire, couldn't stop the cars blowing up, and even if anybody lived through that, there they'd be in their jammies, freezing to death. It wouldn't take long. She couldn't guess what the temperature was, but it felt like forty below. Or like she expected forty below would feel.

At least *she* had somewhere to go. Sam's Bronco. He'd said there was still some gas left. All she needed was enough to run the heater until the highway was plowed and she could drive out.

But Flagg and the others—if any of them survived— where would they go? The studio? She'd taken care of that. Thrown the stovepipe into that creek. They'd never find it, and they sure as hell couldn't light a fire in that stove without the stovepipe.

Help would come eventually, but not until the highway was clear and traffic started moving. The lodge would be burned out by then. Nobody could see it from the highway, so nobody would see the ruins.

Of course, Flagg might head for the highway, come after her. Damn the bastard! If he'd just stayed the hell out of this thing—

No. He wouldn't survive. Not *this* time.

She resumed her labored tramping, groaning as she shifted the duffel bag from one shoulder to the other. Must weigh thirty pounds. But she couldn't leave anything of hers to be found later in the ruins of the lodge.

Nobody would ever know she'd been at the lodge or that she'd ever set foot in Oregon. If the police started asking questions when she presented her marriage license to A. C. King's executor, well, she'd just tell them to talk to her mother. Letta Wilder, librarian, widow of distinguished black orthodontist Dr. Carver Wilder. Letta would lie for her. She always had. She would swear on a stack of Bibles that Demara had spent this weekend with her, while Lucas went to Oregon to visit his family. Demara knew her mother, knew Letta always believed anything her beautiful, glamorous daughter told her.

Demara had considered turning to one of her patrons, as she liked to call them, for an alibi. But she couldn't trust a white man—not any of those rich, respectable bastards—to lie for a black woman. They were willing to keep her in style and talk about her fabulous looks and fabulous performance in bed. Some even told her they loved her. But she couldn't count on any of them to lie to the police for her.

No, she'd depend on the one person who'd always come through for her. Her mother. And after the estate was settled, maybe they'd move to Hawaii. Or Greece. Maybe she'd buy that villa on that gorgeous little island near Thíra with the pink beach. Dry and warm, all year long. Hell, she could buy the whole damn island.

Oh, God, *warm* sounded good.

She was not a stranger to suffering. After all, she had the guts and stamina and iron ambition to make it to the top in the modeling business. It had meant deprivation in the form of ceaseless dieting, hard labor in the form of relentless exercise. It had meant hours of sultry smiles when she was so tired she could barely stand up. It had meant people ordering her around, bitching at every tiny flaw, prodding at her and fingering her like she was a Barbie doll. If she hadn't been so well paid, it would've qualified as cruel and unusual punishment.

But one form of suffering she had never had to endure was cold as intense as this. Everything seemed to be shutting down inside her. Everything except whatever it was that made her hurt. Her feet, her hands, her face, her lungs, everything hurt.

She cast the beam of the flashlight forward along the lines of fence posts and let out a cry of triumph. She could see the square gate posts rising higher than the others, then the new lines of fence posts extending left and right along the highway. Couldn't see the gate. Buried in the snow. Or maybe nobody had bothered to close it.

She quickened her pace, but she couldn't keep it up for more than a few clumsy, painful strides. Jesus, how was she going to explain a case of frostbite to her mother?

No, it wouldn't come to that. Just keep going.

Poor Lucas. She had to admit she'd miss him. He was a lot of fun, until he'd got himself in such deep shit with the IRS. But she'd warned him. Told him they'd never get away with it if the police didn't find his body in the rock slide. He didn't believe her. Said it would cost a fortune to move all those tons of rock.

Well, maybe it would. But they'd do it.

And they'd find Lucas King's body.

The snow seemed whiter. She looked up at the sky. It was dark blue, pink in the east. She couldn't see any clouds.

In a way, she was sorry the blizzard had stopped. That would've definitely taken care of Flagg and the others. But then *she'd* have no way out. Had to take the bitter with the sweet, and she'd had a lifetime of that, a lifetime of having other people in control. She'd made a fortune by the time she was eighteen, and her father had controlled that. And lost it. Then died and left her holding a deep and empty bag. Then there'd been Charlie. Investment counselor, he called himself, and she'd made more money, worked like a slave—a big, beautiful, nigger slave, she thought bitterly—for another five years until she couldn't get the top jobs anymore. Fresh meat. Young meat. That's what they wanted. And Charlie jumped ship like a rat. Told her those investments hadn't panned out. We're in a *recession*, darling. Maggoty white bastard. Left her with the dregs. And she'd had to take the dregs since, all the rich bastards, rich white bastards. Except maybe Maxie. He would've taken care of her. But he was dead.

The gate posts. She had reached the gate posts.

She began laughing through harried gasps, but as she staggered forward, the laughter turned to wheezing sounds closer to sobs.

A ridge of snow stood between her and the highway.

Must be seven feet high, and it ran along the highway in both directions as far as she could see, as far as the flashlight beam would reach.

"Shit!" She shouted the word in a rage of frustration, repeated it over and over, threw the flashlight at the white barrier.

The snow swallowed it, leaving only a dimple in the pristine slope, and she shuddered, pulling in deep breaths of frozen air, clenching her numb hands in the leather gloves.

The snowplow had already been through, and it was the snowplow that threw up this endless ridge of snow. When? Last night? But more snow had fallen since and closed the highway again. She hadn't heard a single vehicle go past.

Shivering uncontrollably, she looked west. The bridge

had to be down there. And Sam's Bronco. She sought a
dark shape against the snow, but saw nothing. Maybe
the light was still too dim.

And maybe the damn truck had been buried under the
ridge the snowplow left.

Well, she'd just have to find the Bronco and dig it
out. At least dig enough to open a door and get inside.
She had to get inside somewhere soon. How the hell
had Flagg ever made it down from that camping place?
Of course the blizzard was just beginning then.

That had been the first thing to go wrong, the blizzard. But she couldn't stop then, and it still would've
worked if it hadn't been for that damned half-breed.
Those people should be locked up on a reservation.

But Flagg hadn't stopped her, and he wouldn't. He
couldn't now.

She looked back toward the lodge. That *was* smoke
rising above the trees, wasn't it? Still too dark to be
sure. Strange, she hadn't heard any explosions yet.
When the gas tanks in those cars blew, they should
make a hell of a noise.

Her chattering teeth reminded her that she had another quarter mile to go. She turned left into what
seemed a white lane between the fence along the highway and the ridge of snow left by the snowplows. She
took two steps, and the snow collapsed under her.

She yelled, flung both arms out, tumbled under suffo-
cating, freezing white that was like a crashing breaker,
drowning her. Burying her alive. In a frenzy, she struggled and flailed, felt a hard surface under her knees, and
with a spasm of exertion she wouldn't have guessed she
was capable of, she pushed upward, screaming for air.

She stood chest-deep in snow, head throbbing with
her heartbeat, every breath a hoarse cry. Only a ditch. It

was only a ditch filled with snow. But damn it, it had felt like death.

The duffel bag had slipped off. She found it buried in snow and hitched it up on her shoulder, grunting with the effort. She saw the gate post and aimed for it, wallowed through the snow, finally reached the post and clung to it, waiting for her pulse and breathing to slow.

At first she thought the low, grinding roar was inside her head. It was so quiet here. So spooky quiet.

No. The sound was definitely outside. A motor. Probably a truck, from the throaty rumble of it. A snowplow. It had to be a snowplow.

Yes! She thrust a fisted hand into the air and waded toward the ridge. She had to get over that ridge. At least *see* over it. But she kept sinking into the snow, slipping backward. Finally she spread-eagled on the slope, packing the snow with her feet as she squirmed to the top, and at last she could see the highway.

A wide, flat ribbon of white curving out of the forest and ultimately back into it. Not a track on it. The rumbling came from the east. It had to be a snowplow, even if she couldn't see it yet, and that meant traffic would be moving through soon. Sooner than she expected.

But she was flexible, always had been. If Sam's truck was buried, and she couldn't drive it out, she'd hitch a ride. Maybe that was even better. The Bronco had been parked at the bridge for a while. A patrolman might've noticed it, taken down the license number. Besides, if she drove out, she wouldn't get far because she'd need gas within a few miles. That meant stopping at a gas station where somebody might remember a tall, black woman in a Bronco.

A tall, black *frozen* woman. Damn, the snow was cold against her body. Couldn't stop shivering. She thought of an island in the Aegean Sea, sun hot on pink sand.

Lights! She could see headlights and yellow warning lights winking through the trees as the snowplow rumbled around the curve.

She had to restrain the impulse to scramble over the snow ridge, to stand out in the middle of the highway and wave, yell for help. Take me with you, take me anywhere, but get me *out* of here!

No. Just hold on. The driver of that snowplow probably lived around here. He was the kind of person the police might question, and he'd probably remember a tall, black woman—frozen or not—outside the gate to the King lodge.

There it was, the snowplow, inching around the curve, a squared-off gravel truck, solid as a tank, with a huge, concave blade angled across the front. It cut through the snow like a broad-bowed ship, the snow crumpling, riding up and out to pile onto the ridge on the other side of the highway. Thank God it was in the other lane. That meant any traffic that followed it would be heading west toward Portland. She'd wait until the snowplow was gone and a few cars and trucks had passed. Then she'd cross the highway, walk west as far as she could, and flag down an eighteen-wheeler. Not so much risk of a trucker being local and available for questioning by the police.

And she had a story for the driver. She was traveling with her boyfriend, and they had a fight, and the son of a bitch dumped her here and told her to find her own way home. Home would be San Francisco. She knew San Francisco. Maxie had owned a condo there. She'd ask the trucker to take her to the nearest bus station. He'd go out of his way for her. And if the trucker was a woman—well, Demara had never met a woman yet who didn't have her own hard-luck story about a man, who wouldn't sympathize with another woman's story.

She squirmed down until her head was below the top of the ridge. The last thing she needed was for the driver to look her way as he passed and see a face looking out over the snowbank. The rumble of the snowplow's motor was so close, her skull seemed to rattle, and she could smell the greasy odor of diesel. Come on, get on past. Damn it, hurry!

But the rumble changed, snorting and chugging, a spasmodic spurt. Shifting gears, that's all. Revving up again now. Jesus, those things were noisy up close.

And getting noisier and—

Closer.

The rumble was a voracious roar, and white-hot terror shot through her, paralyzing her.

Demara Wilder King looked up, and all she could see was the vast blade six feet away and a chromed grill like the gates of hell. And riding high above it, a tiny, shining silver bulldog.

CHAPTER 29

The concrete floor was awash in water: snow that had melted into slush a few yards from the fire and had turned to ice outside the garage doors. Conan filled his shovel, nearly lost his footing on the ice, and did loose his load. Grimly, he pushed the shovel into the snow again. He'd scooped away a scallop at least ten feet into the drift. He turned and made his way cautiously over the track-pocked ice until his feet slapped through water, and smoke enveloped him. The yellow glow led him. He threw the shovelful of snow, heard a hiss of steam, but didn't stay to see if it had any effect. Back for another load.

He was aware of the other occupants of this Dantean nightmare only as vague shapes coughing and gasping as they ran in and out of the smoke. Sometimes he wondered if he was dreaming. Or hallucinating. He wasn't sure when he began to realize that the smoke was thinning, when he could no longer see the yellow glow behind it. His eyes were so inflamed, he couldn't see much, anyway.

Another load. Once more into the breach . . . and back again.

Sometimes he thought he was laughing, but he was only coughing.

And another load flung into the smoke. Back across the water and slush and ice. Damn! Nearly went down. Shouting. Someone was shouting. Too many shouting at once. Couldn't understand a word. He plunged the shovel into the snow.

All that kept him from falling flat on his face was the handle of the shovel driven into the snowdrift. He leaned against it precariously, hearing the shouted words in his head, as if his mind had needed a moment to sort them out and play them back.

It's out. We did it. It's out. Thank God, it's out.

Conan turned, saw the wraiths emerging from the smoke, clothes and faces dark with soot, like miners abandoning a coal shaft.

It's out.

The fire was out.

He was suddenly shaking, quivering; a strange darkness that wasn't smoke moved in on him. Knees were going out from under him.

Might as well sit down.

He collapsed into the snow, sat with his knees drawn up, left arm folded against his body. The pain he hadn't felt since the moment he saw Demara ready to ignite a pyre of death hit all at once. His hands, his feet, his left shoulder, all a torment that stopped his breath.

He looked around, seeking a focus outside his pain. Sky pale with dawn. His watch read 6:30. The survivors all in various states of physical and mental exhaustion. Lise washing her face in snow. Tiff and Loanh leaning

on each other, Tiff still coughing. Dramatically. Mark
with his robe flapping about him as he stared numbly at
the garage. Will, his red hair turned gray with smoke,
on one knee, head down, and he might have been pray-
ing. Or only too weary to stand.

A brave company, and Conan wondered if Demara
could understand or even imagine the courage that had
defeated her.

Lise straightened and stood swaying as if she were
poised on the edge of a chasm, then she reached out to
her brother, touched his hand as it came up to meet
hers, until finally they embraced in anguished tears. The
others moved toward them and the solace of their
shared grief, and Lise stretched a hand out to Kim,
Mark reached for Tiff, and she for Loanh, and Loanh
for Will, and they wept. Together, huddled together in
the gray light of an icy dawn.

Conan, watching in the shell of his aching body,
thought about Demara, about her defeat. Sooner or later
she would be found, and she would pay the only price
that could be exacted of her. Was that justice? He didn't
know. Certainly it wouldn't lessen by a single tear the
price of grief still to be paid by these survivors.

It was Will who concluded this intense, fragile en-
counter with a brisk, "It's *cold* out here, in case you
hadn't noticed. Everybody inside and get warmed up, or
I'll be treating all of you for hypothermia."

The circle dissolved, and the sooty refugees drifted
toward the lodge through the garage, where smoke
lurked in a smoggy haze. All but Will and Lise. Arm in
arm, they walked over to Conan. Will studied him clin-
ically, then offered his diagnosis: "Conan, you look like
hell."

"That sounds about right."

"Conan . . ." Lise gently touched his swollen, reddened hand. Then abruptly her eyes widened in alarm. "Heather! Oh, God, she'll be terrified!" And with that she ran for the lodge, sprinting heedlessly through the ice and water on the garage floor.

Will watched her with a bemused smile. "Now we both know who comes first with *her*." Then he sobered. "You can't stay out here and freeze your butt. You figure you can walk?"

"Probably." Conan extended his right hand, keeping his left arm tight against his body. "I just need some help getting my frozen butt out of the snow."

Immobility had eased the pain in the last few minutes. It returned with a wave of dizziness when Will helped him to his feet, and he didn't balk at accepting Will's support as they crossed the ice to the garage.

Will said, "As soon as I get you inside, I'm heading for the highway to see if the snowplows—" He stopped, frowning up at the garage doors. "Conan, how'd you get those doors open?"

"I didn't. Lise hit the switch. . . ." Then he laughed, which was inadvisable at the moment. Lise had turned on the switch that activated the automatic doors—and the doors had risen, a miracle he hadn't even noticed in the panic of the fire. "Will, the power's back on!"

"I'll be damned. Could've been on for hours. We wouldn't have known, sitting up in your room with all the lights off."

Conan heard a faint rumbling, and as he traced the furrows of Demara's tracks to the curve in the snow-buried road, he saw what at first seemed a figment of his harried imagination—a moving drift of snow propelled by a truck spouting diesel clouds. He found himself shaking again, but this time it was with relief. "You won't have to hike out to the highway to find a snow-plow, Will. Here comes one now."

Will stared at it, openmouthed. "Art must've told somebody we were up here. And the driver'll have a CB. Damn, I think we're saved!"

Conan managed to keep up as Will hurried him past the XK-E—where he noted ruefully that he should have put the top up before leaving the car in a burning building—and past the wrecked generator. The wall behind it looked as if it had been eaten away by a voracious, black rot in a swath twenty-feet wide and extending to the smoke-dark ceiling. The stench of wet charcoal and even an overtone of gasoline made the remaining smoke seem denser, more toxic.

Inside the atrium, Will shouted to Mark, who was on his way upstairs. "There's a snowplow outside! It'll be here in a minute or so."

Mark produced a singularly un-Republican whoop, then called down the hall to Tiff. There were further shouted exchanges as Tiff conveyed the news to Loanh and Kim. In the ensuing rush down the stairs and to the front door, Conan said to Will, "I can make it into the living room. Tell the driver to radio the county sheriff and—"

"Yeah, Conan, I already had that figured out."

"And ask him if he saw a Bronco driving out. Or if he saw Demara on the highway. Oh—and tell the sheriff's department to call the nearest Medical Examiner." When Will gave that a questioning look, Conan added, "For your patient upstairs."

"Hell, I forgot about him. Okay." Will headed for the door. The others were already wading into the snow on the deck, and as Will joined them, closing the door behind him, Conan wondered what the driver would think when he saw this unkempt, sooty troupe.

Lise wasn't among the greeting party. He found her sitting cross-legged with her back to the cold hearth, hugging Heather to her, her disheveled hair shadowing her downcast face. She was weeping.

He crossed to the north windows and opened the drapes, a slow process with only one good arm and two miserably inadequate hands, but the wan light of the new day dissipated the cavelike darkness. The snowplow had reached the front of the lodge, and the cheering refugees were greeting its driver like a liberator entering a concentration camp. In the distance, Mount Hood, clad in new snow, hung in misted space, and except for the edging of pink on its eastern flanks, it was almost the same delicate blue as the sky, and that vast mass of snow-garbed rock seemed as translucent as blown glass.

Conan made his way to the armchair at the east end of the fireplace and collapsed into it, his breath rushing out in a long sigh. Lise watched him with concern evident in her reddened eyes, but she made no move to rise, not with Heather panting and trembling in her arms, pressing her exquisite head into the curve under Lise's chin. The bandage on the sheltie's leg was frayed and stained with blood.

"Sweet lady," Conan said softly, "it's been a hard weekend."

Lise nodded, stroking Heather's head. Outside, the truck's motor idled under a shouted exchange. Lise listened a moment, then her eyes closed. "Oh, God, how am I going to make it through this day?" She began weeping again, containing the sobs in terrible silence.

Conan could think of no answer to that question; he knew no words capable of assuaging her pain. He watched with a degree of awe as she reclaimed her steel control, putting aside the pain. For now.

She said, "I had a strange dream last night. Well, early this morning. I dreamed it was spring, and I was in a mountain meadow full of bright blue wild camas, and Dad and Al and Mark and Lucas were there. But they were all children, maybe eight or ten years old, even Dad, and they were laughing and running in a circle through the grass. The odd thing about it was that *I* was old. When I looked down at my hands, they were wrinkled and thick with arthritis. Yet it wasn't a *bad* dream. There was something . . . peaceful about it." She looked up at Conan. "Before the others come back in, I have some questions."

"I'll answer any I can, Lise."

"You knew it was Demara. When I came up to your room, you said it was Demara who had outflanked you again. How did you know?"

Conan caught himself before he shrugged. "When we gathered here after my shoot-out with Clemens, I showed everyone the money I found in his parka. I said those were hundred-dollar bills, but I didn't say how many there were, nor did I mention a total. But later, Demara pointed out that all of you only had my word for it that Clemens didn't have the twenty thousand dollars with him when he arrived. So how did she know the exact amount if *she* didn't give it to him?"

"Elementary," Lise said with a brief, bitter laugh. "But why the fire? Why try to kill *all* of us?"

"Probably because she thought all of us knew too much. That was my doing, I'm afraid. The rock slide would've been chalked up as an accident, except for my survival. That and the fact that I shared the results of my rather primitive investigation forced her to change her plans. She knew if any of us survived, there'd be a police investigation. But if our deaths could also be attributed to a tragic accident—like a malfunctioning generator causing a fire that ignited the gas tanks in the cars and brought the lodge down on our heads in a flaming mass—then she'd be free and clear, probably with an alibi to establish that she was never here at all. No one outside the family saw her here. The Rasmussens left before she arrived."

Lise nodded, murmuring to Heather, "You're safe, love, don't shake so, please." Then she fixed Conan with a direct gaze. "Demara said the murders—Dad's and Al's—were Lucas's idea. Is that true?"

Conan wanted more than anything to invent a comfortable fiction that she could believe. But she was asking for the truth.

"Yes, Lise, I think it's true. I also think Al's death was incidental to Lucas's plans, as mine would've been. A. C. was the intended victim."

"Why? For Dad's estate? For the money?"

"With Lucas, it was probably more complicated, but essentially . . . yes. For the money."

She didn't move for a long time, and there was in her eyes no light or life. Finally she asked, "Who do I grieve? Someone I never knew, someone I created in my mind, the mirror self that was me under the skin? With Dad and Al, there's no doubt who I've lost. I knew them, my father and my brother, and I loved them. Warts and all. But Lucas . . . I thought I knew him best, I thought we were so close. Maybe that's what I'll have to grieve, that what I lost never existed." She shivered, looking down at Heather. "It's so cold in here. So hellishly *cold*."

Outside, the truck's motor revved out of idle, and the rumbling surged, then gradually diminished. The front door opened, and the family came into the atrium, talking among themselves, yet oddly subdued. All of them headed upstairs.

Conan closed his eyes, waiting, and a few minutes later Will appeared with a blanket and his medical case, his hands and face scrubbed clean. "I guess I need to do a little doctoring here," he said as he knelt to look at Heather's bandage. "Heather, you're the only patient I've ever had who tried to eat my dressings."

Lise kept stroking the sheltie's head. "Oh, Will, she was so scared."

"She had every right to be," he replied huskily. Then he touched Lise's tear-streaked cheek. "You okay, Lise?"

She took his hand in hers. "Don't worry about me, Will." Her gaze shifted to Conan. "But you do have another patient to doctor."

"Mm? Oh." He rose and leaned over Conan to feel for a carotid pulse, then pressed a palm against his forehead. "Well, you're not shocky. *Mark!*"

Conan winced at that bellow, which was aimed over his head. He heard footsteps in the atrium, but it wasn't Mark's limping gait.

"Oh, Kim," Will said in a quieter tone, "Would you get a fire going in here? I've got a couple of patients to tend to."

Kim was still in her smoked, plaid wool robe, but like Will, she had washed her face and hands. Still, the soot clung to her pale hair, and her eyes were puffy and achingly red. "A *couple* of patients?" She knelt by Lise, studying her with frank concern. "Lise?"

"Not me," Lise said with a fleeting smile. "Heather."

Conan, Will, and Lise all stared as Kim tenderly petted Heather and said in the kind of singsong tone reserved for babies and pets, "Oh, you poor, sweet baby, you're going to be all right now." Then she added, "She reminds me of a collie I had when I was a kid. Lassie. What else? The only dog I ever had. Dad didn't like dogs." Then she rose and with cool efficiency began gathering kindling and laying a fire.

Conan caught Lise's eye and smiled, then looked up at Will. "Did the driver radio the sheriff?"

"Yes. Talked to the dispatcher. They'll send a couple of deputies out. Should get here in an hour or so. With all the storm emergencies, they're shorthanded. Yes, I asked Ed—the snowplow driver—if he'd seen the Bronco or Demara. I want to look at your shoulder, so that means getting some clothes off you." Conan grimaced at that, and Will added, "Either I get them off, or the medics'll cut them off later, and since you don't like cutting up other people's clothes . . ."

Kim frowned as she shook out the match with which she had lit the kindling. "You mean A. C.'s clothes? Go ahead and cut, Will. He wouldn't mind."

Will began cutting, and finally Conan sat naked from the waist up, shivering while Will listened to his heart with an icy stethoscope.

Conan asked irritably, "Will, what did Ed *say*?"

"About Demara?" He wrapped Conan's right arm in a blood-pressure cuff and pumped it up. "Didn't see her." Will paused while he released the pressure and studied the falling needle. "Not bad. You're heart's in good shape. Must be all that smoking. Anyway, Ed said he saw the Bronco parked by the bridge yesterday when he came through the first time. He got out to see if there was anybody in the truck, but there wasn't, so he went on about his business." Will put the cuff in his case, then pulled up a corner of the blood-soaked bandage.

Conan asked, "Did Ed see the Bronco today?"

"No, but he was coming from the east. Hadn't got to it yet. But he said he didn't figure anybody could drive it out without some major excavation, since it got buried in the snow he was shoveling off the highway." Will pressed the tape down and delved in his case until he came up with a syringe and a small vial. "Demerol, in case you're wondering, and it's all I can do for you now." He plunged the needle into Conan's right deltoid.

"Will, that's strange he didn't see Demara. I mean, how far could she get on foot in snow a yard deep?"

Kim stared into the fire. "I hope to hell they find her."

"They will," Conan assured her grimly. "She's the kind of person who stands out in a crowd. People remember her."

"Yes. People remember her."

Will unfolded the blanket and draped it over Conan. "You might as well relax. Nothing else to do till the chopper gets here."

"*What* chopper?"

"The Life Flight chopper. The sheriff's dispatcher patched me through to Emmanuel. That's the fastest way to get you to a hospital."

"I don't need anything as dramatic as a helicopter, Will."

"Maybe not, but *I* do. I have to check on Jayleen."

"Who?"

"Jayleen. First pregnancy, remember? Hell, she's probably had the babies already. Twins. She's having twins." He looked at Lise regretfully with those words, but she only nodded.

Conan closed his eyes, too spent to balk at leaving his fate in others' hands. He'd just rest a little while, let the Demerol take effect.

It seemed no more than a minute later when he looked up to find himself flanked by two efficient young people clad in jackets with LIFE FLIGHT embroidered on the pockets.

The helicopter's rotors throbbed, lifting it from the lawn in a whirling, miraculous cloud of white, dazzling in the light of the rising sun. Lise King stood on the deck with Mark's arm around her shoulder in a comfortable embrace that surprised her. He had always seemed to find touching people, even those he loved, difficult.

As the chopper tilted westward above the white hills, and the cloud settled in a sparkling mist, Lise felt an irrational terror. It was, she knew, something she'd have to get used to. Rationally, she understood it: two people she cared about had departed in that racheting machine, and she was terrified that she'd never see them again.

Like Dad. Like Al. Like Lucas.

Mark's arm slipped from her shoulder. "I'm going to check the thermometer again, Lise." She nodded, still watching the empty sky, as he stumped along the snowy deck and around the corner of the lodge.

Not everyone you love is bound to die every time they leave you, Lise. So her rational mind assured her. But she knew it would take a lot of safe returns before the part of her mind that commanded fear was satisfied.

Conan wouldn't be returning to the lodge. She wouldn't blame him if he never set foot here again or accepted an invitation of any kind from her. But he would. As long as she continued to paint, he'd come into her life at intervals to revel in her work. It was a rare relationship, and one she treasured. Every artist needs someone whose admiration is unconditional.

Will would be back. Safely, she insisted to the fear within her. This afternoon, he'd said. After he got Conan to the hospital, after he checked Jayleen, after he checked the storefront clinic on Burnside and his clients from the unforgiving streets.

But Will Stewart *would* be back. There was very little she could count on in her life now, but she could count on Will.

And her work.

That would keep her sane in the following days and weeks and months. And perhaps years.

"Lise!" Mark was hurrying toward her, panting and excited. "The temperature's gone up nearly thirty degrees since I looked an hour ago. It's up to *eighteen*."

"Mark, the temperature always goes up when the sun rises."

"Not that *fast*. What we've got here is an honest-to-God chinook. At this rate, all the snow'll be melted off by tomorrow."

He seemed inordinately pleased at that prospect, and Lise had to admit that it would be a profound relief to have this snow gone. Usually she found in a snowfall endless material for paintings that drove her to frenzied creation. But not this snow.

She could only deal with this snow when it was gone.

Yet what would her world in this cherished mountain fastness be like then? Not as it had been. Nothing would ever be as it had been. Too much was buried in this snow.

Mark said, "Come on, let's go in. Still too damned cold out here."

She started to turn away, but a movement on the freshly-plowed road stopped her. "Someone's coming."

"Hey, that's Art's old pickup, isn't it?"

"Looks like it. And that's a police car behind him."

"Must be the sheriff's deputies. Oh, Lord, I'm not looking forward to trying to sort all this out with them."

Lise shivered, the cold closing in, despite the crystalline sunshine. She wondered how anything that had happened during this endless weekend could be sorted out, could be understood.

She looked to the immaculate presence of the mountain and opened her eyes and mind to the ancient power in its massive planes, clothed now in snow that held captive in its shadows exquisite blends of color. Cerulean, yes, and ultramarine. A hint of alizarin crimson, sometimes a cast of ochre. The essence of the mountain was in the colors in its shadows, but she'd never found all of them on her palette.

There was solace in that. The mountain would solace her with its unattainable color. And one day, she knew—or perhaps hoped—she would discover the color of the wind that plumed off the summit into the depth of the sky.

One day she might even understand that life lived in death in the presence of this mountain.

One day she might understand.

Look for the mystery novels of

M. K. WREN

in your local bookstore.
Published by Ballantine Books.